DRAMA DRAMA DRAMA

CORI COOPER

GRANTSVILLE, UT

Copyright © 2025 by Cori Cooper

Coristories.com

Cover Art by: Amber Cooper

Cover Design by: Cori Cooper

ISBN: 978-1-0882-0534-1

To: Becky (Cutchen) Greer and all the Drama we created in high school!

CB-14 forever.

And yes, I still use Sprees.

PROLOGUE

FADE IN:

EXT: BEATEN DOWN VEHICLE - DAY

Pathetic old sedan that has been laughed off the highways of California for almost twenty years and has never fully recovered. Its self-esteem is as saggy as the back fender. One headlight isn't working and the other is dim. Physical attributes are metaphors to years of abuse.

INT: AFTERMATH OF A STUPID LONG ROAD TRIP, EMPTY WRAPPERS AND ANGST SCATTERED EVERY-WHERE

Three personages. A father (TERRY) in the driver's seat, a mother (TERI) in the passenger seat, and languishing in the back-seat is a teen girl (CARMEN) who is so charismatic and gorgeous it will be a tremendous challenge to find an actress who will be able to fit the part. So, yeah, good luck with that. Snacks are running low, morale is even lower. At least for CARMEN. The Parental Units are immune to their offspring's tortured sighs.

EXT: As the light fades into the west, the sedan sputters along a dusty highway that is so cracked and faded that there are no longer stripes on the road. Every few feet the sedan hits a pothole that jars the prehistoric vehicle so much it makes the fabulous teen girl's (CARMEN) face wrinkle into lines that might permanently damage her angelic features. The parental figures are oblivious.

(CARMEN) rests a hand on the window, but draws it back quickly. The window is hot to the touch, not the good kind of hot that begs for catcalls, the horrible kind that makes a person's hair limp and unmanageable despite copious amounts of celebrity hairspray that Raoul sells for ninety-five dollars a can at his ridiculously overpriced salon in Beverly Hills.

EXT: THE LIGHT OF DAY

The sun doesn't just shine in this desolate place, it torches everything it touches. It's not illuminating the landscape for attractive ambiance and necessary photosynthesis, it wants things to burn. If the role of villain hadn't already been cast by the father (TERRY) and mother (TERI), the sun (SUN) would absolutely get a call back.

EXT: THE LAND OF DESOLATION

Dust devils swirl in the distance. Sad little scrubby brush bushes that have lost all will to survive dot the edge of the road. The scenery is flat, dry, dirty, and uglier than mediocrity. Nothing can thrive in conditions such as these. The setting is a powerful metaphor for (CARMEN)'s life from here until the end of time.

ACT I SCENE I

My life is officially over.

And no wonder. Whenever a person is forced from their natural habitat—the life to which they were made and born, everything and all that is familiar—into the crypt of broken dreams, slow demise is the only path forward.

More to the point, the humans who call themselves my parents have chosen to move from Los Angeles—the city of angels, bright lights, fancy restaurants, shopping, culture, theaters and, duh, Hollywood—to a town too small for a traffic light. This is nothing short of a flipping Greek tragedy.

A very, very, bad, bad, bad idea.

I have explained the situation to my so-called guardians about a million and a half times over the last six weeks. I made masterful powerpoint presentations, covered their mirrors with notes, and put together an original choreographed skit, but all I got in return was good-natured shrugs and way too many chirpy affirmations that eventually I would learn to love the small town as much as I love the big city.

I can't even with that.

Anyway, this is their fault. These orchestrators of my birth are the very beings who exposed me to a world of glitter and fame. If they didn't want me to drown in a sea of despair at the thought of moving, they should never have inhabited California in the first place. It is entirely because of them that I can't adjust, cope, and overcome. They should see that turning my back on the birthplace of all my hopes and dreams to settle for crop fields and dust is beyond ludicrous.

They can't though. They are too busy peering through rose-colored glasses and donning hats of nostalgia to see that they are making me run the gauntlet of the very same experience they had and despised.

Well, it's the same, except opposite.

My mom and dad grew up in a small town, specifically this small town, so obviously both of them were brainwashed from a very young age. They left it for Los Angeles, by choice I might add, which is also the opposite of what they're doing to me. And they never learned to love or even tolerate the city, yet they expect me to embrace this small town.

Put down roots, braid my hair in pigtails, and start wearing plaid.

My parents have been trying to run back to this horrible little mess of a habitation for at least half of my life. They're more delusional than they look if they think I'm not going to do the exact same thing with Los Angeles the second I graduate from high school.

I don't want to live in a town where everyone knows your name and the name of your grandfather and his grandfather and *his* grandfather. I want to go back to the promised land where nobody cares.

It's so deliciously selfish.

I thrive in a city where waving and smiling at someone results in words that make your ears burn. A place where you need an appointment to go clothes shopping and you spend more money on shoes than the nameless masses spend on their cars. A glorious metropolis where driving from one location to the other is done at outrageously high speeds or a pace that resembles a parking lot.

There is no in-between.

Oh, Los Angeles, I will miss you until the day I die.

Which might be soon.

"Look at that!" I fling my arm between my parents' seats and aim it out the windshield.

My best friend, Skylar, yelps in protest. The arm I flung was attached to the hand holding my phone where she is making this journey with me on Facetime.

For as long as the data holds out.

"That's the shopping mall," Mom says.

Dad glances at her with a smile that makes me want to gag. "We're almost home!"

I turn the phone so I can see Skylar. "This will never be my home."

"Never." She shakes her head solemnly.

Mom goes on as if I said nothing. She is getting increasingly proficient at ignoring me. I'd be worried about the lack of attention if my whole life wasn't falling into tiny little pieces all around me. That's slightly more consuming at the moment.

"It's the only one for about thirty miles, so I imagine that's where we will do the majority of our shopping for clothes and shoes."

I imagine I would rather wear a dress made out of paper bags from the Piggly Wiggly than adorn myself in rags from such a tumble-down building.

My mother has no soul.

"Carmen," Skylar breathes. "I'm so sorry. This is worse than I thought. I'm going to flip the station to Enya." She reaches out of view for just a moment, and the haunting melody of melancholy fills the car.

"Skylar, will you turn that down please?" Dad calls over his shoulder as he passes a tractor going the same speed I usually walk. "Enya makes me sleepy."

Skylar does, with a host of sympathetic glances in my direction.

"It was a valiant effort, Sky. All that is left for us to do is stare out the window in abject misery." I turn Skylar to face the windshield and let my head drop like a stone onto the back of the seat.

Dad snorts, Mom nudges him, and I don't spare a thought for either of them. They don't deserve it. They made their choices, and now I get to make mine.

There are a few moments of haunting, low-volume-Enya-filled mourning before anyone speaks again. Far too few moments in my opinion. I need more time to contemplate the perfect graveyard of buried hopes that is about to become my life.

"Oh, Terry, look! I forgot about that!" Mom's face melts into mush. She reaches over to clasp Dad's fingers.

"Carmen, can you turn me around?" Skylar asked. "Your Mom and Dad are holding hands, and it is severely traumatizing me."

"Oh, ew." I aim the phone out the side window and follow it with my eyes so I don't have to see them either. My parental figures should know better than to do stuff like that in public.

"Carmen, sweetie, did you see the butte?"

"The what?" I didn't see a single thing this entire drive that even remotely resembles a beaut. The only thing that has changed in the last hour, scenery-wise, is that we drove over a rise and a lumpy wannabe mountain popped up out of the middle of some bushes, like a hairless old man. There is for sure nothing beautiful about that.

"Look, sweetie, there." Mom points, and I aim Skylar in that direction to see if she can tell what my mom is talking about.

"Does she mean that hill?" Skylar asks. "The squatty, bald one?"

"That is the butte," Mom explains. "It's really—"

"What's that green stuff all over the side?" I wrinkle my nose. It's like a fat dude wearing a bright green tube top. No one should ever have to witness something like this. "Why are you staring at it with misty eyes of yore?"

Mom laughs and leans into Dad. "Is that what I was doing? I'll have to tone down those misty eyes of yore."

"Carmen!" Skylar says, as calmly as she is able in the face of such torturous circumstances. "Your parents are touching again. Can I please look at something else?"

Dad's chuckles fill the car as I acquiesce to Skylar's request and press the phone against the side window so she can take in the abysmal scenery. Now she can feel my pain on a more personal level.

Mom finally stops laughing and turns to face me, wiping her eyes on the sleeve of her sweater. "It's *John Deere Green*."

"Excuse me?" I'm pretty sure she quit speaking English just now.

"It's a country song, by Joe Diffie. When your dad and I were in high school, it was really popular, so someone climbed the butte and painted the words, 'Billy Bob loves Charlene' in letters three feet high."

"In John Deere green," Dad adds with a laugh.

"It's cute." Mom smiles. "And it's iconic to our town, like the Hollywood sign."

"No." Skylar gasps.

I turn the phone so we can exchange horror-filled expressions. The disbelief all over Skylar's face is like a mirror to my very soul.

Oh, no, my mother did not...

She could not...

She...

"Does your mom really think that a pretend mountain painted with retro country music lyrics is the same as the HOLLYWOOD SIGN?" Skylar whispers.

Yes.

Yes, she does.

That's it.

This is proof eternal that I have been abducted to an alien planet by inhuman forms posing as my parents.

It's official.

I'm not going to live to see my eighteenth year.

There is no way I will be able to flourish in a home with parents who really think this freaky Billy Bob paint is at the same level as the Hollywood sign. I cannot survive in a town such as this. I will waste away like a tumbleweed and end up tossed across the highway at five mile intervals.

The tragedy overwhelms me.

With a groan of agony, I fling myself back in the seat and throw my arm over my eyes. Something on the seat jabs into my back in the most uncomfortable way, but potential chronic back pain is a secondary problem.

"Are you hungry? Do you want some more corn nuts?" Mom holds out an individual pack of plain, boring corn nuts. I will not take it. Even if I was languishing in the dunes of the Sahara with nothing to eat or drink,

I would not take those corn nuts as a matter of principle. One should know better than to console their suffering offspring with an unflavored bag of stale corn.

"Corn nuts cannot administer to a mind racked with eternal torment," I wail into my arms.

Dad holds out his hand. "I'll take some."

"Carmen, stick with me, we are going to get through this." Skylar tries to console me, but it is no use. Those are just words. Words which are easy for her to say, because she still has her life.

I am beyond consoling. I close my eyes and tuck my face into my armpit.

Oh, yikes.

That was a terrible idea.

When Mom and Dad first announced that we were moving, a day I marked in black on my calendar and think of only when I listen to my "horror movie" playlist, I went on a bathing fast. Well, first I went on a hunger strike, like Ghandi, but I apparently lack the willpower to do that for long enough to make a difference.

Especially when faced with a cupboard full of Oreos.

Next was the speaking fast. Not like I spoke quickly, that's not what I mean, more like I fasted from speaking. That one went better. I managed five weeks without speaking a single word to either of my parents, but then they tricked me by making an offer I couldn't refuse. Premiere tickets for Skylar and me to go to the first screening of the new DTRJ movie.

They are diabolical.

We went, and I loved it, but then I had to do something else to demonstrate to my parents what this move was doing to me on the inside.

Hence, the bathing fast.

The consequences are putrid.

I try to endure the stench for a few more breaths. Just a few more will make my point I think, but I can't do it. I turn my head to the side and gag.

Where's the Febreze? There's always some around here somewhere, Mom likes the smell of clean linen.

I fumble around the floor, then poke my head under the seats. It isn't there. Now I distinctly remember Mom taking it into the truck stop bathroom with her.

Sigh.

I must speak.

With Herculean effort, I squeeze out the words, "Mother, where did you put the Febreze?"

She hands it back without looking at me. Her and Dad are too busy babbling about a field, and that tree, and, oh look, a bench.

Ugh!

For such intelligent, educated people, my parents are tragically unobservant. Don't they see me deteriorating in their backseat? Don't they even care?

Of course they don't. Why would they? The celebrated team of Terry and Teri just got an obscene amount of money granted to them for research so they could finally leave California and move back to Podunk, USA. Their dream. How could they possibly see through the swirling heart-shaped clouds around their heads to notice how much I suffer?

What about my dreams?

I'm just their only offspring.

What do I matter?

"Maybe you should fast from something else." Skylar watches me administer the Febreze liberally. "Like, maybe you could fast from saying the word 'nugget.' That shouldn't be too hard."

I squirt the Febreze twice more, refusing to look at Skylar, and then resume my position, arms flung overhead, back draped awkwardly over the seat, face tucked into armpit, and then, I force another groan.

"Oh, look!" Dad swerves the car as he points to something out Mom's window. He chuckles as he rights the car. "Did you see that, Carmen?"

I roll my eyes. "You mean, did I see how you almost crashed us into oblivion? Yes, yes I did."

Dad shakes his head. "No sweetheart, I meant, did you see that elk? It was the size of a Buick, standing right on the white line."

"Oh, Terry!" Mom clasps her hands under her chin. "It's been so long since we've seen wildlife."

Skylar laughs in disbelief.

I sit up in order to correct the blatant wrong that we all just experienced. "Whatever, Mother, you have driven through downtown LA at rush hour. You've seen wildlife. Chaos. Like nothing this place has ever seen. If you want wild, you better head back to the city."

"Oh, Carmen." Mom reaches over to rub my arm. "You are so silly. You are going to love this place. I promise."

Well, that's one promise Mom is about to break, because I already decided to loathe this place. Unadulterated loathing. Pure and strong. Seriously, I don't care if Timothee Chalamet has a second home here (he doesn't, I follow him on Instagram), this place is Death Valley to me.

Emphasis on the death.

I aim the screen at my face so Skylar can see the gravity etched there. "I will never love this place."

"Never," she echoes.

"Honey," Mom whispers so low she's almost mouthing the words. "I bet your phone is close to being out of batteries. You've had it on for hours. Why don't you let Skylar go now?"

"Portable charger." I hold it up for her to see. "I made sure it was full so Skylar doesn't miss a moment of this gut-wrenching road trip into the fiery depths of Hades."

"Yeah," Skylar adds. "Though you could have spared me that truck stop bathroom. I'm going to have nightmares for the rest of my life."

Mom sucks in a sharp breath.

"I didn't take her in the bathroom with me, Mother." I roll my eyes. "I just showed her the facility so that she would be able to sympathize with my mortal pain, and then I put her in my purse with the sound muted."

"Thank goodness," Mom says, then covers her mouth part way and tips her head towards me. "But, what I meant is, it would be nice to enjoy the rest of this drive as a family."

"Hint, hint." Dad grins.

I gasp, my hand pressed into my heart. "Skylar is family."

"She is, of course she is, practically our second daughter in every way, but, Carmen, sweetie, you've been on the phone with her since we left Los Angeles. We're almost home now, and this is important to us. I'd like to savor this moment as just our *little* family."

I turn the phone to face me again. "This is not my home and never will be."

"Never," Skylar says.

"Carmen Elizabeth Hurst–" my dad begins, but doesn't get to finish because Skylar interrupts him.

"No, it's cool, I need to finish up this history test anyway."

Mom's eyes widen. "Skylar! Have you been in school all this time you've been on the phone?"

"Yeah," she says, like, duh.

Mom can't even answer because she's too flustered to choose words that make sense.

"I'll call you as soon as we get there." I wave to Skylar.

Dad shakes his head. "We'll be there in about seven minutes, Carmen."

I ignore him. "I'll miss you, good luck on your test, tell Jace I love him."

Mom sighs.

A black and blank phone screen replaces the face of my smiling best friend, the only person who understands how much agony is twisted into the fibers of my being. A sense of loneliness washes over me like a wave of polluted ocean water. It almost steals my ability to breathe in and out.

Only six months, two weeks, and three days until I turn eighteen and can start living my real life again.

Act I Scene II

Dad drives us through a town that time forgot and turns the car around a corner. My parents are practically giddy in their seats, squirming like kittens. He pulls into the driveway of a pathetic hovel, then swivels in his seat so he can see both Mom and me at once.

"This is it! Home!"

Mom sighs, and they kiss. It would be movie magic worthy if it wasn't in front of a ramshackle building, on a tree-lined street, in the middle of who knows where.

And also if it wasn't my super old and super weird parents who were doing it.

I push my door open and stand up.

The scent of horse manure smacks me in the face. Even if I wanted to pretend it was a passing thing, an unfortunate circumstance of something unspeakable residing upwind, I can't do it because of the huge field of rummaging beasts directly across the street.

They are most obviously not temporary.

So, like, this is my forever smell?

Fabulous.

I never thought I would miss the powerful aroma of Caron Poivre or Chanel Grand Extrait, but I do.

More than I can say.

My parents are still occupied, so I trudge up the tulip-lined walkway by myself. I pull out my phone and hit the Facetime app to dial Skylar. Her face appears almost instantly.

"Are you there already?"

"Yes." I turn the screen around so she can see the front of the house.

"What is that thing?"

"Our new abode, apparently."

"It looks like a storage shed," Skylar says, "or a pool house. A really, really crappy pool house that got flooded and left for years."

"You are not making me feel better." I twist my wrist so I can glare at her.

"Sorry, I bet it looks much better on the inside. I'm sure the previous owners spent so much time updating everything else they didn't have time to fix the outside."

Yeah, she wasn't about to hit a jackpot with that bet. The previous owners were my grandparents. My dad's parents to be precise. They lived in this house for a hundred thousand years without upgrading it. I seriously doubted they would do it now that they are retired and pretty much done with the place.

I explain all of this to Skylar in as few words as possible.

"Oh, I don't remember you telling me that. So you already know this house?"

I shrug. "As well as anyone can know a habitation they visited a mere three times in their whole existence."

I only have vague memories. Fuzzy, disjointed memories that don't fit together at the corners. We spent some Christmas holidays here, with Dad's parents, his atrocious younger brothers, and their horrific off-spring. Frankly, those are the kind of childhood memories people spend years burying. It only takes one gassy rendition of Jingle Bells to suck the magic out of Christmas morning, and I can recall more than two.

"Is the door unlocked?" Skylar interrupts my thoughts. "I want to see the inside. I'm sure it's better. It has to be better. It can't possibly be worse."

It is unlocked.

I push the door open and step inside, with instant regret.

"Oh, ew!"

"What?" Skylar asks. She is so lucky technology hasn't invented a smell-o-vision app.

"The house reeks! It's like years' worth of stale socks dipped in eggnog!"

If I thought I was stinky from not bathing, I was grossly deceived. I didn't know what bad really smelled like until this moment. Why did I leave the Febreze in the car?

"Are you serious? That is disgusting!" Skylar favors me with a revolted look, then lets out a horror movie scream. "What's in the corner? Is that a mouse? It's a mouse. I think it's a mouse. It's dead. Carmen, you have to get out of there. Right now!"

I don't stop to think or check if there really is a mouse or if it really is dead. I just whirl around and stomp back to the driveway. My parents have finally extricated themselves from the vehicle and are staring all around with wide-eyed wonder.

Oh, give me a break. Nothing around here is worth looking at that way.

"What's Skylar shrieking about?" Mom stretches her arms over her head.

I fling open the car door and rummage around until my fingers lock on the Febreze. "The house smells like death, and Skylar is pretty sure she saw a decaying mouse in the corner."

"She probably did. Mom and Pop took the cats with them when they moved," Dad says.

"What are you doing?" Mom takes Dad's outstretched hand and they turn toward the house.

"My duty." I hold the Febreze high, like I'm brandishing a sword.

Mom nods. "Okay."

"I can't look." Skylar covers her eyes with both hands. "Tell me when the mouse is gone, I'm turning off the camera."

I tuck my phone in my back pocket and lengthen my stride to reach the front door before my parents do. As much as I detest their life choices, I also love them fiercely and don't think they should have to endure the full frontal assault on their olfactory senses the way I did when I first entered the house of terror.

I push the door open wide and pull the trigger on the Febreze as I walk forward. In especially vile spots, I twirl a circle to cover more area.

Dad starts hacking the moment he steps inside. "That's plenty, Carmen. You can stop now… Stop!" He wrenches the bottle from my hand. "And that isn't a dead mouse in the corner, it's just a pile of dust bunnies."

"Dead bunnies!" Skylar screeches.

Mom plucks my phone out of my pocket. "Sorry, Skylar, Carmen has to go. She will give you a call tomorrow."

"Hey!" I reach for the phone, but Mom already has it zipped away in her purse.

I cross my arms over my belly. "That was cruel and unusual."

"You'll live."

I have my doubts.

The Febreze is already starting to wear off, and Dad hid it from me when I was preoccupied with the phone.

Savage.

I pinch my nose with two fingers, making my voice sound as though I've contracted a nasal cold. "Who's been taking care of this place anyway, now that Grandpa and Grandma are no longer with us?"

"Carmen, please, you make it sound like they've passed away!" Mom stoops to pick up a leaf that blew in the front door.

"They might as well have! Retiring to some weird town fifteen miles away isn't exactly a step up, you know?"

Mom and Dad exchange a look. They have a battle of the eyes for several minutes, then Mom puts her arm around me and steers us toward the hallway.

She apparently lost.

"Why don't we take a look at the rooms, you and me? That sounds fun, yes? You can have whichever one you want."

She makes it sound like I have all the choices in the world, but I know full well there are only three bedrooms in this house. Mom and Dad will get the one with the bathroom attached, and I'll have to settle for Grandma's old sewing room with the lime green carpet or Grandpa's study with the panoramic view of the pig farm behind the house.

However shall I decide?

Mom stops between the two rooms. "Your pick."

I give her a wounded look as I push open the closest door. Into the old study we go.

"Surprise!" Mom claps her hands.

Okay, I was not expecting this. The room is completely redone. Gone is the dark wood paneling that made it look like a cave and the stacks of musty books all over the floor because Grandpa has an aversion to bookshelves.

In their place are white ship-lap walls, pale yellow curtains, a white down comforter, and new beige carpet with flecks of aqua. It's still small and musty, for sure not my bedroom back home, but it's not the worst thing I've ever seen in my life.

"Do you love it?" Mom grabs my arm. "Grandma wanted to be here to see your face, but they have that livestock auction this afternoon. She's been so excited."

I sniff. "I don't totally detest it."

"Well," Mom grins, "I will call that a success." Then she pats my arm and leaves me to inspect the room on my own.

I launch myself onto the mattress to test the springs and stay there longer than I intended because the bed is actually really comfortable. Though, the comforter smells faintly of cow extract. Most likely, Grandma washed it then hung it on the line to dry, and that's where it picked up all the smells. I can only hope it will fade in time.

I reach across the bed for the nightstand drawer handle and tug it open. My intention is to determine if it is big enough to house my journal and screenplay of the week, Shakespeare's Much Ado About Nothing. There's a Bible tucked into the back corner, all new and shiny. I pick it up and roll onto my back, my head half hangs off the bed as I inspect the book. Grandma wrote something on the cover page, but I can't read her loopy cursive, so I toss it back in the drawer and kick it shut with my foot.

I cross the room to the closet and push the sliding doors away from me to reveal the interior. It's narrow and dark, newly painted and clean. More importantly, it's an adequate size for my clothes and costumes.

Now I want to start organizing this space. Not because I accept the situation, but because I miss my stuff and want to liberate it all from the confinement of cardboard boxes. I leave the room behind and hurry to the front of the house to see if the moving van has arrived yet.

It hasn't.

I sit on the concrete step to wait for it. Cold seeps through the back of my jeans like the icy fingers of death and makes goosebumps appear all the way down my forearm. I wrap my arms around my legs and rest my chin on the top of my knees.

"Well, howdy, there."

I shriek and scramble to my feet. My hand automatically goes for my belt loop where I keep the travel-size bottle of pepper spray Skylar bought me for Christmas last year. I yank it free and aim it at the figure walking up the driveway with my finger poised on the button, ready to fire at the barest hint of aggression. "What do you want?"

The person is actually a guy.

A cute guy.

A cute guy that looks like he's my age. He stops walking and holds his hands in the air. "Don't shoot. I'm unarmed. Unless you think Nana's chocolate chip zucchini bread is a weapon." He extends one arm to show me a loaf of bread.

I narrow my eyes. "Why are you bringing that over here?" Not only is it completely disgusting to put a vegetable in bread with chocolate, but it's also the perfect way to disguise poison or some other nefarious substance. Then, once my guard is down, he strikes.

The guy adjusts his baseball cap with one hand.

"Don't move!" I jab the pepper spray toward him, careful not to push the button.

He stops moving. "What d'you have there, anyway? It looks like lip gloss."

"I'll ask the questions around here, cowboy. Now, answer this one. Why are you bringing cucumber bread to our house?"

"Zucchini."

"That's what I said."

"No, actually, you said cucumber. Cucumber and Zucchini are completely different vegetables. They aren't even in the same family."

Now I know he's a nutso. Vegetables don't have families, they're vegetables.

"Enough talking. Listen carefully. You're going to walk backward until you get to the end of the driveway and then go away as fast as you can, or I'll pepper spray your face off."

"Carmen? Why are you yelling?" Mom comes up behind me, but I don't move from my aggressive stance to look at her. "What in the world are you doing?" Her breath tickles my neck.

"Saving your life. You're welcome." I straighten my arms to steady the bottle. I had no idea holding three ounces in front of me could feel so dang heavy after a few minutes. My arm muscles quiver like a minor earthquake.

"Who's this?" Mom puts her hand on my arm, which just makes it that much harder to keep the pepper spray trained on the guy.

"Howdy, ma'am." He tips the brim of his baseball cap like he's a nice, normal person. "Name's Elijah, I go by Eli. Nana sent me over with a loaf of zucchini bread to welcome y'all to the county. Said to tell you she's sorry. She's canning tomatoes or she would have come herself. Now I'm thinking it's a good thing she didn't." He stares at me pointedly.

"For heaven's sake, Carmen, put that pepper spray down. What a way to welcome a guest."

"He's not a guest, Mother," I sputter, leaving my arms where they are. "He's a perpetrator. Why else would he be over here?"

"Like I said, just delivering some bread," Elijah—if that's his real name—says.

Mom smiles at him, then glares at me. "There, you see. I highly doubt this nice young man came all the way over here to rob us blind in the middle of the day. Will you please put that pepper spray away?"

Mom is so naive. We've seen all kinds of atrocities committed in broad daylight in the middle of crowds of people. She's foolish to let her guard down just because she grew up in this town and is all rosy-colored about it. There's nothing to support the false assumption that the city is dangerous and the country is safe. People are still people, in my opinion.

"Carmen Elizabeth Hurst, are you listening to me?" Mom reaches for the pepper spray. "We don't have much in the house yet, but you are welcome to come inside for a glass of water. It was so nice of your Nana to think of us. So hospitable."

You can't just go inviting random people into your house. Has she learned nothing living in LA?

I look at Mom like she's crazy.

Because she is.

And then comes the series of unfortunate events. Totally accidental and completely not my fault.

First, Elijah thanks my mom and steps forward.

Then, Mom tries to wrench the pepper spray out of my Hulk grip.

I hang on tighter to keep her from succeeding.

Dad comes outside to see what's taking Mom so long and startles me so bad my finger presses the button on the pepper spray.

Still aimed at Elijah's face.

A strong breeze kicks up at the same time and...

Can I just say, again, that it wasn't my fault? If Elijah wasn't there in the first place with his pickle bread, nothing would have happened. It just isn't normal to visit your neighbors.

In California, we lived in the same house for almost sixteen years, and I still have no clue who our neighbors were. It makes no sense for someone to stop by and welcome you to a neighborhood with home-baked treats. It's weird. I didn't know people actually baked outside old TV sitcoms from the fifties.

See, not my fault that I am a product of my upbringing. If my parental figures wanted me to be more trusting and stupid, they should have raised me in Mayberry instead of LA.

Mom and Dad escort Elijah, coughing and gagging, into the house to rinse off his face. Well, after Mom confiscated my pepper spray, that is. She reeled back her arm like she was pitching for the Dodgers and flung it over the fence where all the beasts are grazing.

So, basically it's gone forever.

Fare thee well, dear pepper spray. Let not this unfortunate turn of events degrade your value, for you have saved many a poor soul from destruction.

Moment of silence.

Which is interrupted by my mother. She sticks her head out the door. "Do you have your phone?"

"You confiscated it without justifiable cause, remember?"

"Oh, for the love..." Mom pats her pockets, then looks around. "Come get your phone out of my purse and google 'how to get rid of the effects of pepper spray to the face' for me. I have stuff all over my hands. And don't you dare dial Skylar. You are currently in deep doo-doo young lady."

Actually, that would be my pepper spray. Personally, I entered that phase of existence the minute they announced we were moving to this actor-forsaken place.

I roll my eyes and follow her instructions to the letter, like a good robot, then hold the phone out so she can see the results. Mom's eyes scan down the list.

"Water, that didn't work. Okay, here, dish soap. We can do that. Mom left some dish soap under the sink, thank goodness." Her eyes leap from the screen to my face. "I suggest you spend your time out here composing an apology monologue for Eli. That was completely uncalled for behavior, Carmen. I can't believe you. Pick that zucchini bread out of the rose bush and bring it in with you when you're ready."

I shove my phone in my back pocket and stomp to the rose bush in question. It takes me a minute to figure out how to maneuver around the thorny branches. Then I fish the bread out and stare at it. I wasn't planning on eating it before, but there is no way in Prada I would now. Thorns punctured the delicate plastic wrap, leaving holes for dirt to eke through.

Dirt and invisible insects.

Tiny, smelly house. Friendly neighbors. Manure, manure everywhere. And vegetable dirt bread.

I hope my parents are happy with their life choices.

Act I Scene III

FADE IN: INT: BARELY ADEQUATE BEDROOM - LATER THAT DAY

"I can't believe your mom threw the pepper spray away." Skylar runs a brush through her hair for the thirty-fifth time. At least, I think it's the thirty-fifth. I was too busy stewing to keep track. "You might need it."

"Right?"

"I mean, who has ever heard of bringing baked stuff to your door? There could be razors in it."

"Exactly!" I fling my hand at the computer screen.

Her hand pauses over her hair. "Was that forty-three or forty-four?"

"Forty-three," I say even though I have no idea.

"Are you sure you can't get it back?"

"There's no way, Sky, no way. I'd have to crawl around in the mud and unspeakables to search for it. In the dark. It has gone the way of all the earth and is lost forever. I hope my mother can sleep tonight."

"You'd think she'd be more worried about your safety."

"You'd think."

"I mean, you are her only daughter and whatever. Was that fifty?"

"Uh-huh."

Skylar puts the brush down and shakes out her long blonde waves. "Now, tell me about this guy you attacked. Was he hot?"

"I didn't attack him, Skylar, it was an accident." I roll my eyes. "And how could he be hot? He lives in Podunk County."

"That doesn't matter." Skylar leans forward and rests her chin on her hands. "Lots of hot celebs live in small towns. Justin Timberlake moved his family to Montana, remember? And Elijah Wood lives somewhere in Texas, or something, I think. And Tom Hanks has a home in Idaho."

That was, like, three people out of a bazillion. And I don't think some of those small town rumors are true, anyway. Probably tabloid fodder. I've never even heard of a place called Idaho. That sounds fake.

"How could I notice another guy, even if he is hot? My heart resides solely in the hands of Jace, and no other, remember that?" I toss my head.

Skylar holds up her hands in defense. "I was trying to find a bright side for you. It's just so tragic you have to spend your senior year in exile."

"I know."

"And the timing? It's just irresponsible parenting to make you move at the start of your senior year of high school. This is supposed to be the best year of your life."

"I *know*."

"And, what is Drama Club going to do without you? Did your parents think of that? We're putting on Wicked and you already had the part of Glinda. There's no one else with the pipes, and we all know Betsy is going to try for it now."

"Okay, stop talking." I rub my temples to keep the headache and the depression from spreading.

"I'm sorry, I really am trying to help."

"I know." I sigh.

After a short silence, Skylar gets fidgety. "Yeah, so, when does school start?"

I sigh and slump down, making the computer screen wobble precariously on my knees. It was really too bad the moving guys drove to the wrong address, or I would have Skylar placed sturdily on my vintage accounting desk Dad bought at auction from Warner Brothers Studio. Those neanderthals took a left instead of the required right at the old fencepost and ended up in the next county.

"School started here over a week ago." I tap the bedspread with my fingers, pinkie to thumb, then back again. "And my mother and father think it's a good idea for me to start on a Thursday even though it is at the hind end of the worst week of my entire life and it would be infinitely more humane to wait until Monday when I've had the weekend to recover from my emotional trauma." I gulp in more air so I can continue. "And even though the only clothes I have are what I could fit in my backpack. I ask you, how am I supposed to make the lasting first impression required of me with so few apparel options?"

Skylar lets out several sympathetic noises. "Does this guy you met... What was his name?"

"Elijah."

"Does Elijah go to your school?"

"Everyone goes to my school, Skylar. There is only one school. There are a grand total of eighty-five students in my new graduating class. Remember, the high school encompasses *four* towns and can still only come up with eighty-five seventeen and eighteen-year-olds to fill it."

I couldn't forget that, though I definitely tried. It haunted my waking dreams. I didn't know what to do in a school that didn't crush me into a mosh pit on the way to each class or have to divide into three proms because there wasn't a venue big enough to host the entire school.

I really have to stop comparing everything to LA, or I'm going to drown in a swift river of regret, completely swept away by rapids of despair.

"I don't know what to say, Carmen. I just feel so sorry for you, I can't even."

Yeah, me too.

I feel sorry for me too.

This would be the best moment for a pity party. I could throw a fantastic one with a disco ball and confetti that Skylar would be talking about for weeks. I would have done it, too, except for that river and rapids thing.

"Tell me, dearest friend,"—I look into the distance—"how do you make the best of a terrible situation? One in which the whole of your being hangs on the edge of a knife. But one breath and it will fall."

"Well..." Skylar looks at the ceiling for inspiration. "I suppose I would start by picking out a fantastic outfit."

Brilliant!

Except for, oh yeah, the direction-challenged movers thing.

"I bet we could figure something out with what you have there." Skylar leans back. "You have great clothes. Even your lamest stuff has got to be light-years better than what those townspeople will be wearing. Let's do a fashion show. You know that always makes you feel better."

"But, all I have with me is black. I have been in mourning for the passing of my perfect life."

"Black is way chic. Timeless. Go get your clothes, I want to see what we can come up with."

I resist for a little longer, then I give in. Skylar is right. Trying on outfits does make me feel better. As I hold up tops and bottoms for Skylar to approve, an idea comes to me like a whole team of lighting artists just infiltrated my brain.

A purpose.

A mission, if you will.

At this new school, yes, in this new town, I have an opportunity to bring some culture and life to their poor, dreary, backwoods world.

Not only is this thought true, because I feel it in the marrow of my bones, but the thought dissolves a portion of my despair. What is an actor without motivation? A cutout, that's what. With a sense of purpose, I might survive the rest of this school year.

Absolute truth.

My mind expands with wonder. Maybe I'm not tossed to and fro by the sadistic winds of karma. Maybe everything truly does happen for a reason. It is possible that I have come to this dreary part of the world for a reason. Perhaps here I can do my own small part to uplift the lives of those who have so little to live for. This could be my chance, the one I've been waiting for all my life.

The chance to make a difference in the world.

"That's it." Skylar claps her hands. "The perfect outfit!"

I walk over to the warped mirror hanging on one of the closet doors and take a look for myself. A short sleeve, mock-neck sweater hugs all the right places and the full black circle skirt makes my waist look even smaller.

"What shoes?" I put off the moment I tell her she is a fashion goddess. She's already borderline conceited as it is.

"What do you have?"

"Rhinestone sneakers and knee-high black heeled boots."

Skylar laughs. "Then I can't believe you even asked."

I pull the boots out of my bag and zip them into place. "Yes?"

"Yes!"

I spin around to inspect from the back. "Tights?"

"You don't need them with those boots."

I smooth the front of the sweater and nod. "Alright, I agree. This outfit is slightly above mediocre."

"Are you kidding me, it's fantastic! Those small-town peeps don't even know. They are so totally about to be Carmen'd."

Carmen'd.

I really like the sound of that.

ACT I SCENE IV

I might look utterly fantastic as I walk through the doors of Hillbilly High School, home of the Beetdiggers, but I am in an atrocious mood.

And my feet hurt.

My mom made me walk to school this morning.

Walk.

She said the fresh air would be good for me. She even said I should hoof it over to Elijah's house and see if he wanted to walk with me. Hoof it. Like that was a real thing. Like people actually walk places in real life. If that were true, there wouldn't be such thriving taxi cab enterprises.

Skylar tried to call a ride for me. Unfortunately, google came back with no listings for taxi cabs. Not for seventy-five miles. Next she tried Uber and same thing.

This is the place which has been forsaken by Uber.

What planet did I just land on?

So, yeah, I had to walk.

All the way to school.

In the mud.

And other things that look like mud but smell entirely different.

Because someone thought it was a good idea to refrain from building a sidewalk on this street.

To recap: I walked two whole blocks to a grimy high school that is way older than my grandparents, in super high heels, while Skylar read to me from her mother's latest motivational self-help book to keep me from flipping out.

It was horrifying.

Now I just want to find a fluffy Anthropologie couch to rest my weary bones.

Also, some lemonade.

Preferably with crushed ice and an umbrella.

I lean down to inspect the caked mud and stuff on my boots. It's going to take so much effort to get all that crap off. Where can I find like five tubs of Clorox wipes?

And possibly a power hose.

"Oh, that is so bad. Your poor boots!" Skylar makes an expressive pout in solidarity to my own. "Hold on, I'm going to put on some Enya."

I'm not ready to admit defeat just yet. "Hold your Spotify, Sky, I just need to find a peaceful and quiet place where I can assess the damage before we begin mourning."

"Do you know where the facility is?" Skylar asks.

"No, I've never been in this building." I blow a strand of hair out of my eyes.

"Ask someone, look, there's a person."

I peek through strands of hair that immediately fall back over my face and see a figure.

"Excuse me?" I grab the arm of the person as they walk by. "Can you point me in the direction of the nearest facility?"

A short girl with blonde hair stares at my hand on her arm, then blinks a couple of times. She has so many freckles it looks like someone took a generous handful and splattered them all over her face.

Poor child.

"The what?"

I speak slower. "The bathroom facility."

"Be a pal," Skylar adds.

The girl glances at my phone in confusion, then shrugs and points. "Oh, yeah, it's right over there. Next to the office."

Perfect, because the office is the very place I need to go after I take care of my caked footwear. I shoo the girl away and flounce to the bathroom door.

"Turn the phone so I can look around. Oh, yikes! Who picked this color theme? It's like Bad Design by Martha Stewart. But let's look on the bright side. How are the acoustics?" Skylar presses her nose against the screen like that will help her experience the full range of the facility.

I smile because I can never resist the opportunity to test the acoustics. There isn't another moment to waste, so I burst out with a power ballad from Wicked while I clean my boots with a cheap paper towel. Skylar joins in on the chorus. The notes surround me, buoying me up, filling me with confidence.

I can do this. I can conquer this school. In LA I was one in a billion; here I could be number one.

"The facility is bright, ugly, and not nearly as fancy as the one here," Skylar says when the song is finished, "but the sound system is way better. Spot on. I think you've found your place to run lines and practice songs for whatever play your lame new school decides to put on. That's something! Maybe this year won't totally suck for you."

"Maybe not." It was way too soon to tell.

A stall door creaks open.

Either the school is haunted, or I'm not as alone as I thought.

"Hello? Who's there?" I hold my phone out like a gun and start to clear the stalls.

"I don't see anyone," Skylar says.

I don't either, but when I push the last stall door open with my palm, there is a small yelp that confirms appearances can be deceiving.

A girl steps out from behind the door, clutching four enormous books to her chest. She sweeps a lock of hair off her forehead and tries to tuck it behind her ear, but it really wants to be in her eyes.

"What are you doing behind that door?" Skylar bellows. I take a step back so the girl can emerge fully. "Were you—*gasp*—spying on us? Who are you and who do you work for?"

The girl's eyes dart from me to Skylar's face on the phone. It is obvious she is too overcome to speak.

"I'll handle this," I tell Skylar.

"Okay, but call me as soon as you're done and tell me everything. Also, do you think I should wear my espadrilles with this skirt?"

"Absolutely." I smile at her and then disconnect the call and put my phone away so I can give the girl my full attention. "*Were* you maliciously spying on me?"

I'm not as upset as Skylar was. No, I wouldn't blame the poor girl for spying. Elijah probably told everyone all about me, and now they are dying to see for themselves. Oscar knows there is precious little else to inspire excitement around these parts.

"N-no." She shakes her head. "I was using the bathroom when you came in and started singing. I didn't want to interrupt." Her voice is so faint I have to really concentrate to hear what she says. Obviously, no one has ever instructed her in the art of diaphragm projection. Her sound is all caught up in her larynx.

"Your voice is so pretty."

"I know, right?" I turn away from her to fluff my hair. "Next time, say something so I know you're in here. I prefer to know when I have an audience."

"O-okay." She nods but doesn't move. I can still see her reflection staring at me in the mirror.

The poor girl is star-struck, obviously. She's used to mediocre people milling around the school in clearance rack jeans and faded t-shirts like the one she's wearing.

I turn around, my face arranged in abject sympathy. "What's your name, honey?"

"Beth," she whispers.

"Beth, do you want me to sign your backpack?"

"What?" she takes a step backward.

"Well, you're just standing there, I figured you were working up the courage to ask for my autograph. You're not the first one." I reach to pat her head, but she ducks out of the way before my hand makes contact. "It happens all the time. Once, my bestie, Skylar, and I were stalking Chris Pratt outside the CrossFit in North Hollywood. It's a gym."

I better explain because the poor dear looks completely lost.

"You know, a gym, where people go to lift weights and get into shape? Anyway, it was a complete waste of our time because he doesn't even use that particular CrossFit gym anymore. People were bugging him so much he couldn't get his workouts done so he decked out his house with a sick home gym with a big screen TV." I wave my hand through the air. "You wouldn't believe how intrusive fans can be. They just don't give celebrities room to breathe! It's so sad, really. And then there's the paparazzi. Let's not talk about them though, horrors! Anyway I don't blame him a bit for staying in. It's obviously done his body good." I laugh, but Beth doesn't join me, so it falls flat. "Anyway, what was I saying?"

Beth shrugs one shoulder.

"Never mind, I remember, Skylar and I were stalking him at the CrossFit, and this ancient old woman who was like thirty-five, asked for my autograph, she thought I was Brighton Sharbino. Can you believe it?"

Beth stares at me blankly.

"Brighton Sharbino?"

She shakes her head.

"She was on The Walking Dead?"

More head shaking.

"Whatever." I brush a strand of hair away from my face. "The point is, I totally get it. You're in awe. Totally understandable, you have nothing to be embarrassed about."

"O-okay." Beth takes another step back. "I-I need to go to class now."

Of course, she does. That is obviously a lame excuse to cover up her over stimulation. It is not comfortable for most people to be exposed to this much amazingness all at once. Poor, poor child. All the signs are there, shifting from side to side, not meeting my eyes, stuttering. I really hope this doesn't happen all day. How am I supposed to get an education if all the students and staff are struck dumb when I'm in the room?

"Fine, go." I wave my fingers at her and turn back to the mirror to check my eyeliner. I did dramatic cat eyes this morning to deemphasize the dark circles my parents caused with their permanent change of venue.

Well, permanent for them, not so much for me. As soon as I've reached adulthood and saved these backward people from their dreary lives, I am so out of here.

The eyeliner lines are still crisp so I don't need any touch-up there. I pull out Midnightmare black lipstick and run it over my lips. There's no telling when I'll have another opportunity to check my appearance. This is insurance. While in mourning it is imperative that my lips stay black to sustain the proper tone.

When I turn back around, the girl—what was her name? Becky?—is still standing there staring at me.

I heave a deep sigh. "I thought you left."

Didn't I explain to her that I really don't have time for fans right now? I need to find my classes and familiarize myself with the high school culture in this pathetic little town.

Oh, that is funny. I am so funny!

Culture? Here?

I don't know what I was thinking.

"I-I was going to, and then I realized you're new, obviously, and you probably need some help finding your classes?"

A likely story. An excuse to hang around me longer and glean off my fame. I've seen this a million times. There was that ridiculous girl back at home who bribed our driver, Skylar's older brother, to find out what I was going to wear to school. Then she wore the exact same thing. It was such a hassle. I had to take extra clothes and change at the last minute every single day.

Though, on closer inspection, this Betty girl isn't very much like the usual wannabe fame seeker. Maybe she really is just trying to help.

That is sooooooo precious.

"Well, I don't know what my classes are, presently. The parental units didn't think it was a worthy enough cause to get my schedule printed ahead of time. I know where the office is though, just next door." I toss my head.

"Yeah, I mean, yes, it is right next door."

"So, thank you and stuff, but I'm good. I know where I'm going and what to do next. You take care now."

I pat her head before she can scoot away, and push open the bathroom door. Next stop, the office, where I might obtain my schedule and zone out during the inevitable dull lecture on the school handbook which will most definitely follow.

Ugh.

The office is uninspiring. Faded wallpaper, ancient furniture, ragged carpet. How do the staff sit in this place all day and not sink into despair? A velvet curtain and some twinkle lights would go a long way is all I'm saying.

The secretary is nice enough but could use a serious pore reduction treatment. When I offer her this crucial piece of advice, she loses her train of thought and just stares at me.

This seems to be a common trend with the people I've encountered this morning. Maybe there's something in the water that makes these people's brains stall. I eye the closest drinking fountain with suspicion and make a mental note to avoid it, and all others like it, at all costs.

On the other hand, that sounds like the perfect excuse to get the parental units to have bottled water imported from California. My parents are scientists, they can't afford to have their brains stall.

"My schedule?" I hold out my hand and wait for the secretary to place the piece of paper in my palm, then I bring it to my eyes.

I can see fine. I don't need glasses. I just prefer to hold paper extremely close to my face for personal reasons.

"Language Arts, Algebra, Physics, no, no, no, no." I hand the schedule back. "I absolutely cannot take physics, it stifles my creativity. Surely, you must know that?"

"No, I wasn't aware." The secretary folds her hands over one another on the desk. "But I do know that your transcript shows that you are one credit shy of the requirements for science."

I reach for her hand and cradle it between my own. "Miss, secretary, lady of the haloed institution of Hillbilly High, you can't possibly know that my parents are celebrated physicists, but—"

"Actually, I went to school with your mom. We were on the debate team together."

Debate team. Oh-my-snore!

"Then you know what I suffer! My childhood has been a veritable whirlwind of science vocabulary. I made a baking soda volcano when I was but a small, innocent child of four. My parents gave me a microscope and rock samples to play with instead of Barbies and Littlest Pet Shop figurines. Haven't I languished enough in the realm of science? My childhood was sacrificed on its altar. You couldn't thrust me into its clutches once more. No, I know you couldn't, you dear, sympathetic creature."

She pulls her hand out from under mine. "Your choices are physics or geology."

So much for sympathy. So much for compassion. So much for humanity.

Apparently, my heart-rending monologue was lost on this secretary with crater-like pores. "Fine, I'll take physics. Let that weigh like a super fatty fat elephant on your conscience."

The secretary eyes me over her glasses and then turns to the computer. "Are there any other problems with your schedule?"

I scan through it once more. Now that my faith in her willingness to help me construct a schedule of classes best fit for my temperament is dashed to pieces that are blowing away from the rotating fan in the corner, I want to make sure I can bear with everything else before I leave her presence forever. When I vacate this office of stale coffee and beige walls, I plan to do so and never return.

Language Arts, whatever, it's a necessary evil.

Algebra, I'll take it, though math and I do not coincide in the same social class.

Physics, bleh.

Lunch period, acceptable.

American Heritage, another instrument of torture, I assume.

Spanish IV, which I already took, but barely passed so it stays.

Speech and debate, ugh. Boring and boring.

If I accept this schedule, I might shrivel up and perish from utter ennui. There is no outlet, no release, no freedom, no expression. The semester stretches before me now like a barren wasteland of rolling sand dunes and the occasional wandering scorpion.

"Pardon me?"

"Yes?" the secretary answers but doesn't deign to give me her attention. It is glued to her computer screen.

"Speech and debate is an elective, yes?"

"Correct."

"Then, can I see a list of other electives? I'd rather not speech, or debate, for that matter."

"Your choices are speech and debate, art, PE, and agriculture."

I wait for her to go on even though it becomes clear that she has already exhausted the list of electives.

Surely not!

"That's all?"

"Yep."

"Those are the only choices?"

"Yep."

"There's really nothing else?"

"Nope."

"No journalism? No woods? No psychology? No philosophy? No creative writing? No pottery? No choir? No orchestra? No band? No JROTC? No foods or home economics? No graphic design? No computer programing?"

I pause to take a shuddering breath. "No theater?"

The secretary sighs as she removes her glasses and wipes them on her shirt. "This is a very small school."

Like I hadn't noticed that. But, she didn't actually answer my question.

"Madam, please, is there a theater program in this school? A drama club? An improv troupe? Anything?"

She actually looks sympathetic as she replaces her glasses on the end of her nose. The expression does wonders for her complexion. "The closest would be speech and debate, Carmen. Which elective would you like?"

I know she says words. I hear them leave her mouth, but somewhere in the air between her and me, they scramble into a mass of unrecognizable goo.

"Carmen?"

My head has disconnected from my body. Somehow I rise to my feet. The secretary calls my name again, but I don't turn around.

I need air.

I stumble out of the office, grateful in my soul that the halls are mostly vacant of Hillbillies, as I am now quite desperate to be outside. I use both hands to push the heavy front doors open. A fresh breeze picks up my hair and blows it into a tangled mess above my head.

No theater program.

No drama club.

Not even an improv troupe.

I fall to my knees, both hands stretching toward the sky, tingling from nail to shoulder in agony. I open my mouth and wail.

"Whyyyyyyyyyyyyyyyyyyyyyyyyyyyyyyyyyyyyyyyyyyyyyyyyyyy?"

Act I Scene V

FADE IN: EXT & INT: MORE HILLBILLY HIGH SCHOOL – YIPPEE-KI-AY

Footsteps come toward me, but I refuse to move from my position of utter despair. When I ran out of air after emoting all my pain into the atmosphere, I collapsed on the steps with my limbs sprawled around me like a starfish. I don't even peek my eyes open when the footsteps stop near my head. I have lost all zest for life. I only breathe in and out because it's an ingrained habit after all these years and my body can do it automatically. Even when it has been crushed by the weight of disappointment.

"Carmen?"

"Bro, is that the girl who pepper sprayed you in your face?"

"What's she doing?"

"Is she dead? 'Cause, dude, it looks like King Kong just dropped her off the roof of the school."

"Should I, maybe, go get the nurse, or...something?"

So many voices! Ugh! Don't they know their questions and hillbilly accents are destroying my vibe of infinite sorrow? A tangy scent that reminds me of horses wafts across my face. A hand lands on my shoulder and shakes me gently. "Carmen, it's Eli, are you alright?"

I groan and fling an arm over my face.

"So she ain't dead," one of the other voices announces. This guy's voice is much deeper than Elijah's and way more hick-ish. "I really thought she was dead as a door jamb."

"When she's ready to move, we'll need to rotate her so the blood can circulate normally before she tries to stand up. If she's been laying that way for more than a couple seconds she'll pass out when she rights herself."

"Good thinking, Professor."

"Carmen, can you hear me? Answer if you can hear me."

I wish he would take his Round-up Gang and get their Wrangler-wearing behinds away from me so I can wither into the concrete on my own time.

Another shoulder shake. "Carmen!"

I push him away. "I'm awake, you heathen. Leave me in peace."

Elijah lets out a long breath. "Did you fall down the steps? Are you hurt? Can you move your legs?"

Apparently, he doesn't understand the finer points of leaving me alone. I open my eyes to explain it to him in greater detail, and instantly regret it. I forgot about that villain, the sun. It bears down on my face like a relentless, charging foe. I have to squint and squeeze my eyes shut multiple times before I can see without my eyes watering excessively. People such as myself were not meant for the outdoors.

I glare at Elijah, who is crouched on the step below me, and pull my torso against gravity to reach a sitting position. The world swirls around me and my head floats toward the clouds.

"I warned you." A twerpy guy with enormous glasses puts his hand on the top of my head and has the audacity to push it downwards. "Tuck your head between your knees and take deep breaths so you don't pass out."

"I never pass out." I wince as darkness creeps into the corners of my eyes, blurring my peripheral vision. "Nor do I faint. Not unless I am playing the part of a damsel in distress who must do so from a place of overwhelming fear. Fear or heartbreak, one of those." I press my fingertips to my temples and concentrate on rubbing small circles until my vision clears.

"Take deep breaths, it will help." Twerp pats my head in a very degrading way.

Just who does he think he is, anyway?

I do what he says, but do my best to make it look like that was my plan all along. I don't want him to think he can just tell me to do something and I'll do it. That has horrible, lifelong ramifications.

After a few moments, the fuzziness clears completely and I feel normal again. Normal enough to remember that there is no drama club or theater program in this school. That almost sends me into hysterics once more.

"Elijah." I whip around to face him, dragging Twerp with me. His hand is still on my head. He loses his balance and plops onto the concrete step beside me.

The other guy, a burly cretin that looks like he spends more time lifting weights than thinking, bursts out laughing. He even stoops over and slaps his knee. It's such an obvious caricature it raises all my hackles.

Amateur.

Though, I suppose that makes sense since there is no proper program in this wretched town to train him on the arts of acting a part. He's forced to become the same version of backwoods weirdo as all his ancestors before him.

I'm sad for him, really. But not as sad as I am for me.

"Elijah!"

He backs away, his eyes wide. "Yeah?"

I scoot across the step and grab his arm to pull myself into a standing position. I wobble for just a moment before the world steadies itself and all is well. "Did you know there is no theater program at this school?"

He swings his arm out of my grip and brushes hair off his forehead. "Uh, yeah. I guess."

"What's a theater program?" the Neanderthal snorts in a really bad English accent "So fancy."

"You knew this school lacked the one thing I live for and you didn't tell me?" I push by Elijah and glide to the stair railing, a good actor always makes use of whatever props the scenery provides. I drape myself over the rail dramatically. "How could you be so thoughtless? So cruel?

"Yes, how could you, Eli, you beast?" Neanderthal nudges Elijah. "Dude, this chick is three donuts shy of a baker's dozen."

"So, she's ten donuts?" Twerp looks confused.

"Sure, whatever."

"Carmen." Elijah extends a hand toward me. "School is starting. You really need to go inside. I'd be happy to walk you to your first class if you don't know where it is."

"I'd be happy to leave her on the stair rail and pretend like we never saw her." Neanderthal adjusts his backpack and looks toward the school. "The late bell's about to ring and I got one too many tardies already."

"Go if you need to," Elijah tells him. "I'll just help her out and then be right there. Will you tell Mr. Blake why I'm late?"

"Sure, dude. Don't know why you're helping her. She's a few clowns short of a freak show, too, you know?" Neanderthal smirks and leaves, taking with him ridiculous levels of testosterone and the essence of whey protein.

"I can stick around." Twerp stands next to Elijah with a worried look on his face. "Do you have your schedule yet?" he asks me.

I sit up and glare at the two of them. Really, this obsession with school and class schedules when my artistic world has shattered at my feet is just unbearable. "No, I do not have my schedule. I went to that place"—I jab a thumb at the school—"to get my schedule and discovered, to my horror, that this school is without a proper theater program. Actually, without any theater program at all. It was the one thing I was counting on to bolster my sunken spirits. How am I supposed to survive the multitude of months until graduation without a theater program? How, I ask you, how?"

Twerp looks at Elijah with raised eyebrows. "I am unsure how to answer those questions."

"Yeah." Elijah adjusts the brim of his baseball cap. "If you want to go, you can. I sort of feel responsible for her, since she lives on my street and all. I don't want you to be late for class, and I don't think this is getting resolved anytime soon."

"It's alright. I have office aide first period. I think they will understand. I'll stay and help."

"Thanks, man." Elijah slaps the twerp's shoulder and they share a manly moment of solidarity while I languish on the railing, which is terribly uncomfortable. I would resign myself to such hardships to follow my muse, but neither Elijah nor the twerp seem to notice or care about the weight I bear under the pain of discovery. They have missed every single one of my cues.

They are both a terrible audience.

Elijah turns his attention back to me and squints his eyes into a thousand wrinkles. "Do you want me to call your mom for you? Maybe you need some, um, support or something?"

Wait a second.

I slide off the railing and jab a finger into Elijah's chest. "Are you fraternizing with my mother?"

"Excuse me?"

It was a simple question. "How do you have my maternal parent's phone number?"

"She, uh, gave it to me."

"When?" I was around the entire time Elijah was at our house, and I don't remember a chummy exchange of the phone numbers.

"After we got the pepper spray out of my eyes. She wanted me to call and let them know I didn't go blind."

I cross my arms. "Is that so?" I hold Elijah in the steel trappings of my most penetrating stare.

"Yeah." Elijah rubs the back of his neck.

Ha!

I knew it!

He's lying his butt off.

"You better tell her, Eli, she already knows," Twerp the wise advises.

Elijah sighs and shifts his weight from one foot to the other. "And, also, your mom and dad asked me to keep an eye out for you. They gave me your mom's cell number in case you had any trouble, or, uh, did anything..."

"Dramatic," Twerp supplies.

Dramatic? So, if I react in a way that illustrates my passionate nature, I'm dramatic now?

That's just—

That's—

That's just.

Ugh!

"Here." Elijah pulls out his cell phone. "Let's call your mom real quick. I think you'll feel better if you talk to her about your, you know, whatever is going on for you."

I glare at him as I snatch the phone out of his hand. He already has my mother's number on his screen and ready to go. I push the call button and bring the phone to my ear.

"Hello?"

"There is no theater program!" I shriek into the phone. "You have consigned your only child to a life of deprivation. How could you relocate to a place like this? How am I supposed to survive here? You might as well move us to outer space without oxygen. If I live through this, which I highly doubt is even possible, I will never thank you or Dad at the academy awards. Never. I hope you're happy." I thrust the phone at Elijah's chest and stomp up the stairs.

"Where are you going, Carmen? She's, I don't, sorry, yeah..."

I ignore all of the chatter around me as I swing open the school doors. Elijah can use his last breath to smooth things over with my mother, I don't care. They have both wounded me mortally, equally, but in different ways. I curse them to a life of MASH reruns.

I stomp to the front office and plop down in the chair I vacated earlier. The secretary moves slowly, like she's covered in sticky tack, to face me. "You're back."

"Yes, I'm back, to withdraw myself from this institution of haunted dreams."

"To...what?"

I speak very slowly. "To withdraw from school."

"Really?"

I nod and fold my hands in my lap.

"Well,"—the secretary turns her swirly chair so she can face me all the way—"as you are not eighteen yet, you can't actually withdraw yourself from school. You need an adult to do it."

"Fabulous, you can go ahead and withdraw me. I give you my permission."

She stares at me for a minute, then reaches for the phone that's been blinking since I sat down. "Front office. Yes, that's correct... No problem... Bye." She replaces the receiver and blinks at me some more. "I meant that your parents will need to do it. Your guardians."

"That's not possible." I shake my head. "My parents are incapacitated at the moment."

"Meaning?"

"Meaning they are so obsessed with their own dreams, they have completely disregarded my own. Their lack of compassion incapacitates them as parents and/or guardians. They are no longer fit for the title. We are at odds."

"Okay." The secretary glances back at her computer screen with longing. I bet she's playing Bejeweled over there where no one can see. If she's more concerned with beating her high score, then *she's* also unfit for the title of school secretary. She should care more about my dilemma than whatever else she has going on. After all, I am the rising generation. I am the future.

"Look, it's plain that you need to talk some things out. We are currently between school counselors, so we can give your parents a call. I've been meaning to phone Teri anyway. I want to welcome her back to town."

That is a contradiction if I've ever heard one, that's like welcoming someone to Dracula's Castle, The Haunted Mansion, or Sleepy Hollow. Welcome to the most horrifying experience you can imagine.

"I am no longer on speaking terms with said Teri." I lift my chin and turn slightly so my regal profile is in full view, not to mention my classic nose. "Terry, either, for that matter."

The secretary taps her fingers on the dented and dinged desktop. It has clearly seen a lot of ill treatment in its days. The antiquated desk is a metaphor for what my soul has been through the last three months. "I'm not sure how to help you, Carmen. Clearly, you're upset—"

I snort. "That is the biggest understatement of all time."

"Well, be that as it may, I don't have someone here who is certified to help you work through this, uh—"

"One-fifth of my life crises," I interrupt, since she is clearly lacking the correct words to describe this tragic scenario.

"Right, that. Tell you what, let me finish this email and I can lend you my ear for as long as you need to process your emotions and get to class. Does that work?"

That is a poor man's solution to a life-altering dilemma if I've ever heard one. "Is that my only option?"

"Well, no, you can obviously call your parents and work this out, or you can go to class now. Your schedule is right there, waiting for you." She nods at the corner of her desk where a lone piece of paper sits, all filled with soul crushing classes.

"I don't like any of those options." I sniff. "And I don't—"

"Carmen?" I hear Elijah before I turn to look at him. "Oh, hey, Ms. Karlmonger."

The secretary nods.

I clear my throat so he will put his attention back on me.

"Hey, so, I just got off the phone with Carmen's mom and she said to remind Carmen they had a deal."

"What deal is this?" Ms. Karl-whatever fixes her gaze on me.

I shrug.

She can't make me answer that. Not if she hung me from the stained ceiling by my expensive boots and used me as a piñata for the kinder-garteners. I'll never acquiesce.

"Carmen's mom said to remind Carmen that she agreed to finish out high school here"–Elijah pauses and shifts his weight—"without making a scene..."

I let out a huff of air.

Make a scene indeed. Is it making a scene to have emotions? What am I, an automaton? Am I just supposed to be okay with all this?

"And then her parents will pay for her to go back to California after graduation and pursue her acting career."

"I see." Ms. Karl-something taps her fingers some more. "Is this true?"

I avoid her gaze by picking at a thread on my black circle skirt.

"Hm," she says, then looks at Elijah. "You may go to class, Eli. Take a slip so the teacher excuses you."

"What about her?"

"She'll be along in a minute."

Eli is obviously at war. Both sides of his goody-two-shoes are vying for his allegiance. Which will he choose? To obey the almighty school secretary, or keep his commitment to my mother? Oh, the suspense is as thick as gelatin.

"So, I, uh, I told her mom I'd help her find classes and stuff. Is it alright if I wait outside so I can do what I said?"

"That's fine. Carmen will be out in a moment."

And, yes, Carmen just loves it when people talk over her head like she isn't right there, sitting in the room, wallowing in the quicksand of despair.

Eli leaves and closes the door behind him. I can see his distorted image through the wavy glass window checking his phone while he waits.

What a Boy Scout.

Ms. Karl-what-what folds her hands on the desk and leans forward. "Carmen, I understand you. I moved around a lot as a kid. It's tough starting at a new school. I'll give you a bit of advice I wish someone had told me when I was your age. When you fight against reality, you lose every time. Put in your time, make it work, and then go live your dream, okay? This situation is what it is. You can't change it. You'll just make yourself miserable trying."

"What if I'm going to be miserable no matter what? Because this place is misery to me?"

"Well, that's your choice then."

None of this was my choice!

"So"—I narrow my eyes—"You just want me to give up?"

"Not give up, give in."

"I don't follow."

"Like I said, make it work, fake it until you make it if you have to. You're an actress, aren't you?" The challenge in her voice makes the hair on the back of my neck stand straight up.

She might be wrong about a lot of things, her skincare routine for one, her clothing choices, for another, but she is right about that one thing. I am an actress. An amazing actress. She has no idea how awesomely I can pretend like this isn't the worst experience of my life.

I am that good.

I tap my fingers against my leg and study the mind numbing beige walls.

Alright, Mother.

If I have to play your game to get what I want, then I will do it.

I will pretend I can tolerate Hillbilly High School. I will suffer through the hay, the plaid, and the "aints", and then I will leave it all in the dust the instant that diploma is in my hand.

Back to LA before anyone in this town can tip a cow.

Done and done.

Act II Scene I

Elijah shows me the way to my first class, language arts, where I endure forty-five minutes of listening to the English language being tortured into unrecognizable garble. Then he appears outside the door to show me to my next class.

"I'm sure my parents don't expect you to babysit me all day. You know, I am perfectly capable of finding"—I peer at the sheet of paper in my hand—"algebra on my own."

"Of course you are." Elijah grabs my elbow and yanks me in the opposite direction. "The math hall is this way."

I follow him around a corner and up a ramp to the brightly painted math hall. Primary colors assault my eyeballs at every glance.

They are way too excited about their math, I think.

Personally, I think math should be optional. It's all well and good for those mindless masses who go to college and get a job, but it's completely pointless for someone like me. When I'm a famous actress, I'll have agents to manage all that noise for me. I don't need to learn why letters think they belong in equations with numbers.

Elijah walks into a classroom and then stops to wait for me to catch up. "This is it. Your teacher is Ms. Buckley." Instead of leaving, he trots over to a desk near the window and sits down in front of the Twerp.

Oh, that's fan-flipping-tastic. I have a class with Elijah, the Babysitter Boy Scout Super Suck-up. Just what I always wanted. I flounce to a desk on the opposite side of the room and plop into the chair.

Someone clears their throat with an exaggerated *ahem*. And just like that, my theater training kicks in. This is the classic call for attention. I turn around to face the girl who stalked me in the bathroom earlier.

Bonnie or Bernice or something.

She whispers words I can't hear over the din of moving chairs and the thump of books.

"What did you say?" I lend her my ear.

She glances in both directions. It is such a sus gesture, I have to wonder what part we are playing now. The tone is that of a spy film, but the chintzy number charts on the walls look like they came from the dollar store and totally wreck the mystique. Especially that one with an owl that insists "Numbers are fun!"

Such blatant lies are totally pulling me out of the scene.

"Hi, sorry, I'm Beth. We met earlier, remember?" She covers part of her mouth with her hand. "You might want to move before—"

"Oh, naw!"

"Too late," Beth whispers, her eyes widen so that the pupils and color almost disappear, leaving so much white.

Standing above me is the biggest wannabe I have ever seen, and I'm from LA, the wannabe capital of the world. I know exactly what part this girl has been cast. With that too-blonde hair and too-perfect ponytail, too-pink lipstick, and too-tight Walmart jeans.

This is the popular girl, the queen of the school. Standing over me with her hip jutted out to the side and her arms folded like she expects me to kiss her unmanicured toes.

Well, joke's on her.

I bow to no one.

"Oh, hello." I smile at her.

"Naw." She snaps her fingers. "This is my seat. See here?" The wave of an arm takes my eyes to the chiseled name on the top of the desk.

I turn my head to read it. "Kelpie?"

A few giggles make her swell like the music before an especially epic scene. She places one hand on her hip and almost breaks a cheap acrylic nail. "That's *Kelsie*. See?" She bends down to point out each letter.

"Sure, yeah, whatever you say." I purposely don't look at the desk. Instead, I examine my own French manicure with gel set nail polish and hand painted daisies.

Kelsie's face turns an interesting shade of pink. "Ms. Buckley? The new girl is in my seat."

The teacher, who has been writing a billion squiggle marks on the board, turns around slowly. Her brown hair hangs in limp curls that barely reach her shoulders. The brown dress she has on looks like it used to house potatoes, and the thick glasses with tortoise shell frames are not doing her any favors. She is, by far, the most tragical thing I have seen since we drove into town the day before.

And I've seen a lot.

"I'm sorry?" The teacher blinks in our direction.

Kelsie huffs and puts both hands on her hips now. "She's in my seat!"

"We don't have assigned seats, Kelsie." Teacher lady looks toward the door. This is the classic cue that the character is in need of an escape. I imagine, from her appearance, that life hasn't been very kind to her. I mean, who would choose to be a high school teacher on purpose? Poor, sad, thing. She is in desperate need of my help.

For multiple reasons.

I sit up straight and extend my arms. "Ladies and gentlemen of this high school algebra class, before you we have the case of the non-assigned seat. I ask you to judge who should sit in it: the new student, so insecure and unsure of her place in your tiny little world, or the girl you have known since kindergarten who used to dip your hair in finger paint and steal your fruit snacks?"

"How did you know she did that?" Beth whispers behind me.

Elementary, my dear.

Murmurs follow, which tells me I have already won. I now address the figure of authority. "Teacher, ma'am?"

Teacher nods, her eyes a little unfocused.

"I propose that Kelpie—"

"Kelsie!" the girl screeches.

"Whatever." I hate it when people interrupt a good monologue. I was just getting going and now the momentum is gone. I continue with considerably less zeal. "I propose that we find another desk for Kelpie, because this one is taken. Would you mind directing her to one that is unoccupied?"

Teacher lady looks around with a dazed expression, then points to a chair a few columns over in the front row. "I believe this one is free."

"Lovely, there you are, all set." I wave my hands at Kelsie. "Go get comfy. It's time we math."

Kelsie's mouth dropped open a long while ago. Now she closes it, then opens it again.

"Kelsie?" Teacher's voice takes on a pleading note. "Please take a seat so that we can begin." Then she turns her attention to the rest of us. "Class, pull out your assignments from yesterday and check them with the key while I finish these equations."

With a huff and a puff that don't change the circumstances at all, Kelsie stomps to the empty desk and sits. When she looks over to glare daggers and poison sumac at me, I grin cheekily and wave.

She flips her head in the opposite direction, no doubt determined to ignore me for the rest of class. Which is just fine by me. I have no use for wannabe mean girls.

"Wow," Beth breathes out the word, but not low enough to escape my notice.

"What?"

She blinks and shakes her head.

"What?" I say again because one can never hear too much of why one is amazing at what one does.

Beth taps her pencil against a boring purple notebook. "I just, I guess, I've never seen Kelsie back down like that before."

Well, duh, of course not. Who in this dorky little town would have the mettle to stand up to her? No one, that's who. They should know this trope though. It's always the new girl that uproots the queen bee and then takes her place as a much more appropriate ruler.

Not that I intend on ruling anything around here.

I just hate to see someone manipulate the spotlight the way this Kelsie obviously has been doing since she was in preschool. Most likely, her mother did before her and her grandmother before that. I bet Kelpie is the reigning Ms. Piggy of Hicksburg County.

And she's so proud.

I smile to myself and shake my head. Ms. Piggy of Hicksburg, come on, that was good.

A squeak of Beth's pencil brings me out of my reverie. I don't think I ever introduced myself to this girl. That was an oversight. How is she ever going to have her three seconds of fame when she spills everything to the tabloids because she knew me back in the day if I never tell her my name?

"I'm Carmen, by the way. It's nice to meet you."

She stares at my hand for a moment, then takes it. We attempt a few awkward shakes before I take my arm back and rest my hand in my lap again. I imagine she's as relieved as I am to have that over and done with. So uncomfortable. I can't wait until I have bodyguards who will shake hands for me.

Beth clears her throat softly. "Can I ask you a question?"

I glance at Ms. Buckley, feverishly scribbling, determined to fill all the white space with Expo. "Sure."

"What happened to your...to your gloves?"

I raise an arm to see. Nothing happened to my gloves, they are fine.

"The fingers are missing." Beth rolls her pencil up and down the desktop. "James told me you wear black because of a tragic accident. Is that how your gloves got messed up?"

Who in the spotlight is James?

"They are fingerless gloves." I wiggle my fingers in her face. "I bought them this way."

Her face wrinkles in confusion. "What's the point of fingerless gloves? You wear gloves to keep your hands warm."

"One doesn't wear fingerless gloves to stay warm. They are for fashion alone, and therefore, they don't have to make sense." I lift my chin. "And no, there wasn't a tragic accident in my past. Your James is mistaken. I wish there was though. It's so much easier to draw on the emotions of real experience, you know?"

Yeah, she has no idea. I've never seen a face so blank.

I sigh. "The reason I wear black is because my parental figures have torn me from the bosom of my beloved Los Angeles, and I have been in mourning for the perfection of my past life."

"Oh." Beth nods. "That makes sense, I think."

The guy behind Beth nudges her with a clipboard, which she examines for a moment. I take this inattentive chance to study her. What part does Beth play in this story? At first glance she is mousy and small, like she's always trying to blend into the wall, but she has interesting views and a flare for the dramatic. I haven't forgotten the way her eyes lit up when she thought I'd survived a tragic accident.

But those glasses, ugh, and her hair? The girl is in desperate need of a make-over.

And suddenly I see myself in the role of the fairy godmother. Glitter trickles at my feet as I brandish my wand into the sky...

"Carmen?"

"Uh huh?" I blink a few times to help me focus back on Beth.

"Why do you have your arm raised like that?"

I glance at my appendage, wielding a wand that only exists in my mind, and slowly lower it to my desk. I use a classic misdirection technique to draw her attention to the clipboard in her hands. "What's that thing for?"

"Oh, Missy is trying to start an Oceanology club. Wait, is it oceanology or oceanography?"

"Oceanography," I say, though I have no idea. I just like the way the "graphy" rolls off the tongue better than the "ology."

"She's passing around a petition. I think she needs twenty signatures to get the club to pass with the faculty."

"Twenty-five." A tall girl with long brown hair swings into the seat across from us. "I need twenty-five signatures and a faculty adviser and then the office will accept the petition. Whew!"

"Who's the faculty adviser?" Beth asks.

Missy twists her hair into a messy bun on top of her head. "Mr. Skype."

"He teaches all the sciences," Beth explains to me.

I nod, but I don't register. My brain has been in a whirl since Missy explained the process for getting a club to pass. Might this also work for a drama club?

I open my mouth to present my idea just as Teacher turns around and calls the class to order in the faintest voice imaginable. I have to strain to hear her over my own boisterous thoughts.

Beth passes the clipboard over my shoulder, and I take it before it can slide to the ground. Silently, I count the names scrawled across hand drawn lines of separation. I don't even feel bad for not paying attention to the teacher since I'm currently counting, and counting is practically math.

There are twenty-three signatures including Beth. I don't see Missy's name on there at all. Is that because she can't sign the petition as the instigator? Or because she wanted to save her own signature for last? That's what I would have done. Like the moment in Anne of Green Gables when Anne adds an "e" to her name on the chalkboard, it's the perfect climactic ending.

If I sign my name, and Missy is able to sign hers, then there are twenty-five signatures. Enough to make a club.

The most ambitious idea of my career takes place at this moment. I whip around in my chair, catching Beth off guard so she drops her pencil to the floor. Missy kicks it back over to her, and when Beth resurfaces from retrieving it, I'm ready.

"What's the protocol for using the facility?"

"Facility?" Beth begins, stops herself, and then nods. "Oh, right, you mean the bathroom?"

I smile, she's getting it.

"You just take the pass. Ms. Buckley doesn't mind if you leave without talking to her."

Ms. Buckley?

Oh yeah, the teacher.

Perfect.

I tuck Missy's petition under my arm and hurry to the place Beth indicated. The hall pass is simply a large wooden number seven that looks like someone made it in woods class while blindfolded. I pick it up gingerly to avoid splinters and prance my way out of the classroom.

On my way to the front office, I dial Skylar.

"Hey, girl!"

"Hey! Hold on." The view is wobbly as Skylar arranges it on the dashboard of her car. "I'm on my way to our morning coffee break with Gabe and Jace. Say hi, guys!"

Gabe says hi, but Jace grabs the phone. "Hey, baby, miss you, and you are missing all of this." He moves the phone up and down the front of his body. He's wearing the tight blue sweater I gave him for Christmas two years ago, and yes, it makes me miss all of that.

"Yeah, well, are you missing all of this?" I pouch my lips out.

Jace whistles. "Why you gotta be so far away?"

I can only sigh. Sighing is the appropriate response to that question.

Skylar yanks the phone out of Jace's hands, despite his protests. It moves crazily around, giving me a dash of motion sickness, then it steadies on the dashboard in front of Skylar once again. "You guys are adorable, seriously, A-list couple. I hate to interrupt, but why did you call?"

I almost forgot because of my unabashed flirting with Jace. "Oh, well, quick catch up, I'm at school, there's no drama club..." I pause while Skylar gets her gasp under control. "And I figured out a way to get them to form one. I just wanted to have someone else along to bask in my awesomeness."

"What are you going to do?"

"Yes, what are you going to do?"

I shriek and jump into the air, which of course causes my phone to fly out of my hands. It lands inside a garbage can perched right outside one of the classrooms.

"Fantastic timing, Elijah." I glare at him and then stalk over to the trash can.

Oh, ew, it's the art classroom. My phone is now nestled amid scraps of paper, plates of glue, partially dried paint trays, and feathers.

I don't even want to know.

Elijah crosses his arms and glares right back at me.

Skylar, Jace, and Gabe talk all over each other as I try to fish them out of the trash can without touching anything that will haunt my dreams for years to come. The side of my finger brushes against something cold and slimy, grounds for a major freak out, but I bite the inside of my lip to keep myself focused.

I hold the phone by the corner not covered in glitter glue. My friends' voices fill the hall. More than one atrocious thing happened to my phone while it was in that garbage can. The volume is now deafening.

A teacher emerges from the classroom nearest me. He must be the one that does disgusting, sticky art.

"What is going on out here?"

My friends hush instantly, and Elijah steps forward. His words come out through clenched teeth. "Carmen is new to town. I've been showing her around the school."

Well done, Elijah. He didn't even tell a lie. A regular George Washington. Or was it Tom Hanks? One of those guys is known for honesty. I just can't remember which one.

The teacher eyes us both suspiciously. I open my eyes wide to look undeniably innocent and bat my lashes. No one can resist the peaches and cream perfection that is my face. Poor Elijah. He will never know what it's like to be adored by teachers and students alike.

And he really should stop grinding his teeth that way, it will damage his pearly whites. Those are money-makers. Everybody who knows anything about Julia Roberts knows that.

Someone calls the teacher from the depths of his classroom. "Well, carry on then. No more loitering in the halls." He raises his eyebrows while Elijah scowls enough to create gargoyle wrinkles in his forehead.

Once the door closes behind Mr. teacher man, I turn the volume down on my phone.

"Are you guys still there?" I whisper.

"Who's the guy?" Jace says, his voice tight.

"I don't know, an art teacher or something."

"That is not who I meant." Jace's voice raises. "I'm talking about Superman back there who is showing you around the school."

Jace is adorable when he's overcome with jealousy, but the thought of him needing to be jealous of Elijah is pretty much sickening.

"That's just Elijah." I push the reverse button so they can see him standing there glaring at me. "You have nothing to worry about, Jace."

"No?"

"No, believe me. If Elijah and a pig were the only things left on the earth, I still wouldn't be interested in Elijah. You are my guy, Jace. You and me, for-ev-er."

"Yeah?" He's starting to thaw, I can hear it in his tone.

"Yeah, seriously, you think I'd be interested in a guy like that? Like Elijah?" I suppress a shudder.

"My name is Eli." Elijah let out a loud breath. "And you know I can hear you, right?"

"I think he's hot," Skylar says. "Is he single?"

"Ew." I turn the phone back around so my friends can look at me instead. Skylar really needs to stop slumming.

"Are you single?" she calls.

I answer for him, flinging my arms out to the side for emphasis. "Of course he is, are you kidding me?"

"Nice." Elijah rolls his eyes. When they finish their 360, they land on something near my feet.

It's a piece of paper.

A piece of paper that used to be wedged between my arm and my side.

My petition!

I stoop to snatch it off the ground before Elijah can get any more funny ideas. My phone slips and my chin hits a button. Skylar's voice disappears. I'll just have to call her later and explain. Right now I gotta focus on my plan before anyone else realizes I'm not where I should be and follows me like an interfering stalker.

Objective: Ditch Elijah and find a copier.

Except...

Oh, curtains.

I have no idea where the copy machines live in this place.

ACT II SCENE II

INT: DORKY TEACHERS' LOUNGE WITH DORKIER SIDE CHARACTER

"Elijah?" I stand up and smooth my hair out of my face.

"Eli." He gives me a look half wary, half annoyed. "What?"

"I need to use a copy machine."

"What for?"

I swoop my hand with the petition behind my back and rock onto my toes. "No reason. Can you tell me where to find one?"

"As soon as you tell me what you're up to."

"Who says I'm up to anything?"

Elijah presses his lips together.

"You think you know me after spending like three seconds with me? That's not even possible. You are so suspicious. I'm not up to anything."

"No?" He raises an eyebrow.

"No."

"Then what do you have behind your back?"

"A piece of paper."

"And what is on that piece of paper?"

Oh, I'm so glad he asked.

"Words." I smile triumphantly.

Elijah runs a hand through his hair, making it tousle in a way that other guys need mousse to achieve. "I'm beginning to think you're the type of girl who makes everything difficult. Maybe on purpose, maybe you can't help it. I don't know. Will you just tell me what you're thinking so I can tell you why it's a bad idea and we can both go back to learning about quadratic functions?"

Well, tempt me, tempt me.

Elijah's long-suffering tone is the mark of a true antagonist. It is my duty as the hero of this tale to rebuff his suggestions. Plus, it really gets under my skin how he makes it sound like he's in the right and I am sooooooo in the wrong. I'm trying to save this school from an eternity of bland, flavorless electives. Maybe he should assume I'm doing something good, for the benefit of small-town, teenage humanity, instead of automatically thinking I'm planning something that needs him to run interference.

"No one is stopping you from living your dreams of quadratic equations. I didn't ask you to follow me out of the classroom. You are free to leave at any time." I add a few flagrant hand gestures to accent my point.

Which was a mistake.

Elijah takes that opportunity to grab the petition.

"Hey!" I try to snatch it back, but he blocks me with his other arm while he examines the paper.

"This is Missy's oceanology club petition."

"Oceanography."

He looks at me with eyebrows drawn together.

I let out a huff of air. "I know it's Missy's club petition, you sadistic worm. Now give it back." I try once again to reclaim the paper.

"What are you doing with this?" His eyes gloss over the page. "And why are you looking for a copy machine?"

My cheeks start warming up like the lead vocals before a musical. I don't have to answer that. I have the right to remain mysterious.

Elijah studies me intently. "If I give you this paper, and walk you to the copy machine in the teachers' lounge, am I going to regret it?"

"Absolutely not!" That I can answer truthfully. He will thank me on bended knee for providing this school with some culture.

"And yet, I have this feeling in my gut." He looks back down at the paper. "It's sort of like when they hike the ball to me and there is the perfect gap to run through, but I don't, because every time I do some big dude comes out of nowhere and pummels me into the mud."

That sounds like a personal problem. "I have no idea what you just said. Why don't you give me back my paper so I can be on my way?"

"Missy's paper." Elijah looks at me. "And I'm not going to give this back to you." He folds the page and tucks it into his back pocket.

Ew, no way I'm going in after it now.

I fold my arms and glare at him. "What is it that you want, exactly?"

"The truth."

A door creaks open and the same teacher as before sticks an arm and half his torso out the door to throw some junk in the garbage can. When he looks up, his face clouds over.

"Mr. Wayas?"

I have no idea what that means. Is it a code word for "you're super busted"? I don't know.

Elijah grimaces. "Yes?"

Wait, so, is Elijah Mr. Wayas?

Elijah Wayas, that name has star quality. It sounds way too awesome to belong to a baseball cap-wearing hick boy from Nowheresville.

It's so wasted on him.

The teacher leans against the door jamb of his classroom. "Is there a reason your tour of the school has stalled in this hall for the last ten minutes?"

"No, sir."

"Where are you supposed to be right now?"

"Algebra, sir, with Ms. Buckley."

"Then I suggest you get back there and save the extended tour for lunchtime or after school." He raises one eyebrow.

The back of Elijah's neck is flaming red like he fell asleep face down on the beach. "Yes, sir."

Except that I can't go back to Ms. Buckley's class yet. If I do, I'll have to give Missy her petition, and I really need the signatures that are on it. "Actually, Mr., uh, guardian of the art room, can you tell me where I might locate a copy machine that I can use? I need to make a copy before I go back to math class."

"No–" Elijah begins, then stops when the teacher shoots him a withering glare.

"I recall telling you a time or two that we don't interrupt ladies, Elijah."

Oh, yes, I like that rule. I'd love to add to it. Like, we also don't take papers from ladies, or follow ladies around, or glare at ladies...

All of these things would benefit Elijah greatly. That look on his face right now foreshadows devastation for either me or the teacher. Maybe both. His laser eyes are swiveling pretty evenly between the two of us.

"Please, go on." The teacher gives me a grim smile. "You need to copy something?" His eyes move around the space between Elijah and myself.

Well, that's just lovely.

I was hoping he wouldn't notice that I didn't have anything on my person that was copy-able. I glance at Elijah while I try to think, and inspiration strikes. "I need to copy the paper in Elijah's pocket. He's carrying it for me because he's such a gentleman."

Elijah's face scrunches like he's in pain.

"That's certainly touching, Ms...?"

"Hurst." I extend my hand, because this teacher seems like the type who would love any demonstration of old-school manners. His hand feels slippery, but I pride myself on the ability to disguise my disgust with a winning smile. I give him the full blast version. It's the smile that won me the part of Dorothy in The Wizard of Oz my freshman year. The school paper wrote it up as "the perfect combination of innocent and vulnerable, the kind of smile that makes a person want to carry her all the way to the emerald city on their shoulders."

Really? I'm blushing.

"I just moved here from Los Angeles."

"Is that so?" Art Teacher Man taps the corner of his mouth. "I used to know a Hurst, Terry Hurst. Great guy. Any relation?"

Ugh!

First the secretary lady and now this guy? Does no one grow up and leave this town?

"Well, that would be my paternal parent." I leave out the part where I recently disowned him.

"You're kidding me?" More enthusiasm. Gross.

"I am not."

Art Teacher Man rubs his hands together, unable to emphasize his excitement in more creative ways. "Your dad saved my butt in high school. I would have flunked out of physics if it wasn't for him. How is he?"

I'm so surprised that a person of authority in this school just said the word *butt*, it takes me a minute to respond. "Fabulous."

"Tell him Arty says hi, I'll stop by and catch up one of these days after school."

My mind reels with one horrifying thought after the other. A teacher, coming to my house, to catch up with my father? An art teacher named Arty? This is too much for my poor, saturated brain. I need some TLC.

Someone schedule me a mani-pedi, stat.

I guess the good news is I won't forget his name anytime soon. Talk about memory association.

Arty extends his arm enough to show the faint sweat circles under his armpits and points down the hall. "See that 'No Bullying' poster? The door right after that leads to the teachers' lounge. You're allowed to use the copy machine in there with a teacher's permission, and you have mine, provided you go straight there and then directly back to class. No more tour."

"No more tour." I shake my head solemnly.

Arty fixes his gaze on Elijah, eyebrows raised.

Elijah mutters, "Yes, sir," with another one of those death-by-eyeballs looks.

"Welcome to our school, Carmen." Arty the art teacher smiles at me, then narrows his eyes at Elijah. "Straight to the copy machine and straight to class, young man, understood?"

"Yes, sir." Elijah all but salutes. He stays at attention until Arty disappears inside his classroom once more.

"That guy does not like you." I jab my thumb at the closed door to the art room. "Why? I had you pegged as the golden boy of this place. I thought for sure everyone liked you."

"No one likes everyone," Elijah mumbles. "Let's just go to the copy room."

"Oh." I skip to catch up with him. "So, now we want to show me where the copy machine is? Now we're all super helpful? Maybe I should have solicited help from the artsy man sooner."

Elijah's lips press into a thin line. He picks up the pace, so I have to practically jog to keep up with him. And these boots are not meant for jogging.

There's a thin waif of a student teacher making copies when we enter the room. Elijah and I have to wait in awkward silence for her to be done. She leaves, hugging a stack of papers to her chest, without ever acknowledging that Elijah or I exist.

I bounce to the copy machine and hold out my hand for Missy's petition.

Elijah moves like a snail in super glue, taking his sweet time to pull the paper out, unfold it, and smooth out the creases. With wary eyes, he places the paper in my hand.

"I really wish you would tell me why you're making a copy of this petition."

"That's nice." I snatch the paper before he can change his mind, and slide it into place on top of the copier. I let the lid drop and press the green button.

Green usually means go, but apparently not today. I push the button like thirty more times as fast as I can.

"Don't do that." Elijah moves me out of the way. "If there's something wrong you're not going to fix it by overloading the system with more commands."

How geek speak of him.

I bump him back with my hip and relish the moment he loses his balance into the coffee maker. While he's cleaning up all the fluttering filters, I press the button a bunch more.

"Why aren't you working?" I shove the machine with both palms. It wobbles for a moment, then settles back in place. I take a step back. "How old is this thing? It appears entirely unstable."

Elijah blows hair out of his eyes and throws a wad of gross paper towels in the trash can. "That machine is older than my dad. You have to be nice to it."

It's a machine. How does it know the difference between nice and mean?

Elijah stands next to me, his head tipped down to look at me. "Please move over so I can fix it."

"What makes you think you can fix it and I can't? I can fix it, observe." I smack the machine with both palms again. Most things just need another good smack.

But I'm wrong.

The wobbly table the printer inhabits decides to wobble its last wobble. One of the legs buckles and the printer is pitched at a forty-five-degree angle, headed for the floor.

Elijah yelps and tries to stop the thing from crashing to its doom, but the printer which is actually older than his great-grandpa, apparently weighs three times as much as well. All Elijah can do is stop the momentum so when the printer does join with the carpet, it does so at a much slower pace.

"Are you going to help me?" Elijah grunts from his full squat half under the side of the antiquated machine.

"What do you expect me to do? I can't lift that thing."

"Not alone." Elijah shifts the printer so he can pull his arm out from wherever it was jammed. "But you and I can. We can't just leave it here. We have to do something."

I reach over and lift the lid where Missy's petition is resting calmly. "You're right, I have to find another copier and get this back to Missy. Did that art guy happen to say if there is another dinosaur machine nearby?"

"Are you serious?" Elijah squints up at me. "You're going to leave me here, like this?"

"It made a big crash. I'm sure someone heard it and is rushing to your aid as we speak."

Right on cue, the secretary lady hurries into the room. "I heard a—oh dear! What happened?" She sprints over to Elijah and tries to help him lift the printer so he can stand.

It's a futile attempt, obviously. I could have told them that ages ago and saved them all the trouble. Not only is the secretary roughly the same size as a walking stick, but the table they're trying to get the printer back on is clearly incapacitated. There is no way it can hold the weight of a feather boa, much less this monstrosity.

The secretary lady realizes this the next moment. "Carmen, would you please scoot that other table over to us? I think if we move the broken one out of the way and tip that one on its side we'll be able to leverage the printer and get it back in place."

I scoff and hold out the back of my free hand. "Do you see this?"

"Yes," she says.

"This is a three hundred dollar manicure."

"So," adds Elijah.

"So," I huff, "I can't push, pull, or lift anything that will risk breaking one of my nails."

Secretary ma'am furrows her brow. "Well, would you mind stepping through that door over there to find someone who can? Elijah and I are sort of stuck here, and it's becoming quite uncomfortable." Her voice is as sticky sweet as Halloween candy.

I'm sorry for her dilemma, really, but with Elijah stuck there glaring at me, I can do what I came to do without interference. This is the most pressing of the two options, I believe, so the task must go on.

"Oh, I would love to, but I need to copy this paper and get back to class. Do you think the copier will still work with it tipped over like that? Or could you tell me where I can find a working one?"

Madam secretary stares at me, her face all scrunched, which is not a good look for her. It makes her appear ages older and much more haggard. She takes a deep breath, preparing to tell me where to go, I assume, but Elijah interrupts. His face is a deep shade of red that isn't doing anything for his pretty-boy features.

"Don't try to reason with her." His voice fills the room like a noxious gas. "It's pointless. All she cares about is herself. Tell you what, Carmen, you get your butt over here and help us out or, one of these days when you're not at home, I'm going to pay your room a visit and introduce every last one of your precious costumes to my nana's mammoth hedge clippers."

"You wouldn't!" I gasp, my eyelashes fluttering so fast I can't see through them. "Also, how do you know about my costumes?"

Creepy just got creepier.

"Your dad told me about your collection when we were scrubbing pepper spray out of my eyes. The ruby slippers with hand-sewn red sequins, the Belle dress with fifty-five layers of tulle, the—"

"Why would he do that?" My father figure should know you don't share information about priceless treasure with complete and totally weird strangers.

Elijah shrugs. "Maybe he was trying to distract me. The point is that I know things and I'm not afraid to use that knowledge."

"Alright, alright, you beast." I stick out my lower lip. "You win this round. What do you want me to do again?"

The secretary takes it from here. In a steady voice, she walks me through the intricacies of moving the not broken-leg table into the place of the broken-leg table. I set Missy's petition on the arm of the squatty brown couch next to the door and follow her instructions flawlessly.

"Now, please go to Eli's other side and help us lift the printer onto the table. I'm sure the three of us can do it."

By Elijah?

That's disgusting.

He glares at me. "Super sharp hedge clippers."

"Fine." I stomp around him and gingerly place my hands under the printer, making sure I'm as far from him as I can be while still touching the thing.

"Make sure you have a good grip," the secretary says. "On the count of three. One."

"Two," Elijah adds.

On three we slide the printer onto the table and then right the whole thing on all four legs. While they admire their handiwork, I look around for some coconut butter lotion to sooth my hands. It is a necessity. There must be some somewhere. My fingers ache from exertion. I massage each one, trying to rub away the smarting.

And then, I scream.

ACT II SCENE III

FADE IN: INT: TEACHER'S LOUNGE AND MORE TEACHER'S LOUNGE - CAFETERIA WITH MYSTERY MEAT THAT MIGHT IN FACT BE ROADKILL.

"What?" The secretary looks around, her eyes wide. "What is it?"

I extend my jagged nail, tears threatening to smear my smoky eyeshadow. "I told you! Look! My nail is ruined." I bring it close to my chest and caress it slowly.

If she is trying to look sympathetic, she's doing a horrific job. There is no way she can know my pain. I wiggle the broken part of my nail to detach it the rest of the way, then stare at it sadly. There is nothing to be done. It has gone the way of all acrylic. But still, I can't bring myself to throw it away. That just seems so final, and I'm not ready to let it go yet.

Elijah straightens and wiggles pieces of the copy machine like it's the most important thing in the world. He doesn't give me a bit of attention. This moment deserves more than a glance, and he doesn't even spare me one of those. He is an insensitive cretin. This is all his fault.

"We should probably copy something to make sure it still works." He scans the room and spots the petition, still perched precariously on the edge of the couch. He walks over and snatches the paper. "How about this paper?"

I can't even with him. My nail has literally broken from my finger into ugly jagged lines and now is the moment he chooses to finally do what I asked? Has he no soul? I need more time to mourn my loss. In the olden days, people took a year at least to grieve the tragic end of one of their fellows. Elijah can't even give me a full minute. If he'd just let me copy the stupid petition in the first place, none of this would have happened.

He places the paper on the copier and presses the button. The machine whirls to life like it's about to launch itself into outer space, and a new piece of paper shoots out of the side.

"And...it works." He holds the page up so we can see the faint scrawl of names. "Good as new."

"Oh, thank heavens." The secretary puts a hand on her heart. "I'm going back to work. You two head to class now."

"Will do." Elijah nods until she leaves the room, then he turns to me with a grim expression. He dangles the paper in front of my face. "Are you happy? Here's the copy, just like you wanted."

"Yippee," I mutter as I stand over the trash can. My broken nail slips through my fingertips into the disgusting depths of the garbage abyss. The victory of obtaining a copy is soured by my loss. Now my hand looks tacky. I'm going to have to remove all the rest of my nails when I get home. That's hours from now!

Hours and hours of suffering.

"Oh, so you don't want this anymore?" Elijah steps closer so he can dangle the sheet over the trash can.

"Don't do that." I reach forward with my non-blemished hand. "I want it."

"And what do you want it for, again?"

How dare he take advantage of my weakened mental state? I can't be expected to come up with witty banter at a time such as this.

"I want it," I sigh, "so I can use it to form a dramatic society at your deficient, deprived, depraved school, of course."

"Come again?"

I let out a huff of air and tuck my jagged fingernail out of sight, but not out of mind. That would be too much to hope for. "I want to dispense culture upon your dreary little lives with the commencement of a drama club. I'm willing to sacrifice my time and precious energy to bring this to your school. You're welcome."

Elijah retrieves the original page from the printer and holds them both up where I can see. "So, you're stealing Missy's signatures? Of course you are. I don't know why that surprises me."

"I'm not stealing anything!" I put my hands on my hips. "I'm using that sheet of signatures to form a club. That's how it's done."

Elijah shakes his head. "No, how it's done is you talk to individuals and collect unique signatures of people who want to participate in the club you're trying to form. How it's not done is stealing someone else's hard earned signatures and claiming them as your own."

"Would you stop saying stealing? It's not like that."

"No?" He raises a very cocky eyebrow.

I don't like his sass. "I would love to explain it to you if I thought you really cared about what I'm going to say and weren't just trying to make me look like a villain. I never play the antagonist, Elijah, you must know this."

"Eli. I asked you to call me Eli."

There are so many things I want to call him.

"May I have my papers, please? I'm sure Ms. Whoever Teaches Math is wondering where I have gone."

"I'd be happy to give these to you if they were yours. But they aren't. Did you even ask Missy if you could copy her list?"

I sniffed. "I don't see how that's relevant."

"Of course, you don't." Elijah gives me a disappointed look and folds the papers. This probably means he's going to put them somewhere, like his back pocket. I have to stop him before that happens. If they disappear from sight into a place that close to his unmentionable, they will be beyond my grasp forever.

All those glorious signatures.

Wasted.

"Wait!" I fling both hands into the air between us. When Elijah's arm freezes on its path to his behind, I drop my arms and fix that winning smile back on my face. "I'm sure we can work something out. What can I give you in exchange for those papers?"

Elijah eyes me warily. "There is nothing you have that I want."

Oh, I seriously doubt that. Mr. Cowboy Man has never left this sleepy town. He must long for excitement. Fast cars, expensive shoes, beautiful women...

"So, you saw that girl I was talking to on my phone?"

He doesn't answer so I go on. "That's Skylar. She's gorgeous and, better yet, she's interested. If you give me those papers, I'll make sure she ends up with your phone number."

His jaw loosens. "Are you serious?"

Victory is within my reach, I can feel it. "Absolutely. Do we have a deal?"

Elijah clamps his teeth together and shoves the papers into his pocket before I have a chance to wail or weep. "I can't believe you're trying to bribe me with your friend. There is something seriously wrong with you, do you know that?"

I stamp my foot. "Just give me the papers, you horrible little boy! I need drama club! I am not going to survive without it!"

Elijah eyes me with such obvious disdain, my ankles begin to itch. He steps around me and opens the door to the teachers' lounge. "Don't worry, you'll figure it out. I have full confidence in your ability to find another way to get what you want."

Before the door closes behind him, he sticks his head back into the room. "And in case you were wondering, that wasn't a compliment."

I wallow in the teachers' lounge until the bell rings and I am forced from my catastrophic moment of impending doom to retrieve my things from the math room. I move through the herd to Algebra, thinking dark, dank, and dreary thoughts. Ten to one, Elijah is not going to show me around this hive of destruction anymore. Which means I can probably expect to be late for all my classes today.

Fabulous.

Usually, I love to make an entrance, but with my nail now defiled, my confidence wavers at the edges like bad CGI. I step into the empty classroom and gather my things from the desk that used to be Kelpie's throne.

"Carmen?"

I screech and whirl around. Apparently, the classroom wasn't as empty as I thought. Ms. Teacher sits at her desk and literally blends into it. I can't actually see her that well until she stands and separates herself from the background.

"I missed you in class. Is everything alright?"

I hug my stuff to my chest. "Peachy."

"I know it's difficult to move and start anew." She takes a few steps forward. "Especially if you're not used to such a small town, it's an adjustment."

Preach, sister, and amen.

"I'm here for you, if you need it. Just let me know if there is anything I can do to help you..."

I snort. "Unless you can boot me off this producer forsaken rock, back to Los Angeles, there is nothing you can do for me." I stare off into the distance with my most forlorn expression. "I am truly doomed."

Ms. Teacher Lady puts a hand on the nearest desk and leans heavily. "You're from Los Angeles?"

"Yes."

She breathes in sharply through her nose. "I can see how this would be an adjustment for you."

I look at her for the first time. Her kindness starts a seed of hope in my soul. She's the first person who has really tried to understand what I'm going through.

Now I can easily overlook her desperate need for an eyebrow tweeze.

I drop my things back on the desk with a thump and collapse into the chair. "You have no idea what my life is like." Then I proceed to present a moment-by-moment monologue of my appalling experiences over the last forty-eight hours.

Ms. Teacher stays rooted to the same spot, with her hand resting on the desk, for the fifteen minutes or more it takes for me to get it all out. At this moment, I wouldn't care if she was a mannequin. This stuff has been building, and I am liable to explode if I don't get a release valve.

"The worst part is, I already had the lead in the school play. We did try-outs at the end of last year, and I earned that part. There were going to be producers there. Our high school is prestigious. Did you know that Laura Valentine went to that high school?"

Ms. Lady shakes her head.

That was a silly question. The poor, pathetic dear probably has no idea who Tom Holland is either. It is exhausting to bring all these people up to my level.

I sigh. "She's the greatest rom-com actress of all time. Or, at least, she was, until that horrible accident. Anyway, she went to my previous high school and was discovered when she played Milly in Seven Brides for Seven Brothers. I was going to be the next Laura Valentine, but, instead, I'm stuck in this ghastly hobo town without a drama club. Did *you* know that there is no drama club here? A soul as perceptive as your own wouldn't be able to abide such a gross oversight."

She shifts from one foot to the other. "Oh, I don't...I don't know anything about drama club. I teach math."

Of course she doesn't have a clue. No one here does. This was point-less. I really should go find a facility and call Skylar to vent my soul until it's time for lunch. She will understand the thorn of affliction that has pierced me to the depths.

"Okay, well, anyway, I should go, and I'm sure you have a class to teach or something."

Ms. Teacher Ma'am adjusts the low bun clinging to the back of her neck like an enormous groundhog. "This is my free period."

"Okay, thanks for listening, or whatever." I gather my things and walk toward the door. She says something as I'm leaving, but if she really wants to be heard, she needs to learn how to emote from her diaphragm. I step into the hall and follow it until I find a women's facility that is unoccupied. Then, I pull out my phone and call Skylar.

When she doesn't answer, I call Jace.

He doesn't answer either.

I toss my phone in my purse and glower at it with all my might.

Some friends.

Real friends have a telepathic understanding. They should know that I walk across the coals of anguish in this infinitesimal town.

They better not be doing something awesome without me.

I play mindless games on my phone until the bell rings twice more. My schedule deems that classes are over for the morning, it is time for lunch.

And not a moment too soon.

I follow the mindless drones to the cafeteria and look around for Skylar before I remember I am not in Los Angeles anymore. That should have been obvious from the shocking lack of Gucci, but my brain is still adjusting to this new reality. It is absolutely normal to have moments of delusion.

I forgot to pack a lunch this morning. Food took the back seat to the atrocity of walking to school. So I am forced into the greasy cafeteria line. There is no fresh salad bar. There is no meat carving station. There are no gluten-free options. What there is resembles the effect of chewing food and then spitting it back out on the tray. It is a mockery to call this mess meatloaf, especially when normal meatloaf is horrifying enough.

I take my sorry excuse for lunch to an empty table near an open window. This is a strategic move on my part to counteract the stench with some fresh air. My hope is that I'll be able to find something I can actually eat with the aid of a strategic cross breeze because I am quite famished. It takes a lot of calories to have one's life ruined over and over and over again in such a short amount of time.

"Can I sit here?" I look up and see the mousy girl from math standing over me with a huge book in one hand and a brown bag in the other.

"Whatever." I wave my hand at an empty seat and pick up the fork on my tray. Even with the breeze blowing away the smell of unspeakable things, I can't bring myself to take a bite.

"Meatloaf day." The girl whose name I can't remember grimaces as she unrolls the top of her lunch bag. "Do you want half of my sandwich?"

"What kind is it?" I have a suspicion about these people and roadkill that will not go away. That might be part of the reason I can't bring this forkful of meatloaf to my mouth.

"Peanut butter and Nutella."

Nutella?

I sit up straighter. I didn't think such a backward place would know of fine things like Nutella. "Do they sell hazelnut spread at Gus's Piggly Wiggly?"

The girl laughs and shakes her head. "My mom places a huge order from Costco online every month."

"I didn't think such a place as this had access to internet shopping."

I also didn't mean to say that out loud.

But the girl isn't offended, or if she is, she hides it really well. She just shrugs and laughs again. "I know we probably seem really pathetic compared to LA."

"Yes!" I grab her hand. "You do, you totally do! I'm so glad you understand. This place might as well be the jungles of Africa or a cannibal island."

She moves her hand to rip her sandwich in half, then gives one to me. "I'd love to go to Los Angeles. I've never been. What's your favorite thing about it?"

"I could never choose." I lean back and look at the ceiling. "I love everything about LA. Everything!"

"The weather?"

"Always perfect!"

"Yeah." She pulls out a juice box and works to unwrap the diabolical straw. "It gets pretty cold here in the winter. How about the ocean?"

"Breathtaking!"

"I've never seen it." She takes a long drink. "Except in pictures, obviously. And, the movie stars? You said you've met Chris Pratt?"

"Yes, and so many others. They are everywhere. It's like the ultimate I-spy!"

"Have you been to Disneyland?"

"About a billion times. There's always an amazing concert somewhere, zoos, theme parks, and swimming. And the food is to die for..." I push the mystery meatloaf away and take a small bite of her sandwich. I'm starving, but the bread looks sketchy, like it's homemade or something. When my throat doesn't contract into final death spasms, I swallow.

It wasn't completely disgusting.

The girl sighs and leans her head on her hand. "It sounds fantastic."

"It really, really is."

A tray thumps onto the table next to me, effectively destroying my reminiscent moment. I look up and scowl. "What are you doing here?"

"Eating lunch." Elijah smiles.

"Not at this table, you troglodyte. Go find a craggy cave where people want you around."

His smile doesn't waver. "Beth wants me around." He nods at her as he sits down.

That's right, her name is Beth. I'll remember it now. Unless it's really true what he says, that she wants him around. I wrinkle my nose. If she does, we can no longer be friends because I've sworn a solemn vow with me, myself, and I to hate his guts until the end of time.

And beyond.

"Is that true?" I squint at her, trying to activate my x-ray vision.

Beth shrugs one shoulder. "I don't mind, if you don't."

"Oh, I mind." I turn to Elijah. "Don't you have some weird groupies that worship your toenails? Why don't you sit with them?"

"I do have pretty great toenails." Elijah scoops a big, nasty forkful of mystery meat and puts it in his mouth.

Without even plugging his nose.

"Oh, ew, stop! How can you eat that?"

Elijah swallows hard and cuts another huge chunk. "It's good. I think they got the possum scraped off the road before it rotted this time. Wanna bite?"

I push his arm away. "No, really, don't you have a student council group, or a sweaty sports team, or somewhere, anywhere, else to be?"

Elijah stops chewing and stares at me all dewy-eyed. "I am seriously flattered you assume I have so many friends. You must really think highly of me to say things like that."

Oh, great, I just threw up in my mouth a little bit.

"Stop teasing her, Eli." Beth shakes her head. "Give her a break."

"I'd love to, I really would, but I just can't." Elijah stands up and waves one arm in the air like he's trying to catch an elusive taxi. "You girls okay if James and Myles sit with us?"

Beth looks at me, and since I have no idea who James and Myles are, I shrug.

This is exactly why you should never shrug an acquiescence without all the facts.

Because James is the mouth-breathing Neanderthal from this morning, and Myles is the thick glasses Twerp. What a lovely lunch hour this is turning out to be.

I should have stayed in the bathroom stall.

ACT II SCENE IV

FADE IN: INT: SAME GROSS CAFETERIA - INTRODUCTION TO MORE SIDE CHARACTERS, THE GOOD, THE WEIRD, AND THE RIDICULOUS.

Beth takes it upon herself to make sure everyone is familiar with everyone else before I have a chance to tell her we've already met.

"Carmen is new in town, so be nice to her. Carmen, this is James..."

Neanderthal nods without looking at me, he's too busy making an obscene amount of noise while he tries to find space for his heaping tray of food by knocking books on the floor and banging trays around.

"And this is Myles."

The Twerp. He sets his Bento lunch box on the table and shakes my hand firmly.

"We met this morning, but I'm happy to meet you again. Welcome to town."

I'm disappointed. I thought the Twerp might be smart enough to realize what an oxymoron that is.

Welcome to *this* town.

Pffft.

Beth breaks a huge oatmeal cookie in half and slides one side over to me. "How was your first morning at school?"

I open my mouth to respond, but Elijah beats me to it. "Oh, it was great. After she ditched math to steal Missy's list of names for Oceanology club, she then pouted in the bathroom until lunchtime."

How in the heck did he know that part about the pouting in the bathroom? I've heard of stalkers, obviously. I know all about them from my celebrity research. But this guy, he's next level.

"Ocean-ography," I say through clenched teeth.

"*Is* it oceanology or oceanography?" Myles asks absently as he opens his Bento box to reveal separate compartments of cubed tofu, black beans, plain white rice, and salad with no dressing. "I can never remember."

"I was wondering the same thing earlier," Beth says.

"Oceanonomy," James says with his mouth full.

Myles shakes his head. "That's definitely not it."

Elijah's face swings from one person to the other, frustration etched all over it. I bet he was trying to throw me under the bus there. Well, too bad for him, no one seems to be driving it.

"Hahaha."

Oh, wait, I didn't mean to laugh out loud.

Everyone looks at me to see what the joke was. I clear my throat and shove a big piece of Beth's cookie in my mouth to keep from explaining myself.

"So, uh, why did you steal Missy's petition?" Myles asks the question like he's asking about my cereal preferences. The Twerp should be a lawyer.

I glare at Elijah. "That is not what happened. I was making a copy of the list, borrowing it, so I could start a drama club."

"A what-a-ma club?" James stops shoveling momentarily to question me.

"Dra-ma." I emphasize the syllables. "Drama, it's the study of the art of theater."

"Acting," Myles clarifies for James.

I have a feeling this is a common occurrence, explaining things to James.

"Like on TV and YouTube and stuff?"

I drop the last bite of the cookie on the table. "YouTube is not acting, you heathen. Don't desecrate the art by comparing it to YouTube. You have pierced my soul with your careless nouns."

James looks at Myles. "What did she say?"

It's Elijah who answers. "Gibberish. Don't worry about it."

Beth makes a click with her tongue that perfectly accompanies the dirty look she gives him. "Do you have a petition for your Drama club? I'll sign it."

"You?" James sputters, spraying goobers onto his tray. "You, in drama-mama-nana club? Seriously?"

"Cut it out, James." Elijah shoves his beefy arm.

Beth looks down at her hands, the mouse once more.

"Why can't she be in the drama club? If she has the desire, there's no reason she can't do it." I rip a page out of my notebook and look around for a pen. Myles pulls one from his pocket and rolls it to me.

"Thank you." I write Drama Club Petition in my best calligraphy on the top of the paper and slide it over to Beth, with the pen. "There, sign. Let's make this happen."

But Beth shakes her head, enthralled with the palms of her hands now resting in her lap. "No, he's right, I can't do it. I can't talk in front of people."

I give a mighty death stare of flaming fire to James and wait for it to scorch his sideburns. I wait in vain. He doesn't even look up from his partially devoured lunch. So I turn a softened look to Beth. "Don't let him bully you. You can talk in front of people. You've been doing it all lunch hour. "

"That's different." Beth presses her lips together. "It's just the guys. Every time I get in front of a bunch of people, I freeze up. I can't remember what I was supposed to say. I've fainted a couple of times…"

"And peed your pants," James supplies most helpfully.

Elijah punches him again. "That was in kindergarten, dude, not cool!"

"Shall I recount the many incriminating things you did in kindergarten, James?" Myles chews his lettuce calmly, but his eyes are like steel. "Eating crayons to see if the colors have different flavors, for example."

This Twerp is growing on me.

"He's right, though, I can't do it. I don't know what I was thinking." Beth picks at her carrot sticks but doesn't eat them.

I know what she was thinking. I could see it in her eyes when she asked me about Los Angeles. She wants to act, she wants to perform, she wants to really live!

I am surprised to find a kindred spirit in this land of woe.

I grab Beth's hand in mine and hold it tight so she can't let go. "I can help you with all of that. I've been taking acting lessons since I was two years old. I know all the tricks—"

"Like the underwear one?" James asks.

Elijah looks ready to punch him again. "What the heck are you talking about?"

James holds up one hand in defense. "Don't look at me like that. There's a thing. It's real, I swear. When you're public speaking and you're crazy-butt scared, you imagine the crowd in their chonies. Ask her. It's a thing."

I take a deep breath and slowly nod. "While the Neanderthal is correct that imagining the audience in their underwear is one way of combating nerves, it is more of a joke than a resource. I don't know anyone of caliber who actually does that."

James blinks slowly. "I don't understand a single dang thing this girl says. Are you sure she ain't foreign exchange?"

Myles rolls his eyes.

"Anyways," I continue. "I can help you, Beth, if you really want to do this. Say you will?"

If I can get Beth on board, I have a foot in this school. All these weirdos have known each other since they were babies. She could help me get enough signatures and we could actually have a drama club!

And then I won't waste away into the dark recesses of oblivion before I can take my place in the Hollywood squares.

Beth's face tugs back and forth between yes and no. I leverage the yes by placing Myles' pen in her hand. "Come on, it will be so much fun! There is nothing in the world like acting on a stage, under the lights, for a crowd of people who hang on your every word."

Beth moves her hand closer to the paper, then back again.

So close.

"But, what if I can't do it?"

"But, what if you can?" I whisper back.

The sounds of the lunch room, including slurps and smacks from James, fade into the background. This is what happens to me every time I take the stage and focus on the character I want to become for those short scenes. Except, here I'm focusing on Beth. I need her to do this. I need her to become more than she is, so I can survive this school year.

"You...you promise you'll help me?"

I raise my right arm to a square. "I swear on the vintage leather-bound collection of Shakespeare's greatest works that I will do whatever it takes to help you overcome your fear."

And help myself at the same time.

Beth fiddles with the pen a moment longer, then glances up at Elijah. "Should I do it, Eli?"

No, don't ask him.

Just sign.

Sign!

Elijah leans back in his chair and clasps his hands behind his head. "If you do, does that mean you'll stop making me and the others dress up in costumes and act out scenes from dorky movies?"

"No, maybe... I don't know."

Myles leans forward. "What do you want, Bethie, really?"

She bites her lip and stares at the lines on the paper in front of her. "I want to act. I've wanted to forever. I love the theater."

"Then sign the paper."

Attaboy, Myles! I knew I liked this guy.

Elijah's voice softens. "If you really want it, do it. You can do it."

"I can do it." Beth squares her shoulders and signs her name on the first line. "There!" She slaps the pen down and lets out a long breath. "There, I did it."

"Awesome!" I hold the paper up to admire her signature. "Now, we just need twenty-three more signatures and a teacher sponsor."

Elijah reaches across the table for the paper. "I'll take care of your signatures."

I swing it out of his grasp. "No way! You'll burn it or knock a fat copy machine on top of it or something."

"A fat copy machine?" Myles asks.

Elijah rolls his eyes. "You don't want to know. Just give me the paper, and I'll get your dang signatures."

"Why?"

"Because I want to help."

"Since when do you want to help me?" I raise my left eyebrow.

Elijah snorts. "Not you. Beth. I want to help Beth. Now give me that paper and stop being a drama monger."

I let him snatch it out of my fingers this time. If there's a chance he really will get signatures, then that's one less thing I have to do. I'm going to take that chance. "Fine. I'll let you do this. Also, who would be a good teacher sponsor?"

"Someone artsy," Beth taps her fingers on the table. "I bet Uncle Art would do it."

Artsy, Uncle Art, seriously? Is everyone in this place related?

"Don't ask him." Elijah looks up with an uncharacteristic fierceness.

"Come on, Eli. You—"

"No." He shakes his head. "I'm not helping with this if you ask him."

Beth sighs while I try to figure out what the Grammy is going on between them.

"How about Mrs. Dunlap?" Myles wipes his hands on a napkin, neatly folds it, and puts it in his empty Bento box. "I think she used to do community theater when she was in college."

"Who's Mrs. Dunlap?" I ask.

Beth answers this time. "She teaches American History, and you're right, Myles, she's really fun. Remember when she had us act out the American Revolution?"

"Betsy Ross couldn't play herself as well as you did." Myles pushes his glasses up on his nose with a smile.

"Only cause we didn't have to say lines." Beth blushes prettily. "I have history next period. I'll ask her."

I sit back and bask in the perfection. It's hard to believe, but I just orchestrated the ideal scenario to make my drama club dream a reality.

Sometimes, I even surprise myself.

I'd be able to enjoy it a lot more if Elijah weren't over there staring at me as if he knows I'm about to do something he's going to regret.

I'm just going to turn my head, like so, and knock him out of my peripheral. This moment is too good to taint with his doubt and negativity. I'm so close to my salvation.

Drama club, here we come!

ACT II SCENE V

FADE IN; EXT: END OF FIRST SCHOOL DAY - GRIMY DIRT ROAD - UNBELIEVABLE

So, that may have been a premature celebration.

Beth finds me at the end of the day, while Elijah is opening my locker because I can't do it with a busted nail. I don't have the motivation.

She walks up, her forehead all scrunched, and before she even opens her mouth, I know what she's going to say.

"Mrs. Whoever said no," I supply with a sigh.

Beth nods and adjusts the strap of her backpack. "She's expecting a baby in a couple of months and doesn't want to commit to anything. I felt so stupid. I didn't even notice she was pregnant."

"Don't be so hard on yourself." Elijah pulls the latch up and then leans in with his shoulder while he tugs backward. The door opens, almost knocking Elijah to the floor. He brushes his hands together and waves at the locker. "You're welcome."

I stare at him. "Are you kidding me? I'm not going through that every time I have to open this thing. I'm just going to have to walk all the way back to the office, ruin my shoes, and request an alternative locker. Preferably one that doesn't require manly grunting to open."

Elijah glares, turns his back on me, and rests an arm across Beth's shoulders. "I didn't know she was pregnant either."

Beth stares at her shoes. "I feel like a complete buffoon. I am a complete buffoon. Once she pointed it out, it was so obvious she was expecting a baby soon. I better not volunteer to do anything else. I will just mess it up."

"Beth..." Elijah squeezes her closer.

She tries to smile. "No. Yeah. Anyway, I just came to tell you we will have to find another teacher sponsor because Mrs. Dunlap can't do it."

Well, that's provoking. I slam the door of the empty locker, just to hear the satisfying crash. It relieves my feelings.

"Who else can we ask? Are there any other fun, young teachers that would work to run drama club?" Even as I say the words I have to suppress a laugh. The fact that there was even one of those in this horrible little institution was a miracle in the first place.

Beth bites her lip and looks off into the distance while Elijah shakes his head. "I can't think of anyone else."

"Come on!" I'm way too close to my dream to give up now. "There has to be someone. They don't even have to be young and fun. What about that art teacher you mentioned? What was his name?"

Elijah's face tightens like someone injected him with one year's worth of Botox. "No."

"No, what?"

"I told you I'm not doing this if he is."

"Why not?"

"Because, okay?" Elijah pulls his arms in and hugs them to his chest. "If you ask him, I'm out."

"Eli..." Beth tips her head to the side. "Can't you—"

"No stinking way. This conversation is over. If 'Arty' is part of this, I'm not."

"I don't think I want to do it either, if Eli doesn't." Beth gives me an apologetic smile.

I let out a humongous breath of air. Of all the unreasonable, stupid things! If I thought Elijah was provoking before, he was doubly so now. It shouldn't even matter to him who the sponsor is. It's just a formality. Someone old and supposedly responsible in case anything goes pear-shaped. I fully plan on running the club myself.

Elijah is just being difficult.

But, I can't afford to lose his help. Or Beth's. I couldn't care less what their reasons were for backing me up on this. The fact is I need twenty-five student signatures and only one teacher. And since I don't know anyone in this nasty abode, the numbers are against me.

Fine. I'll just find another teacher.

I hope Elijah's happy.

This is going to be so much unnecessary work. I've only met four actual teachers today and two of them were substitutes. Since I spent the morning in the facility, I don't know who teaches those two periods I missed. This makes my grand total of teacher options, two. The math teacher who barely speaks, and Arty who is powerless against my winning smile and would have been the perfect choice except that Elijah is being a pain in my left toenail.

Sigh.

"Why–" My phone rings in my bag, interrupting my train of thought. I drop my books on the floor at our feet and grab my phone. The world suddenly seems brighter when I see who is calling.

"Babe!" I turn on the video so I can see Jace and his chiseled features. That always puts me in a better mood. "Great timing, school just ended. What are you doing?"

Jace doesn't smile. "The question is, what are you doing?"

He is so melodramatic sometimes. It's the byproduct of his artistic side. There's practically a law that says handsome men are supposed to be dark and brooding.

This applies to handsome high school guys as well.

"I'm just chilling. Beth and Elijah are here. Say hi, guys." I turn the phone so Jace can see them. I mean, him. Only Elijah is standing there now. Where did Beth go?

"I only see a dude," Jace says.

"It's Eli." Elijah does that chin lift thing that guys do to say hello and adds, "Nice to meet you too."

"Let me see your face, Carmen."

I flip the phone so I'm looking at Jace again. "You wouldn't believe the day I just had, babe. Not only is there no drama club in this school, but the food is horrific, and the only way Elijah could get my locker open was to do a musical dance number with a top hat and cane."

Elijah's eyes widen and he steps around behind me so he can see Jace again. "That is not what happened. There was no top hat or music. I did NOT dance. She refused to open it herself because she broke a nail. She's being dramatic."

I push Elijah away so he'll stop breathing on the side of my neck.

"Carmen, can I speak with you, alone?" Jace folds his arms and looks pointedly to my left where Elijah stands.

"Subtle. I'm out." Elijah hefts his bag on his shoulder and walks off without another word.

"Is he gone?"

I glance at Elijah's retreating back. "Yes."

"Carmen, what is going on with you and Superman?"

I snort. "Elijah is not Superman. Are you kidding me? He has blond hair and no abs."

"I knew it!" Jace points at the screen, at me, really. "I knew there was something going on with you two. How else would you know anything about his abs?"

Wow, Jace is in a mood. "Duh, Jace, you can tell when a guy is ripped. Like, for example, one look at you, and I can see that you spend hours at the gym. I don't have to actually view your abs to know they are there." I laugh and shake my head. "And vice versa for Elijah. Even if he could find a weight room in this Oscar-forsaken place, he wouldn't have a clue how to use it."

"You're trying hard to convince me there's nothing going on with you two."

"Because nothing is." The thought was so vile, my shoulders hunch over in preparation for an onslaught of nausea.

"I don't know what to think, Carmen." Jace narrows his eyes. "On the one hand, you'd have to be an idiot to turn me down for that guy, but on the other hand, I can't deny the facts in front of my face, because on the last hand, every time I talk to you today, you're with Superman."

The Superman reference is making my neck itch. "Jace..."

Wait a second. Jace just said things were on three hands. How is that even possible? This conversation is ridiculous. I stoop to gather my books and head for the exit. "What do you want me to say, Jace?"

"The truth. Why is that guy everywhere you are today?"

That was an excellent question. "Apparently my maternal parent thinks I'm going to cause havoc at my new school and asked Elijah to babysit me."

"So?"

I turn around to push open the front doors with my back because my hands are all occupied. "So what? I don't get what you're asking."

Jace sighs heavily. "So what if your mom asked him to watch out for you? She asked me to do the same thing once—"

"Really?" That is actually so sweet. I didn't think my mom liked Jace enough to do something like that.

It makes me dislike her a teensy bit less.

"—but that doesn't mean I have to do it."

Significantly less sweet than I originally thought.

"The guy is sus, Carmen. I don't know a single dude who does stuff for a girl without expecting something in return."

I stop walking underneath a huge scraggly tree that about a billion people have tagged with their initials and hearts. "And what exactly do you think he wants in return?"

"What do *you* think he wants?" Jace fires back.

The correct answer was he obviously wants to make my life miserable to match his own sad existence. But since Jace is my boyfriend, and I love him like Scarlett loves Ashley, I stop all the excess brain chatter to really consider his question.

And since I always do my best thinking out loud, I include Jace in the narrative.

"It's a tiny school. He's in a lot of my classes, and the school secretary asked him to show me around. He did it because he said he would and also because it makes sense. We're headed in the same direction most of the day."

Jace grunts.

"When I talked to you and Skylar earlier, Elijah followed me out of class because he suspected I was doing something nefarious, which I wasn't, of course, but if he has this misled conviction that he needs to look out for me on top of a naturally suspicious nature, it makes sense that he would follow me and see what I was doing. And because I know you're going to ask, all I was doing was making a copy of a petition to get signatures to start a drama club."

"There's no drama club? Where are you, exactly? Timbuktu?"

Actually, I think there's probably a thriving theater program in Timbuktu.

I just shake my head and continue. "I saw him at lunch, because, again, the school is minuscule. And then, the only other time was after school."

Just now, duh.

"See, nothing clandestine. Nothing untoward. It's all completely innocent." I start walking again, hugging my books to my chest because the wind goes right through my sweater. I'm going to need to buy a real coat.

Oh!

Online shopping!

This thought puts a spring in my step.

"Why do you look so happy? Is he there with you?" Jace demands.

"No, I–" It takes way too much energy to walk and explain myself. I stop walking again and lean on the nearest street sign. "What is your problem, Jace? Are you really concerned I'm going to fall for some flake in hillbilly hills? Or is there something else going on?"

Jace runs a finger through his hair and happens to glance at his arm. He's captivated for a moment by his bulging bicep. It literally makes him lose his train of thought.

Usually, it would have the same effect on me, but I'm winded, my feet hurt, and I have a bunch of homework just itching to chisel away at my will to live.

"What?" I snap.

My tone startles Jace so he drops the phone. It takes a few minutes of fumbling to get it all to rights again. Jace peers through the screen with pursed lips. "Carmen, you need to moisturize. Your skin looks freaky."

I try not to roll my eyes and succeed, though barely. "Thank you for that insight. What were you going to say?"

"When?"

"When I asked you if you're worried about me falling for a moron like Elijah or if there is something else going on." I swallow a sigh.

Jace stares blankly at me then shrugs. "I totally have no clue."

"Really? You don't remember what you were going to say?"

"Nope, it's gone."

"Well, how about you just answer the question now?" I do calf raises to keep myself from freezing on the concrete. My toes feel like someone soaked them in the Pacific for three hours.

"What question?"

"Jace!" I toss my hair out of my eyes. "I need you to be here for me. This relationship isn't going to work long distance if you can't stick with me long enough to answer a simple question."

"That's it." He nods.

"What's it?"

"That's what I called to tell you."

I am completely lost. "What did you call to tell me?"

"What you just said."

Okay, was he being dense on purpose?

A weight of weariness settles on my shoulders. I'm just going to have to suck it up and walk while I talk. I suddenly want nothing more than a hot bath and my snuggy. "Let's start over, okay? Why did you call me, Jace?"

"This is exactly what I'm talking about." Jace throws his free arm in the air. "You don't listen to anything I say. This isn't going to work, Carmen."

Wait, what?

"What's not going to work?"

"This, you and me, this long-distance thing. It's not working. I can't do this anymore."

It had literally been less than forty-eight hours. "Are you serious?"

"I'm serious. I wanna break up."

I stop walking again. "Ja—"

"Don't try to talk me out of it. This is best for both of us. Now you can be free to hang out with Superman all you want."

"I don't want to hang out with Superman!" I switch the phone from one hand to the other. It's shaking so much I can't focus on Jace's face. I thought it was because I'd been holding it out in front of me for so long that the muscles are all tense, but this other arm shakes just as badly. "I can't believe you're doing this! What about all those things you said about being there for a few months until I'm back in California? That I'm worth waiting forever for? You said you love me, you jerk! All of that can't just disappear after two days."

Unless there is something severely wrong with Jace, which I'm beginning to think is the real problem here.

"This is another thing," he goes on. "You're so emotional. Like, all the time. It's exhausting. I can't even with you anymore. Let's just be done."

"Are you–" The screen goes blank before I can get the words out.

What?

He hung up on me?

Seriously?

My hand drops to my side, my phone hanging so limp it's liable to fall any minute, but I can't find the motivation to care.

Jace did not just break up with me!

What about our plans to be Hollywood's next power couple? We were going to star in a movie together, like John Krasinski and Emily Blunt. We already wrote our acceptance speeches and edited them with Grammarly! I've put so much into this relationship, I can't believe that selfish cretin just threw it all away!

I don't know whether to cry or chuck something really hard, so I just stand there, gaping at the trees.

For about three more seconds.

Then something plows into my side, knocking me to the ground.

Act III Scene I

FADE IN: INT: DILAPIDATED OLD HOUSE -
ADEQUATE BEDROOM - STARTLING REVELATION

I lay face down in the dirt on the side of the road. There is grass on my tongue, mud covering my front teeth, and something heavy draped across my back. A now familiar scent fills my nostrils. I reach back and slap with both hands—at an incredibly awkward angle, by the way—and spit all the stuff out of my mouth so I can shriek.

"Are you crazy? What do you think you're doing?"

Elijah rolls his torso off my back and lands in a kneeling position. "Are you okay?"

"No, I'm not okay! I just got plowed over by an insane stalker! Would you be okay?"

"There is nothing wrong with your mouth, so that's something to be grateful for." Elijah dusts off his arm. "And just for the record, I'm not insane. I didn't plow you over, and I am not stalking you."

"Ha." I spit again. There is a decidedly bitter taste in my mouth. "Then how do you explain the fact that we are sitting in the mud and my Dior skirt is totally ruined?" I gasp. "There's a hole. It's not just ruined, it's decimated! How could you?"

"How could I?" Elijah coughs in disbelief. "You mean, how could I save your life? You were standing in the middle of the road, fruitcake. Just standing there waiting for a semi or something to squish you into a pancake. If your mom hadn't asked me to go find out why it was taking you so long to get home from school, we'd be reading about you in the newspapers." He stops to catch his breath and barks out a humorless laugh instead. "Actually, that's what you want, isn't it? Your picture printed all over the news. So, maybe you're right. I should have just left you there."

I was standing in the middle of the road? I shift through my memories of the last few minutes and seriously can't remember. Everything that happened after Jace hung up is a hazy blur.

Even if I was standing in the middle of the road, Elijah didn't have to tackle me. Whatever happened to politely asking someone to move their buns? I sniff and stand up as modestly as I can in a torn skirt and, yes, broken heel. Skylar gave me these boots. She is going to cry when I tell her. I gather my things from the four corners of whoever owns this yard and hold my head high.

I need to cry desperately, and I refuse to do it in front of Elijah.

I turn away and limp toward the house my parents have deemed home. What a mockery of the word. When they see me, I hope they have remorse for all the ways they have effectively ruined my frail existence in the last two days.

Stupid town.

Stupid Jace.

Stupid Elijah.

"Hey, where are you going?" Elijah jogs to catch up with me. "That's it? You're just going to walk away?"

I suck my lips into my mouth and don't answer. If even a sigh escapes, it will be followed closely by a torrential downpour.

"Hey." Elijah grabs my elbow. His voice is much softer and harder to ignore. "I'm sorry I yelled like that. You're just, really, frustrating."

Well, that was a fabulous apology. I pull away from his grip and continue on my pathetic way.

"Carmen." He appears at my side once again. "That came out wrong. It's not your fault I yelled. I am sorry about that. Are you okay? You're limping."

There is now only one house between me and home. Mom is waiting on the front porch, her hand shielding her eyes as she stares off in the opposite direction. Even though I want to throw her in the garbage for moving me here, my heart zips into my throat at the sight of her.

I hate to admit it, but I really, really need my mommy right now.

I pick up the hobbling pace, trying to ignore Elijah with all my might. He finally stops talking and walks silently with me until we reach the mailbox.

"Mrs. Hurst, Carmen is here. She's fine."

Which is the biggest falsehood of all time.

I really didn't know Elijah had it in him.

"Carmen!" Mom clasps her hands together under her chin, then runs down the driveway toward me. She squishes my face into her shoulder, and smells so perfectly familiar and homey, like that awful ivory hand soap she insists on using even though I buy her expensive body spray for every birthday, that I can't hold in my anguish any longer. I burst into tears so explosive that I lose track of everything around me except Mom cooing in my ear. The next thing I know, Mom is running the bath for me with my favorite lemon rosemary bath salts, and the day melts into oblivion.

Well, until a couple of hours later when I sit down at the kitchen table with a bowl of popcorn and a mug of hot cocoa to tell Mom and Dad every single detail of my horrendous first day of school.

That's all I really needed to do, vent, because once I get it all out, I feel tremendously better.

Also, chocolate helps a lot.

Obviously.

I tap the bottom of my cup to get the residue of marshmallows to slide into my mouth and try to ignore the jubilant smile on Dad's face. It took up permanent residence the moment I told them Jace and I are through. I would be offended if I didn't currently agree with him that Jace is a nimrod.

"Honey, I know things look bad." Mom pats my hand still resting on the table. "Everyone has setbacks, that's just life. The important thing is how you choose to face tomorrow."

Mom is a wealth of inspirational phrases. Most of them end up cross-stitched on overstuffed pillows or vinyled to bathroom mirrors so I won't be able to avoid absorbing them. The joke's on her though. I've mastered the art of brushing my teeth with my eyes closed so I don't have to read that garbage.

Today Mom's perky affirmations are exceptionally disappointing because I thought my day from the shadow of Mt. Doom would convince my parents it's time to move back to Cali. We gave it a good run. It didn't work. It's time to go home.

"Does Arty still teach there?" Dad reaches for the marshmallows and adds another handful, even though there are only a couple of drops of chocolaty goodness left in his mug.

I rest my elbows on the table. "Yeah, I forgot, he said to tell you hi."

Dad rubs the stubble on his chin with one hand. "I haven't seen that guy in years. How is he?"

He's a teacher in the town that time forgot. How did Dad think he was? Eking out a miserable existence, obviously.

I shrug. "And the secretary, Ms. Something or another, said she went to high school with you, Mom."

"What's her name?"

Like I remember that. "It was long and sounded like a guy. That's all I know."

Mom taps her chin. "Hm, maybe I'll walk with you tomorrow so I can pop in and say hello."

Oh, that is a fabulous idea. Walking to school with my mommy. We can hold hands and skip together.

What is wrong with my parents?

"Art Wayas." Dad stares off into space. "Did I ever tell you about the time we almost blew up the chemistry lab?"

And that is my cue. No way I'm taking this blast to the past with my parents after the day I've had. It's barely palatable when I'm the best version of myself.

I push my chair back and stand up. "I'm going to go call Skylar."

Dad's still talking, and Mom is so engrossed in his inane story of yesteryear that they barely look up when I leave. Which is just fine by me. Now that I've worked through the trauma of the day, I am free to hate their stinking life choices once again.

My fingers trail along the hall wall as I make my way to my room. No, not my room, the room which I have been assigned to make habitable until I'm old enough to leave forever and never look back. I push the door open and flip on the light.

My down comforter is spread over the bed. My antique desk is in the corner with my replica of the leg lamp from *A Christmas Story* perched on the corner. The corners of my eyes sting as I walk to the closet and open it. There are my costumes, all snuggled in the back corner while my glorious arrangement of clothing swings happily toward the front.

If chocolate soothed my soul, this has mended it. I'm convinced a girl can face practically anything with an array of clothing options such as these.

I fish my phone out of my bag and dial Skylar.

"Carmen! Are you alright?"

It takes me a minute to process what she's asking. I haven't had a chance to talk to her since that ill-fated encounter in the hall this morning. She can't possibly know all the things that happened to me since then, can she?

"I cannot believe Jace dumped you already! I thought he'd last in this long-distance thing for at least a week."

Oh, that's what she's talking about.

Also—what?

"He's already attached like a squid to some foreign exchange student. She can't even say his name, she calls him 'Cage'."

I do not have it in me to listen to this anymore. Even though I want to ask Skylar how she knew Jace would break up with me. I thoroughly did not see that coming. I am dying to know, but for me, the pain is still too near.

"Sky!" I shout over her ramblings. "I don't want to talk about Jace, or whatever. I called because my clothes are finally here and I need an outfit for tomorrow."

Skylar sits up straight in her pink director's chair and waves her arm like fashion royalty. "You have come to the right place, my darling. Commence with the choices."

That's more like it. I'm always glad Skylar is my bestie, but especially now that she's transitioned so quickly from Jace to clothes. It's nice to have at least one person in my life who knows what is truly important.

I walk through each item in the closet once, then go back through and wait for Skylar to tell me what I should wear.

"The red top, the long-sleeved one with cutouts to the wrist, for sure. Do you still have those slinky black pants that look like leather? They make your booty look fantastic."

I pull them off a shelf and hold them up.

Skylar claps. "Perfect! Watch out guys of... What's the name of that town again?"

"Who cares?" I drape the clothes over my desk chair. "I'm not wearing any of this for them."

"How was school today, pumpkin?"

I don't want to talk about that either. "It was school. What's going on there? Anything new? Besides Cage and his petite femme. I don't want to talk about that, remember?"

Skylar goes off on an informative monologue about who just got a nose job, Ania Cruise, but I already knew about that. Who just got a nose job that was botched beyond recognition, Jasmina Michaels, which I didn't know about and find hilarious. Who is dating who, tactfully excluding Jace, and the drama club preparations for Wicked, which I just decided I don't want to hear about either.

I pull out some nail polish that precisely matches my sweater for tomorrow and consign myself to half-listening for the remainder of our call. Skylar's list of things to talk about is so diminished, it's not really worth my full attention anymore.

"Oh, Carmen! I totally almost spaced this. I can't believe it! Guess what?"

"Hm?" I transform my boring pinkie into a shiny, glamorous red. It looks so fantastic I must hold it aloft and admire it.

"Mr. Call announced to the drama club that The Los Angeles Acting Academy is opening enrollment for the first time in like twelve years."

The nail polish bottle slips out of my hand and almost tips onto the carpet. I grab it just in time. The only sign that anything went amiss is the droplet of red nail polish that just landed on my big toe. "Are you serious?"

"Yes! I am totally serious! They are looking for new talent, so they're holding a nationwide monologue contest. You have to go to the website and fill out an application. If you win, they fly you here in January, as like, a finalist, and you compete for a full-ride scholarship!"

I heard the words she said before and I hear her confirm them now, but I am having a difficult time processing. It can't be real. Dreams don't come true, do they?

LAAA is the acting school of my soul. It is super hard to get into because they accept students by referral only. That's part of the reason Skylar and I used to follow Chris Pratt around. We were looking for the perfect opportunity to wow him with our skills so he would write us a letter of recommendation to LAAA.

Well, that and his abs, obviously.

I'm positive it would have worked if not for that unfortunate boba incident and the consequential restraining order.

Both Skylar and I have trained ourselves to recite a monologue in an instant with the slightest provocation. We can also spout off a heart-rending acceptance speech without even thinking about it.

"Car, did you hear what I said?"

I blink and look around. Just a moment ago I was wearing a Valentino, walking the red carpet to accept my Academy Award. Now I sit with red nail polish colored outside the lines, that is never coming off my skin. They weren't kidding when they labeled it rapid-drying.

"No, sorry. What did you say?"

Skylar laughs and shoos me with her hands. "Get off the phone and look this thing up. I think it's your chance."

My chance.

My chance to go to the same acting school as Laura Valentine.

My chance to leave Hobo county for LA.

My chance to get back with Jace.

I have to win this scholarship.

I will do whatever it takes.

ACT IV SCENE II

Apparently, whatever it takes is parental permission, if under eighteen, which I am, and an official drama club recommendation.

I'm glad Jace and I broke up because now I can focus. Instead of spending energy on the care and feeding of a long-distance boyfriend, I can throw myself into what really matters.

Drama Club.

My mission is clear. I have to get this drama club thing going, and fast, so I can fill out this application before the end of September deadline.

I close my computer screen and go find my mom for Elijah's phone number. I'll just ignore how creepy weird it is that I'm asking my mother for the phone number of a fellow student. In a disturbing way, I'm getting used to the complete insanity of my new reality.

I enter the number into my phone and put the name KingPain instead of Elijah. The nickname is Truth. But it also serves a dual purpose. If, perchance, someone got ahold of my phone, they wouldn't know that KingPain was Elijah. That could be the description of a number of people in this town. I can't have anyone in my future life knowing that

I corresponded with Elijah. He isn't the image I want to be associated with.

I push the call button and count the rings while I pace my bedroom floor.

"Hello?"

"Elijah, it's Carmen."

"Eli." He sighs.

"Whatever, did you get the signatures for the drama club petition?"

"Yes."

"All twenty-five?" I admit, I don't believe him. How could he possibly coerce that many people into signing that quickly? It for sure wasn't because of his winning personality. That everybody-loves-me farm boy routine is so contrived.

He probably bribed them.

"Yes, all twenty-five."

"Fabulous. I will be there in the morning to pick it up."

"I can just bring it to school."

"Oh, I'm sure you can." I roll my eyes. "That's not the point. I need that paper right away, so I'll come pick it up first thing."

"Why?"

Why, indeed? Why was he so stinking nosy?

"Why, what?" I clip my words so they sound short and snappy.

"Why can't you wait until school starts? What's the big deal?"

"Because, Elijah." I heave a great sigh. "I need the list to show the teacher I'm going to award the honor of being our sponsor first thing tomorrow morning."

"You didn't exactly answer my question."

"Then you didn't ask it correctly."

Now it's Elijah's turn to heave a great sigh. "Let's try this, then. Why does all of this have to happen first thing tomorrow morning? You know it will take a few weeks for them to approve the club? It's not like you'll be on stage, living your dream, by tomorrow after school."

Which just goes to show how little he knows me. Even if it is true that it usually takes the school that much time to approve a club, I refuse to accept that. I will be on the stage, living my dream, by tomorrow afternoon, or I'll pick every particle of dried and cakey manure off Elijah's cowboy boots with my now stubby, but beautifully painted fingernails.

"I'll be there at seven," I say.

Elijah is silent for so long, I almost hang up the phone. Then his voice comes through, sounding distant. "Who is the teacher you're coercing?"

"I'm not going to tell you." Because I don't have any faith left in his ability to stay out of my business and not ruin everything.

"I thought so." Now he sounded angry. "Are you going to ask Arty? Because I was serious when I told you I'm out if you do. I will feed this list to my sister's pig right now."

"Simmer down." I roll my eyes. Wow, seriously, he has no business making fun of me. Boy is seriously melodramatic. "You've made your position very clear. I'm not asking Arty. I'm going to ask Ms. Math Teacher Lady. The super quiet one."

"Ms. Buckley?"

"Sure, yeah, her."

There is a brief silence. "Does she act?"

"I seriously doubt it. But what she did do is offer to help me adjust to a new school, and this is what I need to fully adjust. A drama club."

Another deep sigh. "I'll see you in the morning, Carmen."

I had my doubts, but Elijah is waiting for me at the door at exactly seven the next morning. Before I have a chance to say anything, he holds up the petition so I can see my hurriedly scrawled, but still breath-taking, title of drama club and the twenty-five signatures after that.

I yank it out of his hand and start perusing the list.

"You're welcome."

I ignore him and keep reading. It's not like I recognize any of the names on here. I guess I just want to make sure they are real names. That he didn't use fillers like Mickey Mouse and expect it to count.

So far, so good.

Except...

"Kelpie signed the list?" I look up. "Does she have the depth to appreciate drama?"

Actually, an attention hog like her probably gets her energy from the stage spotlight, like solar power, only stronger.

Elijah shrugs. "I guess so."

She's playing her part well. I'll just have to come up with a creative way to oust her before it goes any further. I've seen enough teen dramas to know Kelpie will do everything she can to thwart my plan.

She and Elijah are competing for the role of archnemesis.

I fold the list carefully in half and wedge it between the pages of my math book. "Bubye, now."

"What?"

I glance over my shoulder to see Elijah's incredulous face. "What?"

"That's it? No thank you? No I appreciate what you've done? Nothing?"

Like he needs ego enforcement. Clearly, he already knows, or rather thinks, he's awe-inspiring enough all by himself.

I pull my Oakley sunglasses out of my hair and put them in place over my eyes. "Sure, good job. I'll see you at school." Without looking back this time, I stroll down the driveway away from him. I half expect the sound of running footsteps or a hand on my arm.

Considering Elijah's past record, it is more than fair for me to think this. So far, in the short time I've known him, he can't keep his butt out of my business.

Today, however, appears to be the exception.

The entire journey to the school, I listen with one ear and watch with one eye for Elijah to appear. It isn't until I walk through the front doors and head for the math hall, that I finally accept he isn't following me.

And only then can I relax.

I wiggle my shoulders to get rid of all that balled-up tension between my shoulder blades and wiggle my neck to ease the stress-induced tightness.

There, I feel like myself again.

Confident and capable, ready to convince Ms. Whatever-her-name-is that she wants to sponsor drama club more than she wants to do anything else in the whole entire world.

Before I enter the classroom, I remove my sunglasses and check my reflection in the lens. They are a little dim for a mirror, but it does the job. I look amazing. Totally and completely ready to take on a math teacher.

I knock on the side of the door jamb before I walk inside.

Ms. Teacher looks up and smiles when she sees me coming toward her. "Carmen, you're here early. What can I do for you?"

Now that is a question I can answer without even thinking about it.

"Oh,"—I flounce into the chair on the outer side of her desk—"I am so glad you asked!"

She blinks and discreetly scoots away from me.

I lean forward to close the distance she just created. "Remember how you said you would do anything to help me adjust to this new school?"

"Did I, um, say that?"

I nod enthusiastically. "Yes, I clearly remember you stating that it was your one wish to do your part to sustain me in my time of need at this alien establishment."

She twitches her head to the side. "I'm sure I—"

"That's why I came early this morning, to speak with you. See, there is something I want to do that would make this, my senior year, in a foreign school with no friends closer than four hundred miles away, marginally bearable. Do you know how Missy is petitioning to start an Oceanography club?"

She nods.

"Well, I would like to start a club too." I pull the page out of my backpack and slap it on the desk between us. The teacher startles and then leans over the paper, her cheeks reddening.

"I want to start a drama club."

Ms. Lady looks up, the red in her cheeks deepens to a maroon color. Either that or she picked the way wrong blush for her skin tone. "That's, um, that's lovely, Carmen. If that's what interests you, I'm happy you found an outlet."

"Yes!" I grab her hand and hold it tightly between both of mine. "I'm so glad you understand. Because you see, all I need is a teacher sponsor for the club, and then it's a go."

She rises to her feet so abruptly that her chair skids into the wall and falls over. I stand too, so we're not at such a disheveled angle.

"You said to come to you if I needed help with anything. Remember?"

She pulls her hand out of my vice grip and turns away, but not before I notice the goosebumps on her arms. So gross. She should have worn a long-sleeve sweater.

"I don't act. Why ask me? I'm sure there are lots of teachers more qualified to sponsor your club. Did you ask Mrs. Dunlap?"

"We did. She's about to enter her confinement and couldn't give us a long-term commitment." I want to revel in my use of the word confinement. It's so rare that I get to use it in day-to-day conversation. "I've given this a lot of thought, and I just know you're the one we need."

She whips around so quickly that I get a little dizzy watching her. "Why would you think that?"

Obviously, I can't tell her the real reason, that I think she's a pushover who will do whatever I say. Best to go with truth number two. No, actually, that truth isn't any better, that Elijah won't let me ask Arty, who will also do whatever I say. Truth number three it is, then.

"We need you because you're a teacher that cares. You want your students to dream and achieve." I point to the cat poster behind her that has this very phrase.

She looks at it for a long time, rubbing her arms to make the goosebumps go away.

It isn't working.

I tear my eyes away and look at her appealingly. "This is my dream, Ms...."

Oh, shoot, what was her name? I'm glad she's still staring at the poster and doesn't notice my mad scramble to look for her nameplate. It has to be somewhere on her desk, right? Isn't that, like, a school law or something to have those things in plain sight in case a student is trying to convince you to do something and can't remember your name?

Apparently not.

I don't see a plate, but I do see a printed email, addressed to a Ms....

"Buckley. My dream. I've wanted to act on stage and on screen since I was a little girl. You can make my dream become a reality. All you have to do is write your name on this sheet and sign it. Then I can go to the office and make my dream come true." I pause for thematic effect. "Because of you."

Ms. Buckley shifts her gaze to my face. "Why do you want to act?"

That is not the question I am expecting. Also, it is the dumbest question in the world. Who wouldn't want to act? Flashing cameras, bright lights, expensive chocolates, red carpets, fancy dresses, dreamy men, not to mention the money. It's like every red-blooded American girl's dream, not just mine.

But, there's something about the way she asks, and the look in her eye, that makes me pause and consider.

Why do I want to act?

Besides all the fame and glamor?

"I just, really love it."

She nods, slowly. "Why?"

I brush away the impatience. This moment feels heavy, significant, like my answer is the difference between agreement and disagreement from Ms. Buckley. It doesn't seem like she'd be impressed with any of the reasons I already listed in my head. The woman wears shoes from the dollar store, I'm pretty sure.

And cuts her own hair.

So, what will persuade her? What is the thing that she cannot refuse?

And no, I don't think "it's fun" is going to work.

"I guess..." I look up at the ceiling for inspiration and then realize that makes me seem more vulnerable so I widen my eyes and pooch out my lips a little bit. "I mean, I suppose it's because that's the one and only place I feel like I belong. My parents are intellectuals and, well, their interests have never aligned with mine. I'm an only child with few close friends."

I wonder if that was too much of a stretch, but when I glance at Ms. B, I can see that it was the exact right thing to say. She's slowly melting, her hands resting on her desktop now instead of clasping her elbows.

"When I'm on the stage, or in front of cameras, I know exactly who I am and exactly what I need to do. I guess…" I let out a wrenching sigh. "I guess you could say that I find myself when I am acting."

There is a long silence, in which I wonder again if I overdid it.

Ms. B finally looks at me, like, really looks at me. Her deep blue eyes swim, but her gaze is steady. She steels herself as if she's about to agree to donate one of her internal organs to my cause. "Alright, Carmen, I will sponsor your drama club."

I squeal and hug her and twirl and spout off a bunch of stuff like she won't have to do a thing except show up, I'll take care of everything, and I promise she won't regret it.

But as I leave the classroom in my rush to the office before the first bell rings, I happen to glance back. Ms. B falls into her desk chair and drops her head into her hands.

Yeah, okay, she might already regret it.

ACT IV SCENE III

FADE IN: INT: SAME DAY - SAME HICK SCHOOL - VISITATION WITH AUTHORITY - UNEXPECTED INVITATION

I t takes me approximately three minutes to get the official approval for my club.

That might have something to do with my refusal to give the secretary lady the petition and my insistence that I talk to the principal directly and my semi-loud statement that I didn't care if he was in a meeting with Angelina Jolie herself, I needed to speak with the principal, but all of that is up for interpretation.

Personally, I think asserting myself to get what I want is an admirable quality.

I don't bother to sit down on the cracked blue chair outside the principal's office when the frazzled secretary leads me there. She knocks softly before opening the door.

"Excuse me, I know you asked not to be disturbed..."

Which is all the opening I need. I push my way through the crack to face the head of the school, the man in charge. He who holds all my potential future happiness in the palm of his hands.

I almost burst out laughing.

His important meeting is with the art teacher.

They both look up with startled eyes. This is hugely in my favor but still needs caution. I switch tactics at the last second. I am enormously skilled at observing a scene and making adjustments as necessary.

This is one of the reasons my old high school tabloid stated my portrayal of Elsa in the Frozen musical was mesmerizing.

"Oh, my goodness, I am so sorry to intrude." I speak to them both but appeal to Arty. "You see, I have a petition for a club that I feel will be massively beneficial to the student population at this fine institution."

"Young lady, we are in a meeting. I'm sure this can wait." The principal lets out a breath through his overly mustached nose.

Arty raises his hand. "It's alright, Bob, we can stand a small interruption."

Ha, I knew he was on my side!

Principal Bob runs a hand over his sparkling bald head and sighs. "Fine, go on."

"Thank you, Mr. Arty. By the way, my father says he's thrilled to know you're still in town and cannot wait to catch up." A little name-dropping never hurt anything. Neither did a little exaggeration. My father might not have said those actual words, but I'm sure he thought them at some point in his life about somebody.

I hold up the paper so both of them can see. "Here in my hand is a petition with twenty-five names of students who would like to see a drama club established at this school. I also have the sponsorship of the lovely Ms. Buckley, as you will see by the signature at the bottom." I set the paper down and slide it across the desk.

Principal Bob picks it up and peers at it over the top of his glasses. Without a word, he hands it to Arty, who has his palm out.

"We will discuss this petition at the next PTA meeting a week from Friday. Then we'll present it to the board and have an answer to you by the end of the semester."

By the end of the semester? Was he mad?

I dropped my face into indescribable sorrow. "Oh."

Arty looks up from the list. "Elijah's name is on here."

I nod, sagging my shoulders and tucking my chin for extra pathetic-ness.

"How in the world did you manage that?"

The correct answer is that I didn't have anything to do with it, he did it for Beth, but of course I'm not going to say that. Hmm, I wonder if I can make this work for me. Beth is quite loveable and seems to know everyone, which means everyone knows her.

"Oh, well, once Elijah saw that his friend Beth has her heart set on learning how to act, he moved mountains to make it happen for her."

Now that I say that out loud, it's highly suspect. Elijah must have it bad for Beth. Why else would he go to so much trouble for someone else? I'll just log that information away for later, when it's useful.

Information like that always ends up being useful.

"Beth does love the theater," Arty says, almost to himself. "Though, I'm surprised she's joining your club. She's so shy."

I nod, slowly, like my head is too weighed down to hurry. "Yes, well, you see, I am a gifted actor. I've taken lessons since I was a small child in Los Angeles." I pause to let the glamor sink in. "I told Beth I'd help her. I know ever so many exercises to combat nerves. I believe I could coach her to reach her highest potential. But, I guess we'll never have the chance to find out." This time I pause for effect.

Principal Bob shifts impatiently.

I heave a great sigh. "Since it will really be such a long time before we get approval to begin. I fear it will take months to get everyone stage ready. There's never been a drama club at this school before, and no one has a lick of experience."

"Surely–" Principal Bob begins.

I don't let him finish. "It's a shame, really. Everyone was so excited. And, since it's my senior year and all, I guess that's it. Oh, well. Thank you anyway. I appreciate your time."

I reach for my petition, but Arty doesn't give it back. "Bob, it's just a little drama club, do you think we could rush this one through, without all the hoopla?"

Principal Bob rubs the spot between his eyebrows. "I don't know, Art. That's not how it's done."

The principal has shown weakness. Now is the time to strike! But, not for me.

I appeal to Arty with Bambi eyes.

Like a true knight in shining armor, Arty parries his rapier.

"Come on, Bob, it's just for fun. Heaven knows the kids could use something constructive to do after school."

Principal Bob looks at the clock and sighs. "Fine, you have approval. Ask Ms. Giles for the paperwork. I want to see it on my desk by the end of the day." He peers at me under his bushy eyebrows.

"Absolutely, sir, I am more than happy to see this Ms. Giles for paperwork if you will just direct me to her."

He sighs again. "She's the secretary, just outside the door."

I contain my triumph with only a Mona Lisa smile. "Thank you, sir."

"Hm." He narrows his eyes. "I suggest you get to class. The bell is about to ring."

I nod and march for the door, my back straight as a proper model citizen. Arty nudges my elbow, and when I look down, he hands me the petition. "Hang on to this, just in case. You may even want to make a copy." He winks.

Principal Bob sighs again, louder and more heavily, which I believe is my cue to go. I step into the hall and close the door behind me. Madam secretary is nowhere to be seen, so I take that opportunity to bounce up and down and squeal softly.

The full celebration will have to wait until I'm outside, away from passersby, and have access to enough room to do a stellar victory dance with high kicks. I tuck the petition into my pocket and skip out of the office into the hall.

"Nice performance."

I shriek and slam into the wall. Even though the nasty thing hurt my shoulder really bad, I cling to it to keep my balance. I imagine falling in this crowd would be the same as Mufasa's fate during the wildebeest stampede.

When the jolt of surprise wears off, I see Elijah leaning against the wall on the other side of the office door, his arms crossed and his eyebrows touching.

I find my feet and smooth down my clothes. If I exude enough confidence, I can forget that I just about climbed the wall like a spider monkey. I can even pretend he didn't startle me. I just like climbing walls for fun sometimes.

"Oh, hello, Elijah."

"Eli." His lips are pressed together.

"Whatever. What are you doing here?"

"Checking on you."

Checking on me, like I need checking on. This is getting really old, really fast. "Did my parents send you?"

"No, I sent myself. I didn't like the look in your eye this morning."

Didn't like the look in my eye, like he knows anything about the looks in my eye.

"Whatever. I have to go to class. I hate to be tardy."

Elijah snorts but thankfully keeps his opinion to himself for once. He falls into step beside me. I completely ignore him and concentrate on making it to class without getting mauled by the other students. For how few people there are in this school, the halls are alarmingly crowded.

And they seriously reek.

Sweat, stale hot dogs, and hay, oh my!

Elijah steps back and lets me enter the classroom first, right as the bell rings. He shoots me a look, then heads to his desk behind Myles. Kelpie is nowhere to be seen, so my seat is secure. I move my purse and sit down.

"Hi, Carmen."

I smile at Beth, then turn around for Ms. Buckley's greeting and homework check.

Oh yeah, homework.

I knew I was forgetting something.

I whirl around and press my palms into the top of Beth's desk. "I am mortified beyond recognition that I completely failed to do my math homework last night. I was so consumed with everything else, it never even entered my head. How much trouble am I in here? Is it to be hot oil or the rack?"

"Um,"—Beth presses her lips together—"I don't think you need to worry about either of those things. But Ms. Buckley is really a stickler for homework. It's worth sixty percent of our grade."

Sixty percent! That was way too much to blow off! Failure to graduate rears its bulbous head, making me see spots. I take a couple of deep breaths, trying not to hyperventilate.

"Are you okay?" Beth asks gently.

I open my mouth to answer, but my voice has gone with the wind. I try two more times before I croak out the words, "I have to graduate."

Beth nods.

"No, you don't understand." I grab her hands. "If I don't graduate, I can't move back to Los Angeles. I mean, I could, but as a penniless pauper. I'd be forced to take up residence under a freeway overpass."

"I don't understand."

Why did I ever make that deal? I close my eyes. "When my parents first announced this travesty of a plan to leave California, I was forced to take drastic action."

"What did you do?" Beth's eyes widened. Her imagination could never do justice to the reality of duct-taping myself to my closet door.

Such a demonstration would have made the point enough on its own, but then I had a reaction to the tape glue and broke out in a weird purple rash. While we waited to be discharged from Urgent Care after careful removal of said duct tape and some soothing medicated cream, Mom and Dad presented the deal. If I would stop protesting their dream plan of returning to their misguided Utopia, they would fund my life in California.

After graduation.

I double-checked numerous times. Graduation was absolutely a requirement.

Beth makes a small movement that snaps me back to the present. I don't remember what we were talking about before I took that mental stroll down memory lane. All I know is the dire circumstance I now find myself stuck in.

"I *have* to graduate with all of my soul. The alternative is impossible. What am I going to do?"

"You didn't finish *any* of your homework?"

I shake my head.

"For *any* of your classes?" Beth's look turns incredulous. I realize it must be hard for her to understand that there might be things happening that are way more important than homework. She grew up in a place where nothing ever happens. Homework is probably a highlight of everybody's day.

"I had a busy day, okay? My stupid boyfriend broke up with me. Elijah tackled me in the street, and then I found out about the LAAA scholarship. There simply wasn't a spare insta-second for me to do anything else. I didn't even have a chance to don my avocado mask."

"Ms. Hurst?"

I untwist myself to face the front again, and there is Ms. B, standing with her hand out. "Homework?"

"I—"

The words are elusive. Ms. B's face is pinched in a way that tells me she isn't going to appreciate any of my prepared excuse monologues.

Which is a shame, because all of them are marvelous.

"Ms. Buckley?" Beth's voice is shaky, but she continues on. "Carmen wasn't in class yesterday, remember? She left in the beginning and didn't come back in time for the assignment."

"Yes, that is true, but I distinctly remember Elijah volunteering to give her the homework."

All three of us look at him. Along with at least half of the class. Do they not have something better to do than witness my shame?

"I gave it to her." He's a little too eager to volunteer that information.

I scrunch my face. "Are you sure? I don't remember you giving me anything."

Except for a minor concussion.

"I left it on the kitchen counter after I walked you home."

"Ooo oooo oooo." A few disillusioned imbeciles coo.

Elijah shakes his head. "Bruh, no."

Ms. B raises an eyebrow at me.

"I, uh, didn't see it? I had such a formidable day, I simply couldn't observe paltry pieces of paper on counters."

Elijah stares at me incredulously and then shifts his gaze to the ceiling. It's hard to tell from here, but I'm pretty sure he just massively sighed for some reason.

Ms. B steps toward Beth and takes the paper from her hand. "Since you are new, I will give you an extra day. In the future, if you fail to turn in your paltry homework papers, you will receive a zero. There are no make-ups."

"No make-up?" How can that be? Everyone knows life is unbearable without make-up. "No second chances? Ms. B? Can you be so cruel?"

She turns away from the person behind Beth and gives me a stern stare. "Ms. Hurst. The world will not give you second chances, make-ups, or do-overs. I feel it is my duty, as your teacher, to prepare you for real life. Turn your homework in on time, or receive a zero."

I gape at her back as she continues to the next aisle. Unfeeling woman. I never would have believed from observing her. Of course there were do-overs, second chances, and make-ups. She is just being difficult.

Well, I will deal with it. If she wants to run her classroom like the military, I will endure. Whether I agree with her methods or not, she has done me a great service with the drama club, and I will be forever grateful.

Some natures are too lofty for school work, and mine, I fear, is one of them. Alas, I will persevere. I guess I'll just have to do my stupid homework.

While Ms. B finishes up her morning ritual, pausing to discuss the ins and outs of cosines with a brainy-looking girl on the third row, I lean over to Beth and whisper, "Normally, I am amazing at math. It is a feat I am quite equal to, but there is so much on my mind at the present, I fear I will not be able to focus on it..." I pause for the words to take on their own meaning. "...on my own."

"Oh!" Beth nods. "Do you want to join our study group? We meet for an hour or so a couple of times a week. You should. I think it will really help you."

The dear girl is a gem. "Oh, yes, that would be grand. You are a lifesaver, Beth."

She blushes prettily. "Today, after school, at Eli's house."

Wait, no!

More Elijah?

Really?

I hide my inner groan with a tight smile. I am an actress after all. "Lovely, I'll be there."

Act V Scene I

I arrive on the front porch of Elijah's house with my math book, notebook, glitter gel pens, construction paper, and markers. Beth said study *group*. In my experience a group means more than a couple of people, which therefore means there is the possibility of many humans gathered to help me make posters for the new drama club. Once we are done melting our brains with math, of course. I already talked to Ms. B and she's good to meet with the club tomorrow after school in the auditorium, so, all we need is numbers.

And to get those, we need eye-catching fantabulous posters that make everyone who sees them feel like they must join the drama club or perish.

A young girl comes to the door and opens the screen with a confused look on her face. "Yes?"

"Hi there, little one, I'm Carmen, and I'm here for the study group."

She straightens her back. "I'm in seventh grade."

"Of course you are." I shift my books to free up a hand so I can pat her head as I squeeze into the house. It's a good thing I did that celery mint diet with Skylar a few months ago because this little girl didn't give me much of an opening to slip through. "Where are the people gathered?"

She wrinkles her nose like it pains her to answer, then lifts an arm and points down a dark hall.

"I assume that means I should travel in that direction until I find them?" I'm unsure, because the look she's giving me makes me wonder if that hall drops off into a pit of alligators.

"Becky?" An older woman shuffles into the living room. A shock of white skin peeks out of the gap between her mumu and the striped knee socks she wears. "Is that your mama home from work?"

"No." Becky shakes her head. "It's just this girl, Carmen, or some-thing."

"Carmen!" The woman roots through her hair for a pair of glasses and tips them on the end of her nose. Then she rushes me and grabs my hand before I can hide it. "Welcome to the neighborhood, sugar. We are so happy to have your mama and daddy back home. They left a hole in this poor town that only they can fill, and then they bring you back with them! Our cup runneth over!"

Her sincerity wafts all over me, but I refuse to be moved. One nice old lady doesn't change anything. There are probably nice old ladies in Hades, but that doesn't make it a place I want to live.

Or visit.

"Come with me, love." She loops her arm through mine and tugs me toward the hallway. "They're all set up in the den with some of my molasses cookies. It may run slow, but it's brain food, I'm quite sure!"

I let her lead the way since she's going where I want to be. I also let her continue to talk, because she seems to be able to do it without any response from me. I'm actually curious how long she can go without encouragement.

Our walk ends abruptly about two steps into a circular room filled with at least four mismatched couches.

"Dear me, is that the oven timer? It is. 'Scuse me, sweet cheeks. Those cookies just don't improve with time." She pats my arm and hurries through another doorway into the great unknown.

Elijah groans.

"Be nice," Beth whispers loud enough for me to hear, whether she means to or not.

"Did you invite her?" Elijah turns his frustration away from me and onto Beth.

"I did." She lifts her chin. "Of course, I did, Eli. She asked for help with math and she's new here. That's a no-brainer." Then she squints her eyes. "Plus, she's my friend."

Elijah groans again, louder and way more dramatic. He shakes his head, then flips a page in his math book like it mortally offended his family's honor. "Considering how shy you are, I'm kinda surprised you're so quick to invite another person over to my house. Especially a stranger. She's only been here like two days, and she's your friend?"

"Why not?" Beth doesn't look up from her book. "Maybe it's friendship at first sight."

"Yeah, I'm pretty sure that doesn't exist."

"And I'm pretty sure you would think it did if you thought of it first."

"Whatever, Beth." Elijah rolls his eyes. "What happened to stranger danger? Now she knows where I live."

I hate that they're sitting there right in front of me talking like I'm not even there. They should know that's the peevest of pets. I refuse to stay silent one more moment. "No one is stranger than you, Elijah." I flip my hair over my shoulder. "Plus, I already knew where you lived. I live like two house away, as you'll recall. If I was going to do something heinous to you in the confines of your abode, I would have done it by now. Beth has nothing to do with it."

"*Eli.*" He glares at me. "And this is really none of your beeswax."

Beeswax? Really? Who even uses that word anymore? We are in high school, not kindergarten.

I appeal to the rest of the people in the room. Myles, especially, because he appears to be less of a blockhead than the average hillbilly. James is shoveling cookies into his mouth in such rapid succession that I twitch my eyes around to look for cameras, because he has got to be doing an episode for one of those YouTube eating channels. There's no other explanation for stuffing his face like that. Kelpie, of course, is sitting there, too, gazing at the males with one swoony eye and glaring at me with the non-swoony counterpart.

Beth places a hand on Elijah's arm. "Come on, Eli, don't be this guy."

They stare into each other's eyes for so long it starts to get uncomfortable. Really, I am seconds away from spouting off the dialogue of my favorite TV movie just to fill the silence, when Elijah finally looks away.

"Fine, whatever, I don't care. Let's just go over the homework."

"From yesterday, too," Beth says firmly. "So Carmen can catch up."

Elijah grumbles many things that should remain under his breath but turns the page back to what, I presume, is yesterday's homework.

I take the seat Beth offers me with an odd feeling. It is something I rarely have for other people, who are so often vastly inferior, but I recognize it nonetheless.

Respect.

What Beth did just now was manipulation almost to my own level. I currently share a beanbag with a powerhouse that could become a serious rival with a bit of practice. I am fully capable of helping her hone that power. In return, she can teach me how to make Elijah grovel. I would enjoy that more than anything.

What is this hold Beth has on him?

For her, he volunteers to help with the drama club, even though I'm a part of it and he clearly hates me. And the feeling is absolutely mutual, by the way. For her, he gives in, he gives up, and he calms down.

It is clear to me that I need to keep this Beth close.

And now, everyone is looking at me.

"What was that?" I ask.

Eli looks at the ceiling and is clearly counting to ten. I can see each number move into place on his lips.

Not that I'm looking at his lips, ew.

"Myles asked what you were working on at your old school."

I was working on the perfect senior year with the perfect lead in the perfect school musical which would surely have led me to the perfect scholarship to my beloved LAAA.

But, somehow, I sense this is not what they are asking. I swallow a sorrowful sigh and give a robotic recitation of the last semester of math in California.

As far as I can remember it.

"Oh, so you're a little ahead of us. That's really good!" Beth gives me a bright smile.

That is good news. That means I don't have to pay all that much attention as they go over the homework from the day before. I mechanically copy equations and, sure enough, remember how to solve them with ease. It all goes so smoothly, even Elijah stops grumbling every time I take a breath and just does his stupid work.

When the group moves on to the next chapter, I breeze through that too, finishing before the rest of them. While I wait, I begin the prototype design of drama club posters. With this, they can recreate a bazillion identical copies that we can hang all over the school. I put extra effort into my bubble letters and deem them remarkable. Now to create an eye-catching border.

"I'm not sure." Beth looks up from Elijah's paper. "Carmen, can you take a look at this?"

"Hmm?" I pause the border to add an exclamation mark at the end of the title. This is necessary to emphasize how fun the drama club will be. Probably the most fun any of these people have ever had in their entire sad existence.

"Elijah got a different answer than me, and I'm not sure where we went wrong. What did you get?"

I slide my paper over to them so they can figure it out amongst themselves.

Elijah glowers at my paper in a way he usually reserves for me alone. "Carmen?"

"Yep?" There is silence that forces me to tear my eyes away from my flyer masterpiece. "What?"

Beth points to my paper and to hers. "We got the same answer."

"Then clearly it's right." I bend my head over the flyer prototype.

"Or, you're both wrong," Elijah grunts. "I'm going to look in the back of the book."

"Don't do that!" Beth slaps her palm on his book before he can get it open to the right spot. "Check with the group first. That's why we do this."

"Is it?" Elijah bites the words with the same vigor James uses to finish the last cookie on the plate.

"What number are you guys on?" Kelpie asks.

"Seven."

"I'm not there yet, give me a minute." She scribbles on the paper madly to make up for all the time she's been scrolling her Instagram under the table instead of working those math problems.

Yeah, I saw that.

Myles brings his paper over and stoops between Beth and Elijah to check his answers.

James, apparently, has slipped into a cookie coma and is now drooling on his homework. With any luck, he'll wake up with an imprint of the word ZERO on the side of his face.

That seems like good Karma to me.

"My answer is different from both of yours." Myles picks his paper back up to examine it closer. "No, I see what I did. Beth and Carmen are right."

I shoot a well-aimed smug look directly at Elijah's head. He blocks it with disbelief. "I'm checking the book."

It takes approximately thirty-two seconds for him to look up from the answer key and another seventeen to admit he was wrong.

W-R-O-N-G

Wrong.

And that would make me?

Right.

Ha!

Elijah's nana interrupts my touchdown celebration dance with another plate of cookies. The small tap the plate makes on the table is enough to wake James from his slobbery slumber. He pulls the cookies close to his chest, knocking several off the pile and onto the table.

"How are we doing?" Nana clasps her hands and smiles at each one of us like we are her greatest pride and joy. Even Kelpie, who has returned to her insta-feed.

"Fan-slipping-tastic!" I grab one of the cookies from the edge James hasn't touched with his grubby paws and take a big bite. I deserve it after my blatant victory. "Oh, bright lights, these are phenomenal." I stand up and wrap my arms around her. "I love you for making these cookies."

"Oh, dear, my goodness, aren't you the most darling girl? I would adopt you in a second if your parents would agree." She kisses my forehead with a cinnamony waft and leaves for some milk so James can unglue his chops.

"Your grandma wants to adopt me." I return to my place on the beanbag with a smug little shake of the shoulders.

"Heard that." Elijah presses his pencil into the paper so hard that it snaps and a piece flies across the room. He throws the now useless stick of wood on the table and slams his math book shut. "I need a break."

"Oh, that's splendid!" I dust crumbs off my hands and reach for my poster supplies. "And exceptionally good timing because I need help making posters for the drama club. Look, it's super easy. I already made an example for you. Just recreate what you see here so we can hang them all over the school tomorrow." I distribute the supplies and give everyone my best stern librarian stare until they reluctantly start recreating.

"Posters for what now?" Myles adjusts his glasses in a very Clark Kent-y kind of way.

"Drama club." I'm pretty sure I already said that, but things like this are worth repeating. "We have a club, now we need members."

"What about all those signatures Eli got?" Beth's forehead wrinkles in confusion. "Aren't those the members?"

"Yeah, so, those were great, but they were just people saying they are interested. Now we need people who are committed."

"My uncle's committed. Didn't do it though. His alibi was skin tight." James nods seriously.

Um.

Okay.

Moving on now. "We'll need to start, like, yesterday with drama club meetings. We are so behind."

"What's the rush?" Elijah asks.

Followed closely by Myles. "You know it's impossible to start yesterday when you're already firmly rooted in today, don't you?"

These guys, they are killing me. Literally killing me.

"I want us to make the first official meeting happen on Friday after school and then we're going to meet every day. We'll skip weekends, obviously, but otherwise, all in until Christmas break. Make sure people know that."

"That's a lot to ask." Kelpie looks up from her phone long enough to be incredibly unhelpful. "People have lives outside your drama club, you know."

Sad, pathetic lives.

They don't even know what they're missing. It's like the whole stinking town is stuck playing the original Nintendo. When I introduce them to the Nintendo Switch, it is going to blow their minds.

And by "Nintendo Switch" I mean, the grand institution of theater.

"Fine, whatever. All in until October first. That will get us through the monologue competition."

At which time I will blow the academy's mind with my stirring performance, win the scholarship, and get the heck out of this stupid town.

"Monologue competition?" Beth asks.

I didn't actually mean to say that part out loud. "Um, yes, that." Obviously, they were going to find out sooner or later, so, why do I feel so hesitant to talk about it?

I mean, it's not like anyone within a hundred-mile radius is actual competition for me.

"Yeah, so, some acting school in LA is having a monologue competition. It's nationwide, so we can all enter. It will be an easy way to practice performing in front of people while we're still working on funding for sets and costumes and things."

Kelpie popped a bubble with her gum and sucked it back into her mouth. "What's the prize?"

Now why did she have to go and ask that? I don't want to tell her what the prize is in case it fills her head with visions of grandeur. I'll have to stall until someone changes the subject. Shouldn't be a problem, I am the master of hemming and hawing. I bet I can drag this out until it's time to go without ever telling her anything else.

"Wait a second." Elijah sits up. "Do we need funding? You never said anything about that. I'm beginning to think this is a mistake."

"Eli..." Beth's pleading eyes are too much, even for me, and I'm not in the blast zone.

"I know, I said I'd help and I'll help. Sheesh, don't give me that look. This is just way more than I signed up for."

"I can ask my parents." Myles shades in his bubble letters with a blue marker. "They like to support local."

Elijah smirks. "Dude, that's perfect."

It sounded perfect, but I really don't like the look on Elijah's stupid face. Plus, I can't imagine Myles' parents have enough money to fund an entire high school theater program. He is also wearing Walmart jeans.

I put my hands on my hips. "What would you ask your parents?"

Myles gives me a stern look. "I would ask them to make a contribution. With their business. They do that all the time for tax write-offs."

Elijah leans forward like he can't wait to see what happens next. I fail to see what the big deal is, but I take the bait out of curiosity. "And, what is their business?"

"Brooks Mortuary." Myles reaches for a green marker and I watch, because he has got to be joking.

James interrupts with the dumbest question of all time. "Are there any more cookies?"

"Did you seriously eat all of those? James! You are disgusting!" Kelpie smacks him on the arm, then takes a pic of the empty plate and James. I could give her the perfect caption if I were so inclined, which I'm not. It would be the perfect blend of funny and biting.

Elijah laces his fingers behind his head and stares at me like a creeper. "Isn't that nice of Myles' parents?"

Before I have a chance to respond, Nana appears like she was just waiting in the wings for someone to ask for more food. She is followed closely by the little sister, Hecky, or whatever her name is, carrying a pitcher of milk.

"We thought you might need some more sugar. How are y'all getting along in here."

James can't respond. His cheeks already bulge with cookies. Kelpie doesn't even look up as she snaps a pic of the full plate and gets to work on whatever lame thing she has to say about it. Elijah continues to stare at me, which I have had about enough of, by the way. Myles works dutifully like a good robot, and Beth colors poster paper with starry eyes.

"We're taking a homework break, Nana," Elijah says. "So Carmen can use us as slave labor for drama club posters."

Oh, that was just adorable.

"Drama club!" Nana claps her hands. "Oh, I loved the theater once upon a time. Did I ever tell you about the summer I toured as Juliet in a traveling Shakespeare Troupe?"

Wow, as fascinating as that sounds...

"Well, thanks for the cookies!" I smile brightly, hoping they will get the hint to go. Especially Hecky. She's staring at me with the exact same expression as Elijah, and it is really starting to freak me out.

"Let us know if you need anything. Come along, Becky."

Becky, Hecky, it's practically the same name.

She smiles sweetly, holding the milk pitcher with both hands. "Can I pour you some milk? It's fresh from this morning."

"No." I turn away with my nose in the air. "That is completely vile." I swear I see hairs floating around on the top. I'm not drinking anything that hasn't been pasteurized or sanitized or any of the izes.

"Okay."

Now, silly me, I thought she meant, "Okay I'll go now and stop pestering you like the mini Elijah that I am," but no, apparently what she means is, "okay, now I'll dump milk over your head."

Because that's what she does.

I scream and launch to my feet. Not only is this shirt I'm wearing actual real silk and now completely ruined, but that milk is freezing. I hop up and down, alternately shrieking at the top of my lungs and glaring at Becky.

If she was within grabbing distance, I would not be responsible for my actions.

But, like a wise little weasel, she retreats right after she enacted her diabolical deed. "So sorry, I'm so clumsy."

She doesn't even try to hide her grin.

Or the air high-five she shares with Elijah.

Nana rushes back into the room at the first ring of my anguish. Now she pats me all over with thin, scratchy towels that have probably never ever even brushed elbows with Egyptian Cotton. I have had quite enough of this family.

I hold both hands in the air, causing the towel on my shoulders to slip to the floor. "I believe," I announce, "this is my cue to exit. I expect one of you will bring the unblemished posters to school tomorrow."

Beth nods, rapidly. "I'll do it, I can do it."

I gather my purse and books, then turn on my dairy-destroyed heel and leave them all behind.

As soon as I shut the front door, the house rocks with laughter. Peasants, really. I can't believe the things I put up with in the name of my art. Well, let's see how hard they're laughing when I accept my third Oscar.

I can't wait for that moment.

Act V Scene II

S omehow I survived my first full week of Hillbilly High School.

It's a miracle really.

But now, it's Friday afternoon, and I am waiting in the auditorium, combating the stench of stale french fries with vanilla lotion. Ms. B sits in the farthest, most isolated corner of the auditorium grading papers. I sent her there, with assurance that I have everything in hand.

Which I do.

Now I can get this thing started the way I want, without any interference. Ms. B might be the responsible party, but I am definitely the one in charge.

Principal Bob already stopped by twice to check on things in the five minutes since school ended. He keeps eying me like he expects illegal contraband to jump out of the rafters and conga line across the stage with a background of explosions. In fact, I have a suspicion he's using the sound and lighting box to spy on me right this moment.

Not only is that disturbing, but it's got to be tremendously boring. It's only Ms. B, me, and Beth at this point, and we're for sure not doing anything noteworthy. He seriously needs to chill out.

And so do I.

I'm blaming my sweaty palms on the lotion, but even I know that's not true. I'm freaking out a little bit here. I'm not sure if I can keep Ms. B involved if it's just Beth and me. In my memory, and believe me, I've racked it, there are very few successful plays involving only two characters.

"Elijah will be here, I'm sure." Beth wrings her hands nervously.

I'm sure too. He's not going to disappoint his precious Beth, and where he goes, Myles goes. So that makes four people. I can't think of any four person plays either.

"I heard Kelsie say she's coming." Now Beth twiddles with the end of her ponytail. "She was talking to Tina and Michelle and Nina, so I'm sure they will be here too. They looked really excited." Her foot wiggles so quickly that I'm concerned it's going to launch into the air at any moment.

"I'm not worried." I plop onto the stage, my home away from home, and lean back as if I am enjoying a relaxing day on the beach. All of my training emerges when I am the most stressed and also when I have an audience. Even if it's just Beth, it's enough. I can rise above all tumult when I know someone is watching. It is one of my greatest strengths.

"How can you not worry? What if no one shows up?"

I raise my palm. "Please, why wouldn't they show up?"

Beth stares at my hand, then flips her gaze to my face. "I wish I had an eighth of your confidence. How can you be so sure of everything, all the time?"

I suppose it could be that I am amazing at manipulating reality to be what I want it to be. Or, it could be a byproduct of growing up in the most dazzling city in the world. Either way, I'm not going to tell her that. There's no reason to bombard her with the realization that she'll never be able to achieve what I have because she grew up in this forest speck.

It's really not her fault, and she is a sweet girl. I wish there was something I could do for her.

Wait!

Maybe there is.

I slip off the stage and take the seat next to Beth. My sudden movement makes her foot speed up, something I didn't think was humanly possible until this moment.

"I'm going to help you, Beth."

Her eyes widen. "Help me what?"

I grip her shoulder so I have her full attention. "I'm going to help you win your heart's desire."

"My heart's desire?" She blinks.

"Yes, your heart's desire. I am horrendously busy, but I think you need this. I don't really understand it. I mean, I think he is an idiot, but it's not about what I want, it's what you want, so I'm going to give you some pointers on how to win Elijah."

"Elijah?" She says the name like it feels foreign in her mouth. "Do you mean Eli?"

"Yes, so, I don't know if you noticed this or not, but he watches you all the time. And he keeps doing things to make you happy. I thought at first that you were just stringing him along, but now I realize you just lack the self-esteem to realize that a guy might actually like you, so I feel it's my duty to point out the painfully obvious."

"But—"

I hold up my hand. "No need to thank me. I am happy to help. Overjoyed, in fact. Or I would be if I were fixing you up with someone less idiotic than Elijah. But I won't judge your taste. At least not to your face. Actually, before we go any further, is it possible you could like someone else and I could help you win them instead?"

"Um…"

"Never mind, I get it. The heart wants what it wants. Okay, so, rule number one, when Elijah shows up in the auditorium, make sure you say hello to him, with a smile, and as an added bonus, tell him you saved a seat for him." I tap my finger against my bottom lip. "Now that I think about it some more, dating is a lot like acting. At first, anyway, until you get to know each other better. Do you have any questions?"

"Uh—"

"Shhhh." I flap my hands and stand up. "They're coming. Remember what I said, okay? Wave, hello, smile, saved seat."

Beth just nods like she's in a trance. I should have given her only one action item. Clearly, she is daunted by four.

The people approaching are not just Elijah and Myles. James is with them, which I should have foreseen, but also a huge red-haired guy I haven't met, a medium sized guy with dark hair, and Kelpie with her crew of wannabes.

The auditorium is filling up.

Just the way I like it.

I head back to the stage and pick up my notes. It's a simple collection of jotted thoughts from last night before I went to bed. I don't really need to review them. I can't read my handwriting anyway, but it feels lovely to have something in my hands.

Like, more legit.

I shuffle my papers so if someone happened to observe me, they would see me focused on my task, but really, I watch Beth to see if she'll follow my advice. I almost let a sigh escape–amateur move–because Beth just sits there like she missed out on the latest Coach clearance event. All frozen and lifeless. I clear my throat until she looks at me, then I mouth the words, wave, hello, smile, and seat.

She gives her head a slight shake, but I nod firmly, widening my eyes for effect. Finally, she sighs and raises her hand. "Eli, I saved you a seat."

"Cool." He and the rest of the guys crowd around Beth while they get settled. It takes an abominably long time for all of them to sit down, but I wait patiently until the moment comes where I can smile at Beth and give a discreet thumbs up.

She doesn't acknowledge if she saw me or not.

No matter. It is exactly three-o-five. I'm not wasting another second getting this thing underway.

Beth and I can talk later.

I clap my hands to get the attention of the room. My drama teacher in third grade could do this just by clearing her throat daintily, but I don't think we're at that point yet.

Also, I don't think Hillbilly Land does dainty.

It takes a while for everyone to quit their mindless jabbering and look at me. "Welcome to the wonderful world of theater!" I announce in my most prestigious voice.

I admit, I expected applause, so when all I get is blank stares, it mildly takes my breath away. I drop the bravado in disappointment and my arms to my sides.

Whatever, let's just move on with this thing.

"My name is Carmen Hurst. I recently descended on this..." I cough so I don't have to supply an adjective. "...town with my parental figures from the grand and glorious city of Los Angeles."

"Ain't that near Tulsa?" James says without even raising his hand.

How dare he!

"No, sir, LA is not even in the same sphere as Oklahoma."

"Oh, yeah, I knowed that! LA. When you said the whole Los Ang-thing, it sounded like that one place near Tulsa where we got them hot wings with my great grandpa."

I raise my voice. "Having lived in LA for the last seventeen years, I have honed and refined my skills at acting, which makes me uniquely qualified to lead you along this path of greatness. Together we will take that seed of acting that is in your soul, however small and withered it may be"—I shoot a glance at Elijah—"and nurture it until it blooms into a thing of beauty." I clap my hands once again. "Now, how many of you have been in a play, one act, theatrical, or the like? Just raise your hands, if you please."

All the hands enter the air.

They have got to be kidding me.

I point to the dark-haired guy lounging in the seat behind Elijah. "What's your name?"

"Eldon."

"Eldon, tell me about this piece of theater you experienced."

"Yeah, so, every summer my cousin comes to visit and she makes us do haunted houses in the basement of my grandparents' house. I'm always a zombie. No, one year I was a ghost, but yeah, mostly a zombie."

A haunted house. That is his great theater experience?

My sensibilities scream in agony.

"Yeah, one year, she even made us put ketchup on our hands to make it look like there were bloody handprints on the walls. Our moms were so peeved, we had to stop in the middle to clean up the walls, but by then it all dried up so it took hours to get all the ketchup off. All that scrubbing also took off the paint so then we had to repaint the wall. We never did finish that haunted house."

And now my sensibilities are writhing on the floor.

"Wow, okay, does anyone else have"—I clear my throat—"theater experience they would like to share?"

Beth shifts in her seat. When Elijah leans over, she whispers something to him. He shakes his head, then she puts a hand on his arm. Physical contact, I'm impressed! I didn't even cover that yet. It was our next lesson, after the waving, hello, smile, seat thing.

Maybe there's something to be said for the natural instinct of a woman to flirt. I can't think of any other way Beth would have known to do that.

Elijah puts two of his fingers in the air.

"Yes," I nod at him. "Elijah?"

"Eli." He takes a deep breath. "Beth just reminded me that we all did that reader theater in Mr. Kirkpatrick's class in fifth grade. You guys remember? Alice in Wonderland."

Murmurs echo through the auditorium's acoustics.

That's slightly better than a haunted house. At least reader's theater and actual theater live on the same planet. But it's still not great.

I don't want to hear any more about their experience. This was a bad idea. It's just making me depressed.

"Well, thank you for sharing. I have a much better idea of what your level is." I catch Elijah's eye and he scowls at me.

Wow, he is so cranky.

The boy seriously needs a girlfriend.

"We won't try and tackle something as monumental as a group performance until we have better skills and supplies. So, for now, we're going to concentrate on monologues." I take a deep breath to launch into my explanation of the revered monologue, but a chorus of questions interrupt.

I let my breath out and clap my hands. "One at a time, seriously, I can't understand anyone when you all talk at once. You." I point to the red-haired guy. "Name and question, please."

"Yeah, name's Zeb, uh, I have a question about that mono thing."

"Yes?" It is getting increasingly difficult to remain patient.

"Uh, what is it?"

"Excellent question," I say through my teeth. "Thank you for asking. I was just getting to that. A monologue—"

"I know about that thing!" James sprays chip crumbs all over the seats in the row in front of him. I imagine everyone is extremely grateful they chose to sit somewhere else. "My cousin had that after he kissed that pig on a dare. He was sick for a couple of years with yellow fever."

What?

"She is not a pig!" One of the Kelpie girls points a finger at James. She's practically draped over the back of the chairs, trying to get at him. "Your cousin is a turd, and he's the one who had mono first. He gave it to her. She had to give her Ms. Piggly crown to that tramp, Vanessa, because of you! Get your facts straight before you go flying off your stupid mouth."

Beth puts a hand over her smile and hunches over to hide how much her shoulders are shaking.

Elijah raises his hand.

"What?" I snap.

"I believe what my friend James is talking about is the virus, Mono. That's what his cousin got." A screeching sound makes him look at the Kelpie girl and reconsider his word choice. "Or already had and shared, or whatever."

"Thank you for clarifying." I try to think happy thoughts, but they are alarmingly elusive at the moment. "A monologue is quite different from that disease of which you speak."

"Virus," Myles says.

"Sure, okay, yeah, whatever. A monologue in theater is a piece of speech that allows an actor to demonstrate their range."

James shoves a bunch of chips in his mouth and then raises his hand. No!

Nonononononononononono.

"Yes?" I point at him.

"My gramps has a home on the range. Also, he has a shooting range on the range. Built it himself to practice skeeting all year round. It's tight."

I have an undeniable urge to pinch the skin between my eyebrows. That's where the biggest headache of all time is threatening to appear. I talk fast so no one can interrupt with any more insanity. "Yeah, so, an actor's range has nothing to do with shooting or any of that stuff. It's the range of emotion they can express, also the depth. A monologue is one of the rare times an actor stands on their own, without any supporting characters, unless they are Tom Hanks in Castaway."

"Wilson!" Zeb bellows, making everyone in the auditorium jump.

Some of them look like they possibly peed their pants.

I am so not checking to see if that happened. I have enough on my plate right now. They are going to have to deal with it on their own.

"Wait, you're saying that you do a monologue all alone?" one of Kelpie's girls asks. I don't bother to get her name, because I really don't care.

"Yes."

She slumps down with a pout. "I only came because I want to do kissing scenes."

Eldon hoots and Zeb raises both massive tree trunk arms into the air. "That's what I'm talking about!"

"So, wait." James sits up straight. "I just had an atomic brain bomb slide. When people kiss in the movies, they, like, don't really know each other, right? They aren't really in love? They're just acting!"

"Uh-huh." I glance at my notes. Literally, I have only covered the first paragraph. We might never get through this.

"So, that means, if I become an actor dude, I get to make out with tons of gorgeous chicks and it don't mean nothing, right? It's just funness. I'm so in the upside down of this thing! Where do I sign?"

"Pig." One of Kelpie's other friends throws a wadded-up ball of something at James.

I wish I had thirty wadded-up balls of something to throw at him. He is completely missing the point. Not only that, he is making a complete mockery of a very precise aspect of theater. Kissing on stage takes way more skill than people think.

This is practically unbearable in every way.

Kelpie raises her hand, and I call on her. If she isn't about to change the subject to something relevant, I am totally done with this whole thing.

"Do you, like, make up a monologue? Or do you have to find one somewhere? And where do you find them? Also, when does an actor use one? I always thought the script people tell you what to say."

Actually all of those are really good questions. Kelsie has surprised me, and that's not easy to do. Maybe I was hasty casting Kelsie as the mean girl. Perhaps she has supporting role potential.

As I gather my thoughts, my eyes swerve to Elijah and his smirking face. He thinks Kelsie's question has stumped me. His doubtful expression is just waiting for me to fail. Little does he know, I can answer that question in my sleep.

"A monologue is used mostly for auditions. You can find monologue sites online where they are divided into categories, making it especially easy to find the one that works best for you." I refrain from dropping the mic and also from sticking out my tongue at Elijah.

It's tough, but so am I.

"Stop and think for a sec," I go on. "I'm sure you can remember a movie or TV show where a character has monologued."

I get a lot of confused faces, at which time I despair of any of them ever comprehending anything, and then...

"Dude!" Zeb punches Eldon in the arm. "'Member on Incredibles? Syndrome was flippin' monologuing? 'Member? When he had all them Incredibles stuck in the blue bubble thingy?"

A smile twitches the corners of my mouth. Okay, for reals, he is absurd, but he's spot on with it.

He gets it.

That's actually kind of cool.

"Right, yeah, that's a good example. Also, in any of the Marvel movies, you're going to find tons of monologues. Anything with a villain will have one. Writer's love to make a villain monologue. So, what we're going to do is spend the future five weeks of our lives deep diving into monologues. We're going to get so good at them, like, amazing. That means your job this weekend is to find one that you like so we can start practicing on Monday."

It would be sooner if I had my way. We'd all be eating, sleeping, and breathing monologues everyday of our lives until I win that scholarship to LAAA.

Beth nudges Elijah, who raises his hand. "Do you have tips on picking a monologue? Like, how do we know what kind is a good fit for, uh, our range?" He raises his eyebrows at Beth, who nods with a smile.

"Oh, that's simple. Just read a bunch of them, try them out, and see what feels natural. It helps if you already know what part you play."

"How would we know what part we play?" Kelsie asks.

"Yeah," Zeb bellows. "I thought you said we're not doing a play."

"Shakespeare said all the world is a stage." I fling out my arm for emphasis. "So we're talking about the part you play in your own life. That's what you determine. When you know who you are, it will be easier to find a monologue that fits you. For sure, you want to feel a zing when you read it, maybe goosebumps, or butterflies in your stomach. The feeling is different for everyone, but it's got to be there or the monologue isn't going to work as well for you."

"Do you have a monologue ready?" Elijah asks with a challenge in his voice.

I roll my eyes. "Duh."

If he knew me at all, he would know I always have at least three memorized monologues in the back of my mind for that moment when a talent scout, studio executive, or big name producer is overcome by my amazingness and asks me to demonstrate my ability. It's best to be prepared at all times.

"I still don't get how this mono thing works. I mean, I get that a villain does them, but I don't get how we're supposed to. I'm like a stuffed possum on a shelf." James crumbles another chip bag and tosses it toward the front row. It veers to the right and smacks Myles in the head.

"Hey!"

He ignores Myles and goes on. "I can't picture it. I'm up a paddle without a leg in this thing."

Now that I know James better, I'm able to sift his true meaning out of all the randomness. That's a W, I think.

"Allow me to demonstrate." I walk to the center of the stage. "We'll walk through the entire process of auditioning with a monologue." I take a deep breath in preparation to project. "My name is Carmen Hurst. I'm seventeen years old, just months from graduating from high school. Today, I'll favor you with Juliet's monologue from Romeo and Juliet by William Shakespeare."

"Romeo and who now?" Zeb says.

I close my eyes and shut out the idiotic question, as well as the sounds and smells of modern day life. No more heaters kicking on, no shifting in seats, no more stale fast food smells. This is ancient times, cobblestone castles and terraces overlooking courtyards. The cover of night with a sprinkle of stars. Velvet drapes and a forbidden crush.

Only when I am convinced I have become the ill-fated Juliet, do I open my mouth.

"O Romeo, Romeo, wherefore art thou Romeo?
Deny thy father and refuse thy name.
Or if thou wilt not, be but sworn my love
And I'll no longer be a Capulet.
'Tis but thy name that is my enemy:
Thou art thyself, though not a Montague.
What's Montague? It is nor hand nor foot
Nor arm nor face nor any other part
Belonging to a man. O be some other name.
What's in a name? That which we call a rose
By any other name would smell as sweet;
So Romeo would, were he not Romeo call'd,
Retain that dear perfection which he owes
Without that title. Romeo, doff thy name,

And for that name, which is no part of thee,
Take all myself."
I lower my head and let the last melodious notes of my voice fade. I imagine there is thunderous applause, just as I always do when I finish a piece. It builds my morale against the silence of the theater. I don't need their affirmation. I provide my own.

Well done, Carmen.

I let out a long sigh to transition back to the present and walk down the stairs to descend among the commoners. "That, my counterparts, is how you perform a monologue."

"What the crap did she just say? I didn't understand none of that." Zeb's face is ashen. "Was that English? Tell me it wasn't English."

James pats him on the back. "Ain't your fault. She speaks in tongues sometimes. I heard her do it the other day. Just about chapped the hide off my ear-ball."

Okay, that's it.

My monologue euphoria has vanished.

I'm done for today.

"Go home, find your monologues, and come back Monday ready to work on them. Byeeeeeee." I wave them off and collapse on the corner of the stage.

Now I want to enact a wrenching death scene.

That feels true to me.

The room clears out in record time, thank goodness. Ms. B congratulates me on a successful first meeting, then scoots on out of there too. The only people left are Elijah and Beth.

Beth looks about as awesome as I feel.

"Well, what do you think, everything you dreamed of?" I give a sharp laugh.

Beth looks up, her eyes full of tears.

"What in the name of the Bard is wrong with you?"

She just shakes her head and lets it drop into her hands.

I slide to the floor and crawl until I can see the underside of her face, squished between her knees.

"I can't do that," Beth croaks, then bursts into sobs worthy of a swoony heroine.

I move back to avoid the waterfall. Elijah puts his arm across Beth's shoulders and glares at me, like this is all my fault. I can practically feel him waiting for me to say the wrong thing and make everything worse.

Well, joke's on him, I played Melanie Wilkes in an extremely abbreviated version of Gone with the Wind. I know how to be sweet and supportive.

Jerk!

I put my hands on Beth's shoulders and push lightly. "Hey, look at me."

She sniffs and raises her head, but just a little. The thing looks like it weighs a billion pounds hanging there off her shoulders.

"I told you I would help you, remember?"

She shakes her head some more, wanting to drop it again, but I hold her shoulders steady so she's forced to stay upright.

"I can't do what you did, Carmen. That was amazing. I felt like I was on a terrace in Italy while you were reciting. It was incredible!" Her eyes light up for just a moment before she droops again. "I'll never be able to do that. I was fooling myself this whole time. I'm just going to quit."

Quit?

In my mind's eye I see the entire club prancing behind Beth as she leads them Pied Piper style out of the theater door. My dreams become the crumbled path on which they trod.

"No, you're not. Remember? You're the girl who played Betsy Ross better than Betsy Ross! I told you I would help you, and I mean it. I'll show you all my tricks. It just takes practice. Like riding a bike or sowing a row or whatever you people do. Acting is like everything else in this world. You can't expect to show up and just be good at it. You have to put in the time and really want it. If you don't ever give up, I promise you'll get good. It's just what happens."

Beth grows very very still. Her big brown eyes lock on mine like she's checking for lies. Lucky for her, there are none. I have fifteen years of acting knowledge in this gorgeous head of mine. I meant everything I said. I absolutely can help her.

"Really?" She rubs her nose against the sleeve of her jacket.

"Duh." I wiggle my head until she smiles. "I have time tomorrow, okay? Let's meet up and we'll get started. I promise you can do this."

"You promise?"

"I more than promise. I guarantee."

ACT V SCENE III

FADE IN: ONE WEEK LATER INT: THE PRACTICING OF MONOLOGUES - NOT ENTIRELY TRAGIC. EXT: (CARMEN) ASSIMILATED INTO THE CULTURE OF HILLBILLY HIGH VIA FOOTBALL GAME WHILE SIMULTANEOUSLY FREEZING HER BOOTS OFF.

Not only did Beth and I spend four hours on Saturday going over stage fright techniques in my backyard where no one but the adjacent pig farm could hear us, but we also met up in Ms. B's class Monday morning before school to practice.

That led to Tuesday morning, and then Wednesday, and so on, until it's Friday afternoon once again, one week since that first monumental drama club meeting.

Everyone has a monologue chosen, a good one too. I didn't even have to intervene. They all showed up on Monday with something that would work and even better, something that will work with their personality.

Even James.

Now they are trying to memorize flawlessly while I take one person at a time and help them insert inflections and, the biggest hurdle of them all, figure out what to do with their hands while they are talking.

That's always such an issue for people.

Ms. B waves good-bye from her corner of the room, and I give everyone their five minute warning. They've developed a habit of lounging around the auditorium long after Ms. B says her farewells. I'm supposed to Facetime with Skylar in an hour, so I have some time, but not forever.

I'm just going to walk the rows and make sure there aren't any food wrappers. Generally, I start cleaning and people start leaving. They're afraid I'm going to ask them to help. Which I will. So it's a great way to clear a room. Plus, it's necessary. I don't want to give Principal Bob any reason to shut us down. He's got a thing with litter, and James stuffs his face with a never-ending supply of snacks throughout our club meetings. He's usually good about picking up his crap, but sometimes he forgets.

I wave Zeb and Eldon out of the way so I can check under the chairs. They oblige by vaulting into the row in front as if they're jumping a fence. I just shake my head and squat to see better.

"So, what do you have going on tonight, Ms. Carmen?" Jeb kneels on the seat and rests his chin on the back of the chair.

Oh, thanks for asking. Skylar and I are going to watch *Clueless* together while we give ourselves mani-pedis.

Somehow, I don't think Zeb wants to hear the actual details. Both because he wouldn't really care and because he wouldn't have a clue what I'm talking about.

The boy is the epitome of *clueless*.

"Just hanging out with my friend."

"What friend?" Eldon asks.

I find a gum wrapper, but it looks faded and torn, like it's been there awhile. I pick it up anyway. "My bestie, Skylar."

"She lives here?"

Eldon scratches his chin. "I don't know any Skylar."

"No, she's in California. We're hanging out over Facetime."

The boys look at each other and shrug. It's alright. I don't expect them to understand. They live in a world where everyone has known each other since they were born. No one ever leaves, so there's no reason to keep in touch over the internet.

"Well," Zeb drawls, "what about you don't do that and you come to the football game instead? It's our first varsity of the season. Except for the scrimmage, but we don't talk about that."

James boos.

"Why would I go to a football game?" I straighten and look at them because I seriously can't think of a single reason.

"To support the team, for one," Eldon says.

James adds, "Because football is the shindiggity."

"And so you can watch us cheer," Kelsie calls, officially revealing herself as a blatant eavesdropper.

And she's not the only one. Her friend, Michelle, adds, "To check out the guys in their uniforms."

Tina pretends to swoon and Nina catches her.

"Is that a thing?" Elijah raises an eyebrow. "Really?"

"Oh, it's a thing," Tina assures him.

"How do you guys feel about that?" Elijah waves a hand toward the girls. "Do you like knowing the only reason girls come to the football games is to check out our butts in tight uniforms?"

Eldon shrugs. "That doesn't actually bother me all that much."

"Eldon." James slaps him on the back. "You're as shallow as a frog on a lily pad. Personally, I feel, dang, what's the word? Like what people do with parole?"

"Violated?" Myles supplies.

"Yeah, violated. My body is a temple, ladies. It's not for your oogling pleasure."

Of course, while he says this he flexes his arm muscles and clenches his...

Never mind.

"Wait, do all of you play football?" Somehow I can't picture Myles out there. He'd get squashed like a June bug on the Fourth of July.

Oh shoot, I think James is wearing off on me.

Elijah seems to read my mind. "We're all on the team, but Myles here is an athletic trainer. He's not in pads, but he's one of us."

Myles gives a stately bow.

"And, all you girls are cheerleaders?"

"Well, Beth isn't," Kelsie says.

Beth ducks her head and tries to hide behind Elijah. It's just so cute how he always defends her.

"She tried out freshman year, but then she freaked out at the first game when she saw how many people were in the stands," James explains, then squirms away to avoid Myles and Elijah pelting him with their backpacks.

I agree, actually. If I had my backpack with me, I'd swing it at him too. I do have a hand full of trash, but if I threw that, I'd just have to pick it up again. Plus, I don't think a frail gum wrapper is going to pack much of a punch.

I just detest it when people talk about someone like they aren't standing right there.

"You should come though. Really, it's fun." Kelsie fluffs her hair.

"I don't know."

"What don't you know?" Eldon asks.

I hesitate. The truth is, sports people have a stigma in my brain. At my school in California, the cheerleaders were nerds. No one wanted anything to do with them unless they were making fun of them. Same with any and all people who played sports, totally shunned. The drama club, on the other hand, was the elite of the school. Everyone thronged whoever was the lead in the school musicals.

Usually me.

But I'm not sure how to tell these people that without it sounding offensive. We might all be part of the human race, but their culture is completely opposite from what I am used to.

"It was different at my school in California. People didn't really go to sporting events. They weren't cool."

They all look at me like I have cow dung for eyebrows.

I shrug. "I'm just saying. It's a good perspective, yes? Just because football and cheerleading are the, um, what was it? Shindiggity? Just because it's the thing here, doesn't mean it's anything somewhere else."

"I suddenly feel small and insignificant." Nina smiles. "Maybe we should quit."

"Maybe you should," Elijah says. "The cheerleaders practically out-number the football players these days. If you stay at those numbers all season, we're going to start running you girls on the field."

"Some of them could handle it." James puffs out his cheeks and waddles like he's three times his actual size.

Tina throws a notebook at his head.

Zeb catches it with one hand and smacks James in the back. "You better watch it."

James just slaps his knee and laughs.

I suddenly feel like I'm on an alien planet. "Okay, you guys, don't make more work for me. Get out of here and go to your archaic sports rituals already."

Elijah starts after the guys, then comes back to coax Beth into coming with him. She shakes her head and hugs her books to her chest, looking diminished. No one likes to be reminded of things they struggle with. Who even cares if Beth couldn't hack it as a cheerleader? She's a really good actor. We just need to get her over that stage fright thing, that's all.

I continue picking up trash like it's my only goal in life so I can give Elijah and Beth a moment alone. They're standing so close, I'm sure something is going to happen. Then I notice Beth's face is extremely red. I rush through the last couple of rows, then join them. It appears that their lovers' tête-à-tête has morphed into an argument.

They probably need an arbitrator.

"Just drop it, Eli. I don't want to go, okay?"

"Bethie…" He stops when I join them with a bright smile that is guaranteed to diminish all contention.

"Hey! I need to shut off the lights and stuff, so I'm going to have to ask you both to leave."

So, it wasn't my most smooth execution, but it would have to do in a pinch. At least it got them to stop griping at each other for a minute so they could glare at me.

Together.

Beth recovers first. "Yeah, sorry, we're on our way out."

Elijah rests a hand on one of the chairs. "You should ask Carmen what she thinks."

"About what?" I ask automatically and then realize I just stepped in it.

"About Eli." Beth glares at Elijah. "Do you think he doesn't know when to let things go? He's always in other people's business."

"Absolutely, I do." I point at her, because solidarity! "But do you think it's because he feels like his life is out of whack and the only way he can find some semblance of control is to butt into other people's business and boss other people around?"

Elijah shakes his head a hundred thousand times.

At least.

"That is not what she was supposed to ask you. She was supposed to ask you what you think about the fact that Beth has never been to a football game other than that freshman one she was supposed to cheer for? And since she spent most of that in the bathroom throwing up, it doesn't count."

"You want to know what I think about that?" Didn't I tell them all just now I don't care a sequin for sports? I thought I made my position very clear.

"Yes," Elijah says, but doesn't sound so sure anymore.

"I think, so what?"

Elijah rolls his eyes. "I should have known better than to ask you."

"No, really, enlighten me. What is the big deal?"

Beth now points at me. "See!"

"Wait a second." Elijah rubs his forehead. "You've never been to a football game before either, have you? What is wrong with you two? You can't go all four years without going to a single game. You'll miss out on a major high school experience. You'll regret it."

I seriously doubt that. I give him a look that makes what I'm thinking very very clear.

Elijah shakes his head. "Just come to the game, you guys. Seriously, Carmen, if you do, then Beth won't be able to say no. It's only one game, just a couple of hours on a Friday night. If you hate it, you don't have to go to another one, and I'll never bug you about it again."

Oh, I hate that he makes good points. Plus, if I go, Beth will have more time with her boy toy. At least, watching him from the stands. That's a thing. I'm pretty sure I saw it in a Taylor Swift music video.

Beth starts to say no, but I put my hand on her arm, still formulating how to agree to Elijah's plan without him thinking it was his idea.

Elijah sighs and rolls his eyes. "Tell you what, you two come to the game, sit through the whole thing, and then afterward I'll take you to Mabel's for pie."

Beth's chin raises. "You are diabolical."

"I know." He grins.

"Mabel's"—Beth remembers that I am a noob and fills me in—"is the best pie in the entire world. It's worth getting mobbed by a stand full of yelling people."

"Is that what we're agreeing to? Getting mauled by rambunctious fans?"

"Pretty much."

"And this pie is worth that?"

It's hard to imagine pie that makes it worth subjecting oneself to such atrocity. I mean, I know my future life of fame and fortune will have that as an occupational hazard, but I'm not there yet. I still need my super buff twin bodyguards from Guatemala: Alejandro and Jorge.

Beth sets her lips in a determined line. "It totally is the best pie in the world. I'll do it if you will." Her eyes plead for a yes. "I could really go for some triple chocolate mud pie after how hard we worked this week."

Obviously, I'm not going to say no, but I hem and haw anyway like I might. It's just kind of fun, to be honest. "Fine, I'll go, but only if this Mabel lady has chocolate chip pie and ice cream."

Elijah nods in satisfaction. "She has every pie you could ever imagine."

Beth told me to dress warm, but she seriously underrepresented the idea. I have never been so cold in my life.

And I have no idea what is happening on the field. It's like sitting through a foreign film without subtitles.

The crowd around us erupts into cheers. I squint forward to see if something happened that makes sense, but it's the same as always, guys lined up facing each other, over and over again, for an eternity.

I totally do not understand football.

"It would be nice"—Beth's teeth chatter—"if there was someone not playing football that we could ask to explain this to us. I'm not following."

"What are you talking about? Aren't these stands full of people not playing the game whom you could ask to explain it to you?"

She huddles into her jacket against a howling gust of wind I can feel all the way in the marrow of my bones. "It's only September. It should not be this cold."

I was wondering about that, as I am unfamiliar with the weather patterns in this part of the country. Of course I knew it would be vile, because this place is the opposite of LA in every way, but I underestimated what frigid feels like when you're sitting on a metal bench.

I guess there is some comfort in knowing it's not supposed to be this cold yet.

Wait a second.

My weather tangent almost makes me forget that Beth didn't answer my question. That is unacceptable. Questions are meant to be answered. Plus, talking keeps my teeth from chattering in a very disturbing way. "Aren't you related to everyone in this whole entire thriving metropolis? Someone in the stands would love to tell you what's going on out there, I'm pretty sure."

Beth laughs. "I'm not related to everyone, Carmen! I mean, I am related to a lot of people, but not to everyone."

"But you've known them all forever. You can't ask someone, like that guy over there, to explain the game to you?"

"I could." Beth wrinkles her nose. "Of course, I could. I just don't want to."

"Why not?"

The crowd erupts again, for no apparent reason—the team looks the same as always out there—and we have to wait for the noise to dissipate before we can talk again. I'm ready as soon as my voice can be heard.

"Why don't you want to again?"

Beth sways back and forth to keep the blood moving. I know, because I've been doing the same thing.

"I just feel stupid when I ask questions. Or say anything, really. I have to explain that I don't understand, and then they have to explain it to me, and then I feel stupid if I still don't understand, and sometimes my words get all slurred up and I can't ask the question in an understandable way. It's just a mess. It's better to figure it out myself or wait for Elijah to explain it to me than go through all that. Plus, I've messed up so many times now, people just expect me to be an idiot. Some people even think I have a condition. I don't, not really. Unless you count the condition that I've given up trying to talk to people because I know they'll think I'm stupid no matter what I say because of the way I say it, so I accept the fact that I am what they think and there's nothing I can do about it. It's easier than trying and failing again."

I stare at her. "You realize you just monologued about your fear of talking to people and you didn't stutter or slur one time. I don't think you even said the world um once and um is a veritable stumbling block for like ninety-percent of humanity."

"Well," Beth shrugs, "that's because I'm talking to you and you're different."

I don't think I like the sound of that. Different sounds unnatural and unnatural sounds wrong. I'd take exceptional or fabulously unique. But different?

Ugh.

"Different how?"

"I don't know." She tucks a strand of hair behind her ear. "You're just, you."

"Yeah, no, I need you to elaborate because I am in the process of coming down with a huge personal complex right now."

Beth laughs. "That's exactly what I mean. You're so...open, honest...real, I guess. I don't ever have to wonder what you think about me because you just tell me. It takes all the pressure off. Plus, you're new. You don't know about the time I fainted while cheerleading and ralphed all over the first row of the auditorium. I can be whoever I am without all the judgment hanging over my head. I wish everyone was like you."

Now that right there was a thought and a half. I adore myself to the Hollywood sign and back, but I don't really want to be surrounded by a bunch of me all the time.

That sounds exhausting actually.

"Well, I'm glad you feel safe with me." The words fly out and I realize I have stumbled into the realm of the profound.

Everyone should have someone they feel safe with.

Skylar is like that for me, and Jace used to be. It is so much easier to just *be* when you feel like the people around you understand you and won't judge and love you no matter how uniquely superior you are.

"I'm glad you moved here." Beth nudges my arm. "I know you aren't glad yet, but I am. Nothing used to happen until you got here. Now it's like things are happening all the time."

"May I sit here?"

I'm so bundled up that I have to crane my neck at a weird angle to see who is talking to us.

"Sure, Arty." Beth scoots over to make room for him on her other side.

"How are you girls this fine evening?"

Fine evening? He's only wearing jeans and a hoodie with the school mascot. He doesn't have a hat or gloves or anything. Either the man is crazy or immune to cold.

I wish I was immune to this crazy cold.

Another gust of wind from Hades rips through the stands. I groan and lean into Beth until it's over.

Arty just laughs. "It's a howler, for sure. How are the boys doing?" He leans over to peer at the scoreboard. "Not bad. Not bad at all."

"Eli's right there." Beth pokes her finger out of her coat pocket. "Number sixty-seven."

"I remember, but thank you."

I've never been to a football game before, so I've never sat in the bleachers with a teacher, so I'm not sure how this is supposed to go. I didn't actually know teachers were real people outside of school. I squeeze my arms to my belly awkwardly and listen to Beth chat with Arty like it's not weird at all.

Wait a second.

I tug her arm and lean in. "You're talking to Arty, no problem."

"Yeah, well, that's because I've known him forever, he's—"

"What are you girls whispering about?" Arty leans over to stick his face in our conversation. "I like to whisper too."

Beth laughs but doesn't tell him. That's privileged information.

"Hey, ask him to explain football," I say to Beth, Beth and only Beth, but my voice carries and Arty makes a funny face.

"Explain football?"

Beth shrugs. "We're a little confused."

Arty laughs and launches into a simple, yet detailed description of the ins and outs of football. The line of guys is to protect the endzone while the other players try to get the ball into the endzone. The Y-shaped things at either end are the goals—for extra points or something. The reason the guys hit each other isn't because they're trying to warm up, they're trying to get to the ball and keep other people from getting further down the field. The guy with the ball right now, he's the nickleback, which I thought was a lame band my dad used to listen to, but I guess I was wrong about that. Anyway, that guy decides what happens to the ball once it's hawked. Like, see, he just threw it to a runner back, that's the guy further down the field, and the runner back catches it, and he runs for the goal and...

Touchdown!

I jump to my feet and cheer with the crowd. My heart beats in sync with the fight song blaring from the nearby school band. I hop and twirl, my feet stomping the stands in unison with everyone around me.

Okay, now I get football.

This is the way I feel at the end of a performance when the applause goes on and on. It's magical.

The game is so much more pleasant after that. The weather hasn't changed, but I forget about it as I'm absorbed by what happens out there and breathe in the energy of the stands.

"Elijah's pretty amazing, isn't he?" Arty's voice has a mixture of pride and something else. Something familiar. Oh, it's wistful. That's what my voice sounds like when I talk about my beautiful, wonderful, perfect life in California.

"He's really good," Beth agrees.

I can't figure out how they know which one he is. All the guys look the same in their uniforms, helmets, and pads. Their numbers are way too hard to see from where I stand.

"Did he get that scholarship, do you know?" Arty glances at Beth, which is the only indication his question is more important that he's letting us believe.

Beth nods. "He chose the scholarship to State, but it's academic only. He turned down the football scholarships. He doesn't want to play in college."

"Why not?"

Beth shifts uncomfortably.

"No need to answer, I know why." Arty's voice takes on a bitterness that must go to his core. "Because his father played in college, and he's determined to never do anything his father did. Thank you, Beth. I know Elijah doesn't like it when you talk to me about him, but I appreciate the information all the same."

"I wish it wasn't so...hard...for the two of you."

Arty looks down at his lap. "Me as well."

A loud buzzer sounds, which means the end of the game, apparently. We won, 28-13.

Act V Scene IV

FADE IN: INT: LOCAL DINER WITH PIE THAT MAKES YOU WANT TO BE A BETTER PERSON - CAST OF SIDE CHARACTERS - SHENANIGANS, SO MANY SHENANIGANS.

"Good game." Arty stands and shakes out his legs. "I'll be on my way. Have a good night, ladies."

I watch for a minute as he weaves his way through the crowd to the bottom of the bleachers.

Beth grabs my hand and I yelp.

Her hands are freezing!

"Promise you won't mention any of that to Eli?"

"Sure." I slip my arm out of her grasp and rub it to warm it back up. I think she's frozen me to the bone.

"Eli really hates Arty. It's stupid. Arty isn't a bad guy. I feel so sorry for him." Her words disappear into the noise of a billion people leaving the stands. The way down the bleachers is jam packed, and people are moving like sleepy slugs. It's going to take some time to clear out.

Time to find out more.

"Yeah, so, what's the deal there? Why doesn't Elijah like Arty?"

Beth presses her lips together like she just put on ChapStick, even though she didn't. "I don't know how much I should say."

"Say whatever you want." That's what I do.

Beth chews on her lip now. "It might help you understand Eli better. So, that would be good. Especially if you stop calling him Elijah. You wouldn't do that if you knew why that bugs him so much."

Fat chance, but I'd love to hear why she thinks so.

"Okay." Beth nods, her mind made up. "I'll tell you. Obviously, you already know that Arty is Eli's dad..."

Actually, I did not know that.

"Uh, no." I hold up my palm to get her to hush a second while I wrap my mind around that. Elijah sure as handprints in the sidewalk doesn't treat Arty like his father. There's a story here. I can feel it.

Now I must know.

I lower my hand and wave it to get her going again. "I didn't know that. Please go on."

Beth's eyes are super wide. "Oh, shoot, I thought you knew! Sorry! I thought everyone knew about it. In some weird way, it feels like you've been here forever. Like, I think about my birthday party in first grade and I'm like, where was Carmen? Why didn't she go?" Beth laughs and pushes a strand of hair behind her ear.

I watch her, trying to identify what I'm feeling. That's one of the drama tricks my teacher loved the most. You tap into your real life everyday emotions and really feel them so that when the time comes to act, you can draw upon them easily.

I think I feel stirred.

Touched.

Affected.

Beth feels like I've always been part of her life.

That's pretty...

Cool.

I clear my throat. "So, you were telling me about Elijah?"

"Oh, yeah." Beth glances at the huge crowd of people still streaming from the stands. We weren't getting out of here for a while. Might as well talk. "Eli's parents separated when we were six, but they didn't get a divorce officially until last year."

Interesting, I wonder why.

"That's got to be awkward, sharing a school with one's estranged father." I cringe. That would be the worst, actually.

"Yeah, it's hard on Eli. I think he always wanted his parents to get back together, and he had such a long time to hope. Anyway, he hates his dad for leaving and for the divorce, but Eli is also way too harsh. Arty really is a good guy. He just made some dumb decisions. He's a super talented artist, but he had the worst luck all the time Eli was growing up. They never had any money. His mom went back to school for her nursing degree to keep the family afloat. It was a real struggle."

I can't really picture Elijah divulging all of this information to Beth unless he felt something for her. It's super personal. I wonder if they are secretly together already. Maybe they have to keep it a secret because of a Romeo and Juliet type conflict with their families.

Well, no, not because of that.

We were just talking to Arty, and he really seems to like Beth. Oh, this is seriously intriguing and kind of romantic, which is one word I never thought I would think alongside Elijah's name. He's, like, the opposite of romantic.

"Eli's mom finally gave Arty an ultimatum, and he left to pursue his art full-time. Eli was so mad, he tried to get his last name changed to his mom's maiden name, but she wouldn't let him. The funny thing is, she probably has the most reason to be angry at Arty, but she isn't. She really loves him and encourages the kids to have a relationship with him. It's sad though, because Eli won't even try, and Becky won't either. She's fiercely loyal."

Yeah, I remember that, actually.

"So, anyway, Arty finally had some good luck about eight months ago. He got an agent and sold some paintings. He came back home with some money and tried to patch things up, but it was too late. They were all settled in with Nana, and Eli's mom didn't want to rock the boat for the kids again. Arty bought a house and got a job teaching at the school this year so he could at least see Eli sometimes, but, as I said, it's too late. Eli is so stubborn." Beth's mouth turns downward.

That I knew on a personal level.

The crowd moves forward a couple of steps. Now we were getting somewhere.

I stretch my hands over my head. "What does that have to do with calling Eli by the full and rightful name of Elijah?"

"Oh,"—Beth lets out a puff of air—"Elijah is Arty's middle name. It's the name he always uses when he talks to Eli. So, of course, Eli hates that name."

"That's heavy." I stand and skip down the last of the steps to the walkway that will take us away from this freezing tundra. I think I actually do understand Elijah a little bit more now.

Not that it makes me like him any better.

"Yeah." Beth gathers the blankets we've been using and stands up too. "It's a mess. I am so getting two slices of pie. That game was brutal. How about you?"

"Yeah, for realsies. I do not actually think I needed to suffer that to have a well-rounded high school experience. I might get a whole pie, just to make a point."

The echo of Beth's laugh follows us until we turn the corner toward the parking lot.

I never thought I'd be warm again, but here I am, crushed into a booth at Mabel's, and I am sweltering. I just jabbed Beth in the ear on accident trying to remove my cashmere sweater that brings out the blue in my eyes but is also causing unsightly sweat rings.

My phone vibrates in my pocket. I pull it out to check who's calling and see that it's Skylar with a video call. There's no way I'd be able to hear her in this place, so I reject the call and put my phone away. I'll check in with her in the morning.

"What are you guys getting?" Kelsie looks tiny, smooshed in between Zeb and James. I feel a little sorry for her. She keeps wrinkling her nose. The smell must be overwhelmingly putrid. It's bad enough from where I'm sitting.

I don't think they planned on six teenagers squishing into one booth when they designed these things. Especially when three of them just played football and smell like the inside of a rotten egg.

Zeb slams the menu to the table, making everyone jump, and announces his preference for chicken fried steak, mashed potatoes with country gravy, and greens.

It's like ten at night. He's either going to puke or have cruddy dreams.

I really hope it's not the first one.

James, of course, has to one-up Zeb with the fried chicken platter, french fries, onion rings, and a whole banana cream pie.

I hope he enjoys his diabetes.

"I'm just going to get a salad." Kelsie daintily puts her menu down and takes a sip of water.

"No, you ain't." James puts his arm around her. "You ain't eating that unnatural rabbit food in front of me. Get something real or I'll force-feed you pork rinds."

This is apparently horrifying for multiple reasons. Kelsie picks the menu back up and scours it desperately.

"Did you girls decide what kind of pie you want?"

Elijah is on the other side of Beth, but his arm stretches across the back of the booth. His fingers snag my hair every once in a while, and then I am forced to risk my beautifully smooth forehead by scowling at him.

"Mud pie," Beth says without hesitation.

"Of course. What about you, Carmen? Need some help?"

"Not from you." I roll my eyes. "I'm old enough to choose my own pie. I want the chocolate chip."

"Oh, yes, holy crud, yes, that's what I want too." Kelsie puts the menu down and gives James a stink eye. "Is that real enough for you?"

"That's as real as windshield wipers. Approved."

"What about you, Eli? What are you getting?" Beth unwraps a straw and puts it in the water where it bobs up and down a few times before it settles.

"I can't decide between coconut cream and French silk, so I'm going to get a slice of each."

"Excellent choices, my man." Zeb grins. "Do y'all think Hailey is working tonight?"

Kelsie shakes her head. "I doubt it. She didn't say anything about it at the game."

"Aw." Zeb slumps over. "Thought that was too lucky. Win the game *and* see Hailey. Karma don't love me that much. Well, anyways, you girls tore it up on the sidelines. I think we play better when you cheer your hearts out like that."

Kelsie has the humility to blush.

"*I* think we play better when Eli talks to his dad before the game and gets super ticked." James tosses his straw wrapper at Elijah, who catches it and looks at it like he wants to murder it in its sleep.

"Did you talk to your dad?" Kelsie sits up straighter. "I thought you never talk to him."

"I didn't and I don't."

"Arty shanghaied young Wayas here when we came out of the locker room for warm-ups. Coach even gave him a pass, so Eli couldn't get out of it." Zeb shakes his head sympathetically. "Seems like everyone's on a mission to get the two of them together."

And that right there is the biggest hazard of living in a small town, especially for most of your life. If Elijah lived in LA, no one would give a flying flip if he and his dad didn't get along. In fact, his story would be one of a million just like it.

"What did your daddy want?" Beth asks in a low voice.

Eli slaps his hand on the table, making everyone jump back. "Is Myles coming?"

Beth puts a hand on his arm. "You don't want to talk about it?"

James puts his finger on the end of his nose. "Bingo. Riles him like a hornet in a mattress."

"Then why did you bring it up?" I enter the conversation. It was a supreme effort to stay quiet this long anyway, but James is just so ridiculous, I can't stay silent.

"I didn't. Don't make me the goat that got scraped by a pin! I was just saying that's why we played so hard. Eli's a beast when he's ticked."

Eli was also turning an interesting shade of purple. I have no idea what kind of CPR is required for that, so I prepare to change the subject when the waitress walks up.

Impeccable timing.

She asks for our orders, then walks away with a swing in her hips. Zeb watches the movement intently.

Well, until James punches him in the arm. He has to reach over Kelsie's head at a weird angle, but he still gets in enough of a wallop to make Zeb grunt.

"You gotta knock off this waitress thing, Zebby," James says. "You're obsessed, like the goose that gandered. Put a chick in a waitress uniform and all she's gotta do is ask what you want and you're slobbering all over her. I don't think you'd like Hailey more than a salamander if she worked at the car wash or the Piggly Wiggly."

Zeb shoves him into the window, so James shoves him back, almost into the aisle, and it would have continued, maybe forever, if Kelsie didn't threaten to throw both of them in the pig pen if they didn't knock it off.

I don't think she could actually throw them in the pig pen, even with that determined look on her face. She's less than half the size of one of them, saying nothing about the two of them together. But the threat is enough to get them to cut it out.

James looks around for something to do—he's apparently at a loss without food to fill his face—and grabs hold of the two mini bottles of hot sauce sitting in a caddy off to the side, minding their own business alongside the ketchup and the salt and pepper shakers. "I challenge y'alls to a hot sauce drinking competition! Loser takes the check."

"Oh, ew, no." Kelsie leans into the booth and pulls out her phone to start scrolling. It's been at least thirty minutes since her face was glued to that screen, she's probably experiencing withdrawals.

"Come on, any takers? Y'all as scared as a calf stuck in a graveyard? Zeb?"

He's watching the waitress talk to the booth in front of us and doesn't answer.

"Eli? Come on, man, I know you ain't scared."

He's still brooding about his dad or whatever and just shoots James a lethal glare.

"Carmen? New girl gotta earn her place. You game?"

I give him the most condescending look I can muster. And I am master at the condescending look. "I don't need to prove anything to you, sir."

"Man." James slams into the back of the booth, making our table wobble. "Y'all are no fun!"

"You didn't ask me." Beth toys with the knife and fork peeking out of a cheap napkin roll.

James folds his arms. "You're joking. You ain't gonna drink hot sauce."

I glance from Beth's determined profile to James's skeptical expression. Is this what Beth was talking about when she said people won't let her be anything other than what she's always been? I didn't understand what she meant, but I think I get it now.

"What, James, are you scared Beth's going to show you up?" I press my lips into a mocking smile. "You as scared as a calf stuck in the graveyard?"

James's face hardens. "That so? You're on like Donkey dot com. I'll even take the green one, it's hotter."

Beth strikes like a snake and snatches the green bottle before James can reach it. He smirks as he wraps his meaty fingers around the red bottle.

Kelsie starts filming. "This is going to be epic! I think it might actually go viral. James and Beth, the hot sauce competition."

Zeb deepens his voice. "Ladies and Gentlemen, boys and girls, welcome to the first hot sauce showdown at Mabel's on Main. Our competitors..."

"Knock that crap off the wall. Let's do this." James flips the cork out of the bottle with his thumb and raises it to his lips. "You ready, Little Miss?"

Beth sets the cork from the green bottle next to her water glass and nods. "Let's do it."

Zeb hits the table with his palm and after the third smack, yells, "Go!"

At first, my eyes dart back and forth between James and Beth, but that gives me the biggest headache in about three seconds, so I focus my attention only on Beth. Instead of the loud gulps and gasps coming from James across the table, Beth is silently draining the whole bottle. The only indication that she's struggling at all is the tear slowly making its way down her cheek.

Beth takes a deep breath and slams the bottle on the table. "Done."

Zeb and Kelsie cheer. Elijah rallies enough to raise Beth's arm in the air. James looks at the last few drops in his bottle and shakes it.

"How does it feel to get beat by a girl?" Kelsie holds her phone out like it's a microphone.

James sets his forehead on the table. "My insides feel like a snake in a wildfire. Anyone got any ice cream?"

Zeb is more than happy to hail the waitress, and she immediately brings James a soft-serve cone.

Beth declines.

After finishing it in about three gulps, James holds out his hand. "I've been jolly gagged. You beat me fair and square. I didn't think you had it in you, Bethie."

Beth just shrugs and goes back to toying with her napkin, but there's something in the square of her shoulders and the turn of her head that just reeks victory.

Zeb and Kelsie are giving James such a hard time, none of them pay any attention to us anymore. Which is the perfect opportunity to make a very good point.

"You just blew expectations, Beth." I nudge her with my elbow. "Not the same old Bethie everyone knows."

A smile curls around her cheeks. "I did, didn't I?"

"Astronomically." And now for the point. "What made you do it?"

Beth shrugs. "I don't know. It just bugged me that he automatically assumed I wouldn't want to compete."

"What did that feel like?"

Elijah snorts. "Seriously?"

"Shushie your mouthie over there." I flip my hand over the top of his head, making his hair fly into the air. "I'm making a point."

"Well, yeah, obviously." Elijah smirks.

He doesn't even know, but he's about to. I zero in on Beth again. "I'm serious though, what did that feel like?"

"Like, um, I don't know, like super annoying."

"What color is super annoyed?"

Beth gives me a strange look but answers. "Lime green."

"Where do you feel it?"

"Um, here." She laces her fingers over her belly. "But it also kind of crawls up my throat."

"And is it hot or cold?"

"How does it like its tea?" Elijah interrupts in a terrible British accent.

No, really, it's horrendous.

"Shush!"

Elijah rolls his eyes and pulls out his phone. Good, now maybe I can make my point already without his stupid commentary.

Beth chews on the top of her lip. "It's hot. Why are you asking me all these questions?"

She hesitated before she said the word questions. I'm sure she was about to add in a descriptor like "weird" or "stupid," but that's okay. She doesn't see where I'm going yet, but she will, and then she'll understand.

Before I can explain, the waitress arrives with her arms full of plates. There are a couple of other waiters in similar circumstances behind her. They go to work distributing everything, and in just a few seconds the table is completely covered. They have to drag a smaller table to the end of ours to fit everything.

I set my pie to the side so it will not distract me from my very important point.

"When you're acting, you have to tap into emotion you don't really feel. That's why I asked you those questions. Now that you know what annoyed feels like and what it looks like and where it shows up, you can generate it on stage at the snap of a finger. See?" I pick up my fork, thoroughly satisfied with myself.

"Seriously, is everything about theater to you?" Elijah has one eyebrow an inch or so higher than the other. "That's either a gift or something you need medication for."

"We should try that out!" James swats a fly and leans forward. He's all wiggly, like a puppy that needs to go out. "Can Carmen make every single thing-a-ma-hickie that happens about drama? I'm gonna say a word. You tell me what it has to do with theater. Strike."

Oh my grammy, I thought this was going to be hard. "That's the term used for clearing the stage when a play is closed."

"What? How'd you do that so fast? No way, I want to try." Zeb glances around the room. The passing waitress gives him a weird look. "Apron."

Oh wow, give me a hard one. "That's the part of the stage that extends past the curtain."

James whistles.

"How about graph?" Kelsie says, her phone pointing in my face.

Easy.

"ChoreoGRAPHy is the sequence of movement in on-stage dances." I wiggle my head and purse my lips to give her viewers some sass.

"You do dancing on stage too?" Elijah's lip curls. "I'd rather eat pickled pigs feet than dance up there in front of a bunch of people. It's bad enough talking."

Pickled what? Ew!

I ignore him. I am extremely skilled at that these days. "Anyways, back to what I was saying to Beth about accessing feelings. This is important. I can see that you need a demonstration to remove the doubt. Watch and learn, people."

I close my eyes and imagine that place inside my chest where it hurts to breathe. A big, black ball of yarn that unravels and then tightens as

I draw air in and then blow it out. My eyes begin to sting, then I open them and look at the ceiling to accelerate the process. Tears run down my cheeks and drip off my chin onto the table.

"She's crying," Zeb says in a hushed voice.

Kelsie snaps a picture with her phone. "That is sick!"

I raise both hands in the air and lower them with a flourish. "Thank you, thank you."

"Wow," Beth breathes, "that looked so real."

"That's because it is real." I cut off the tip of the chocolate chip pie and bring it to my lips. "I've really felt those feelings that make me cry, I just have to tap into them." I put the fork in my mouth and my eyelashes flutter. "Oh my Grammy and Oscars too. This is the best pie in the entire world!"

"Told you," Elijah says, reaching his fork toward Beth's pie. She takes some of his French silk as retaliation.

The sounds of the people around me fade as I savor each and every bite. There is not one single thing I can think of to improve the experience. The slice is not small, but I feel sad when the last bite disappears. I'll have to remember this moment when I need to generate the emotion of contentment and awe.

"The chocolate chip is the best, isn't it?" Kelsie offers me a smile of solidarity and I raise my hand for a high five. The smack she gives is strangely satisfying.

Forks scrape empty plates. It's alarming how quickly Zeb and James put away all that food, and before I know it, Elijah pulls on his jacket, Zeb thanks the waitress, Kelsie puts her phone away, Beth grabs her purse, and James pays the bill.

"How much should I do for a tip? I don't want to rip the girl off to high heavens."

"Here." Zeb tosses a couple of bills onto the table. "I'll contribute, she was worth it."

The rest of us follow his gentlemanly example, but I imagine with different motivations. Zeb stares at the pile of money, his eyes lighting up. "You guys go on, I'm going to make a scavenger hunt for the waitress to find her tip. It's going to be amazing!"

I feel like I should find out what he's talking about and intervene, but a wave of sleepiness settled over me once I finished my pie. I just want to go home and snuggle with my blankets.

"It's fine." Beth sees the look on my face. "He always does something like this. Once he put the tip under a urinal."

"What?"

"No, I mean, it was fine. James found it and made him put it somewhere else. See, James is sticking around. He'll stop Zeb from doing anything super crazy. We can go."

I'm too tired to argue, so I follow Kelsie, Elijah, and Beth out of Mabel's. When I look over my shoulder, James scribbles furiously on a napkin and Zeb folds dollar bills into origami.

Act V Scene V

FADE IN:TWO WEEKS LATER INT: HILLBILLY HIGH SCHOOL - MORE ASSIMILATION - UNEXPECTED TURN OF EVENTS

I swear I blink and two weeks have gone by. My life has become a whirlwind of monologuing during drama club, extra work with Beth, normal school work, and math group. (Beth talked me into giving it another try, granted they move it to Beth's house so Becky can't douse me with anything. I agreed. They really are hopeless without me.)

I'm getting ready for school on Friday morning when I realize Skylar and I haven't talked in ages. We've texted and messaged and liked each other's posts on social media, but real time, nothing. This is a gross oversight. I vow not to let myself be so overwhelmed with the minute details of daily life that I neglect my bestie anymore.

I dial her number with a video call. As soon as I see her face, I let loose.

"Skylar! How are you, babe? What have you been doing? What's going on? Did Janelle really get her, you know, done?"

Skylar opens her mouth, then closes it tightly. "How do you know about that?"

"Instagram." I laugh and flip a lock of hair over the side of my head to tease the underpart. This cow pokey climate is wreaking havoc on my volume.

"Oh." Skylar folds her arms. "Well, did Instagram also tell you that I am seriously done with you?"

My arm holding the comb drops to my side, leaving the comb wedged in my hair. "No, it did not."

"Well, it should have, because I am. Done with you. I am so done with you. I only answered the phone so I could tell you I want my Taylor Swift tee back and that you are the worst."

Okay, I know I haven't put as much into our friendship as I should have. I let myself get too busy. All of that is true. But there's more to it than that. I can't be the worst because I'm not the only person who didn't try to call or video the other person this whole time. Skylar has been just as MIA.

I remind her of this small fact in a few short sentences.

"Carmen!" Skylar presses her hands onto the screen. She must be on a computer because her phone is way too small to fit those hocks of ham. "I've been waiting and waiting for you to reach out to me. So that I know I still matter to you. But it's become painfully obvious that we're growing apart. I just don't see how I can be friends with someone who blatantly overlooks colossal turning points in my life."

Colossal turning points?

I search my brain for what those might be. Obviously, she's been wearing a bra for like six years so that's not it. She has her driver's license. Her first pair of high heels were in the sixth grade. The first time she colored her hair was in seventh. Her first kiss was with Weston Callaghan in eighth. What else is there?

"I have no idea what you're talking about." I work the pick out of my hair and brush it over to check the effect. It looks good so I go to work on the other side.

"That right there is the problem, Carmen. You are not present for me."

Wow, really?

"Are you present for me?" I shoot right back.

"Excuse me?"

"No, for reals, this goes both ways, Sky. Do you know why I haven't been calling as often?"

"What?"

I repeat the question.

"You tell me," Skylar says in her stalling voice.

"No." I shake my head. "You tell me. What have I been doing here that has totally filled up my every waking hour?"

"I can't possibly imagine." She leans forward and blinks, then pulls out a tube of mascara to pump up her lashes. "You are in the outskirts of nowhere. What do you possibly have to do?"

Excuse her?

"That's my point, Sky. You should know. As my bestie, you should have a clue what's been going on in my life."

"Maybe I would if you called me more."

I should have called her more. She's right. But she should call me more too. Friendship isn't all on one person.

That's why it's a ship.

Skylar makes a derisive noise. Basically, she snorts. "I mean, come on. You're in a town that has, what, two working streetlights? You're just biding your time until you come home. You're not doing anything important. I, on the other hand, just had a life-defining moment, and you weren't there for me." She blinks back tears, and I know I've lost.

My breath stalls for a moment. "What happened? What moment defined your life that I missed?"

"I don't know if I should tell you."

I am not going to grovel, so I just wait. Skylar doesn't have the ability to hold in surprises or secrets for very long. I'm sure she'll crack soon. I brush smoky gray eyeshadow across my eyelids.

"Okay, I'll tell you!" Skylar holds a piece of paper so close to the screen it never unblurs. "It came over email late last night, but I printed it out so I can show everyone."

I tip my head and squint to see if that helps me read the type.

It doesn't.

"What is it?"

"Thanks for asking, this is my acceptance to LAAA for the fall semester!" She flings the paper in the air and does a chair dance that culminates in a dab.

Which I think is excessive.

"How...?"

She didn't tell me she'd applied. I thought we were going to do that together when I moved back.

"It's such a funny story." Skylar jostles her screen as she settles into place. "You know that girl Jace dumped you for?"

I shake my head "No."

Obviously, duh. How would I know her when I'm stuck here?

"Well, her godmother has a niece who is the nanny for Scarlett Johansson."

Oh my heck, really? Everyone has a connection like that. If everyone used their convoluted connection, then everyone would get into places like LAAA and it wouldn't mean anything anymore.

And that would make it lame.

I respond slowly, wrapping my head around a new thought. "So, this girl told her godmother to tell her niece to tell Scarlett Johansson to recommend you to LAAA?"

"Yes!" Skylar bounces around some more, coming dangerously close to another dab.

And if she dabs again, I'm going to lose it.

"That's it? Just because she said? You didn't have to do anything to get in? Did you apply or perform or..."

"Nope!"

"Oh, well, that's...nice," I say in a stilted voice. I've never had to choose my words carefully around Skylar. This feels so alien. But I can't tell her what I'm thinking. I just don't think she'd take it well if I reveal that I think that's the stupidest thing I've ever heard.

Sure, I would love a recommendation for LAAA, but not for such an absurd reason. I want to get in because they think I'm an amazing actress.

"I know! Isabelina is soooooooooooooo nice. She is just darling with her accent and all. You will really love her, Carmen. We can all hang out."

Yeah, sure I will. We'll all hang out together once I get back to California like one big dysfunctional family. I can sit in the back seat of Jace's lifted hummer and watch them make out at stoplights like Jace and

I used to. She can use her super darling accent to steal all my friends and dump me out on the curb.

Super fun.

I chew my lip, completely wrecking the gloss. "I guess I didn't know you and Jace's girlfriend were so tight."

Her face is stern like she suddenly doused it with maturity. "No, you didn't."

"Don't do that!" I jab my lip gloss brush at the screen. "You have as much responsibility to tell me what's going on in your life as I have to ask."

Skylar sighs and shakes her head, her hair brushing her shoulders. "You know what, Carmen? I don't like your sass. I know you have your hands full with cows and stuff, but that is not my fault. Don't make me your emotional whoopie cushion, alright? I think we need some time apart so you can reevaluate your priorities."

And just like that, the screen goes blank.

I walk into Ms. B's classroom still reeling from Skylar's epic hang-up. Even though I know what happened, I can't wrap my head around it.

She, like, actually hung up on me.

After accusing me of being selfish. Me! I've put so much work into helping others with their monologues, stage fright, and math homework, I haven't had a chance to spend any time on my own.

If that's selfish, then I don't even know what is happening right now.

"Hey, Carmen!" Beth sits at the desk across from Ms. B. She waves a freckly arm holding the printout of her monologue. It does lift my spirits a tad to recognize that she's been working on memorization. Yesterday

I told her we've gotten as far as we can without the words in her brain. And here she is, all prepared.

See, there I go, help, help, helping again.

There is something wrong with Skylar.

"Are you okay?" Beth purses her lips. "You look upset."

"I am upset." I drop my stuff on the ground and slump into the chair behind her. "I just got off the phone with my former best friend in California."

"Skylar?"

I blink in surprise. Beth remembered Skylar's name? That's...something. "Yes."

Beth looks concerned. "What happened? Is Skylar okay?"

What happened is Beth.

I only mentioned Skylar's name in passing a few times and Beth remembers that. Beth doesn't even know Skylar and still wants to make sure she's okay. What is Skylar to Beth? Nothing, that's what. And still, Beth asks. Why does Beth care what happened to upset me when it has nothing at all to do with her?

Because Beth is a good person who cares about other people.

"Oh, I'm sorry." Beth's eyes widen. "You don't have to tell me, you know, obviously, if it's not something you want to talk about. I just thought, if it will make you feel better, you can tell us."

I glance at Ms. B who watches me carefully but nods.

"I can talk about it. It's not that. I'm just surprised you remember Skylar, that's all." That isn't all, but I can't process this mind melt right now on top of everything else. I prop my cheek up with one hand. "She just called me to tell me she got into LAAA."

"What's that?"

It's so weird that after all this time I still keep forgetting I'm not in LA anymore. "It's the most prestigious acting school in the United States. Tons of famous people went there. It's been my dream since I was a little girl."

"And your friend got in? That could be good though, right? If she got in, you can get in too."

That's the plan. Like, the whole purpose of this monologue competition thing. But that's also not what's bugging me about Skylar's acceptance. I finally realized what it is on the walk to school.

"LAAA is super prestigious. With few exceptions, they will only allow students with genuine talent into the school, who also have the backing of someone super famous. It's elite. The application process is crazy."

At least, that's what I used to think.

"That should be easy. I bet you know tons of famous people."

Beth is sweet, but, oh, so naive.

I shake my head.

"No? I thought because you talked about Chris Pratt and stuff..."

"No." I grit my teeth.

"Sorry, I don't mean to assume." Beth looks down at her paper and starts to study it like her life depends on it.

I imagine my face is Halloween-scary. It's not Beth's fault though. "No, Beth, it's not you. I just, I don't know Chris Pratt or anyone else. I just follow them, you know? I've never spoken to anyone famous, actually."

"Oh."

My shoulders slump forward. "That makes me way less interesting, huh?"

"No!" She puts her arm across my shoulders and squeezes. "You're interesting because you're you, not because of who you know. That's why you're my friend."

Does she mean that?

Sincerity is kind of Beth's thing, but it's so hard to wrap my head around it. Is she really my friend just because I'm me?

"What's really bothering you?" Ms. B speaks up for the first time. She sips her tea and studies me over the rim. Sometimes I sympathize with dissected frogs when I'm with Ms. B. "Are you jealous your friend got into your dream school and you did not?"

My head jerks back as if Ms. B hit me with those words instead of just saying them.

Was I jealous?

"No..." I press my lips together. "No, I don't think that's it. I mean, yes, I want in, but not like that. I think what's bugging me is that Skylar got in without an application or a video of her acting performance. They don't even know if she *can* act."

"Can she?" Ms. B sips her tea, and the steam gathers around her face, warping it slightly.

"Yes, I mean, she's been in every play I've been in. She's had some really good parts, too, so she has skills. Here's the thing though. This is supposed to be an amazing acting school. It's where Laura Valentine went for Oscar's sake. It's bothering me that they will take someone they know nothing about based on the word of a celebrity that knows nothing about them either. Does that make sense?"

Beth nods slowly. "You're not jealous. You're confused."

"And disillusioned," Ms. B adds.

I try those descriptions on and find that they fit perfectly. "You're right, I am. And disappointed. I expected more from LAAA."

"Well,"—Ms. B sets her mug down and shuffles some papers—"that's probably your first mistake."

I want to ask her what she means by that, but the room is filling with students. "Beth, I'm so sorry. We were so busy talking about my junk, we didn't get a chance to work on your monologue."

Ms. B looks at me sharply.

Beth shakes her head. "Don't apologize. We're friends. If you're having struggles, I want you to be able to talk to me about it. We have tons of time to work on my monologue." She smiles and gathers her things to head to her seat.

I watch her go.

Is that what we are?

My friend, Beth.

For sure it's not like my other friendships, but as the words settle deeper into my mind, I realize they are true. Or, at least, I want them to be true. Beth is the most loyal, kind-hearted person I have ever met. Being her friend sounds pretty amazing.

"Excuse me, miss, you are in my seat."

I look up to see Elijah standing over me. "Sorry, I'm moving."

His face changes into a look I can't define.

"What?"

"Nothing. It's just that I don't think I've heard you apologize before."

I smirk. "Yeah, in the years and years and years that you've known me?"

"No." He narrows his eyes thoughtfully. "But for sure in the days and days and hours and minutes that I've known you. Remember, you didn't even apologize when you pepper sprayed me in the face."

"Admit it, you were acting like a creeper."

"I was bringing welcome zucchini bread from my grandma."

"And you don't think that's creepy?"

Elijah laughs and shoves my arm. "No, I don't."

I move out of the way so he can sit down. "Well, then you're weird, Elijah."

His shoulders move up and down dramatically. "Are you ever going to call me Eli?"

"Probably not."

I turn toward my seat, but Elijah grabs my hand and pulls me closer. My face is in direct proximity to his minty breath. "Hey, before you take off to save the world, I just wanted to tell you." He looks down at our hands and lets go like I suddenly morphed into a poisonous reptile. "I just wanted to tell you thank you for all the help you're giving Beth. She's loving this drama club, and I don't think I've ever seen her so happy. So, yeah, thank you."

Well, that was convenient. I've been overcome with curiosity about Elijah and Beth's relationship and haven't been able to get either one of them to spill the spotlight. They are both remarkably good at avoiding the subject, or changing it, when I try to bring it up.

I plop into the seat in front of Elijah so I'm not awkwardly crouching over his desk anymore. "I've been meaning to talk to you about Beth." I glance over to make sure she isn't paying attention and also that no one else is near enough to overhear this sensitive subject.

"What about her?"

"Do you think she's pretty?"

Elijah wrinkles his nose. "Yeah, I guess."

That was not an enthusiastic declaration of everlasting love. I need to work with him on emoting.

"Come on, she is, isn't she? And she's so nice, right?"

"For sure, yes, Beth is the nicest person I have ever met."

That was more like it, though he could definitely put some more feeling into the words.

"Have you ever thought about...you know?" I introduce the idea slowly so his mind can grasp it. Sometimes this technique works so well that people even end up thinking it was their idea. Then I raise my eyebrows and nod knowingly.

"What?"

"You know." I dart glances at Beth.

He shakes his head. "No, I don't know. What?"

I lean forward to whisper, "Dating her. Have you ever thought of dating her?"

"Beth?"

I nod.

"Have I ever thought of dating Beth?"

I nod more vigorously.

Elijah runs his fingers through his hair. His usual hard look is replaced by an amused one. "Why would I do that?"

"Why wouldn't you?" I plow on enthusiastically. "She's pretty and smart and kind. You said so yourself. You would never find another girl like her anywhere. Plus, you're both small-town people. It works."

"Carmen," Elijah rests his hands on top of each other and stares me down, "I realize that you think people in small towns are slow and stupid. You buy into the stereotypes about cow tipping and eating roadkill. But I thought you were too smart to believe people actually date their cousins."

What is he even talking about? That doesn't have anything to do with anything.

"I'm not talking about dating your cousin. I'm talking about dating Beth."

"And Beth's my cousin."

The surprise is actually enough to unhinge my jaw. My mouth falls open as I look back and forth between Elijah and Beth.

Now that he says it, it's painfully obvious. He's protective. She can talk to him without trouble. They've known each other forever. Arty and Beth were tight. I think I even remember Beth calling Elijah's grandma Nana.

So, now I feel stupid.

"I think I should have known that," I say.

Elijah nods but can't talk because he's so busy laughing that his face is bright red.

"Well, if you wouldn't mind keeping this conversation between the two of us, that would be greatly appreciated." I sniff and straighten my shoulders.

Elijah still can't talk.

"I missed a joke, I see." Myles walks up then, and I scoot out of his desk chair. "Care to share?"

I glare at Elijah, waiting for him to sell me out, but he just covers his mouth with his arm and shakes his head.

"As long as I'm not the subject." Myles sits down. "I am happy to see the two of you getting along amicably. I've been hoping you'd reach a truce. Fielding your arguments is exhausting."

Act VI Scene I

After school, Ms. B sits in the left front row instead of her usual place in the back. I'm not a bit surprised. Over the last few weeks, she's stopped bringing papers to grade and has been inching closer to the stage every day.

And who could blame her? The stage has a magnetic force from which I am convinced none of us is immune.

"Quiet, people." I wave my hands around.

Zeb brought me a blow horn to use to call everyone to order, but I've only had to use it once. Now I merely glance at it and everyone gets quiet.

"Today we're going to do something a little different."

There is a general sigh of relief.

I thought so.

Yesterday at practice I sensed that people were getting annoyed with their monologues. That's the cue to switch things up.

I hold up a basket filled with pieces of paper. "In here I have scene descriptions. We're going to play a game like charades to increase our acting tool box." I glance at Beth, who is wilting in her seat. "It's not mandatory. Obviously, we need an audience just as much as we need players. So, if you want, come up on stage, pick a scene, and then pick a buddy."

"Can we pick a buddy first?" asks Tina, Kelsie's friend who hates James with a fiery passion. I can just imagine the scene that would go down if the two of them were paired up. The auditorium would need weeks to recover.

"No, and you'll see why. The scenes are for only two people, but they'll require a mix of boys and girls. You won't know which your scene requires until you have it in your hand."

"Oh, yeah, that makes sense." Tina smiles at me, then goes back to French braiding Michelle's hair, the one who joined drama club for the kissing scenes.

Association is amazing. I want to high-five whoever came up with it. I never would have been able to sort all of Kelsie's friends without this unique ability since they all look pretty much the same. It's easy to remember their names when I remember that Tina hates James, Make-out Michelle, and Nina the Knowledgeable because she thinks she knows everything.

Although, Nina isn't here today. Apparently being a know-it-all doesn't get you out of detention when you spend all of history class putting on nail stickers and then tweeting pictures of them to your peeps.

"Who wants to go first?"

Eldon raises his hand and makes it to the stage in a couple short steps. There is no end to his Energy and Enthusiasm. More association.

Snap!

I hold out the basket and shake it until Eldon chooses a paper. He unfolds it fast and brings it close to his face to read.

"Scene: you are in the grocery store and run into your crush but you keep messing up your words because you are so nervous." He looks at me with question marks.

"Now you need to choose a buddy, or ask for a volunteer," I encourage.

Eldon leans forward. "What if I don't have a crush on anyone here?"

"Then act."

"Oh, yeah, I knew that." He folds the paper and puts it in his pocket. "Kelsie, wanna help me out?"

Her face lights up as she prances to the stage. They arrange themselves across from each other, then they both look at me.

They don't know what to do.

I step back to take in the two of them and everyone else in the seats. "See, this is why this is such a good exercise. First, you have to set your scene. What does the grocery store look like? Where are the shelves? Are you pushing a cart or carrying a basket? Where do you meet? Frozen food, vegetables, deli? And do you bump into each other or does Eldon see Kelsie first and then freeze because of those nerves? Really imagine the whole thing before you start."

Eldon nods more enthusiastically the longer I talk. "I got this. I'm walking by a canned food display, right here." He points stage right. "When I see Kelsie, I get flustered and knock the whole thing over." Eldon drops to his knees, then mimes picking up cans. "While I'm trying to clean it up, she comes over to help, but we keep fumbling over cans and knocking more stuff over until it's a big mess and we're both laughing. Then I forget to be nervous and ask her out. Yeah?"

I glance at Kelsie who nods excitedly. She takes a step toward Eldon, then almost trips on a cord that's running the length of the stage. I catch her hand and steady her.

When she's stable, I let go and walk toward the wings. "Move away from that cord. You've got your scene. Go for it."

Eldon rubs his hands together. "I knew all those haunted houses would come in handy. Do we just use our normal names or should we make up new ones?"

"Let's just use your normal names for now. When we're more practiced at the scenes, we'll add characters." I cross my arms and watch their scene unfold. Eldon is a ham and a half, but it works in this situation. They have the auditorium ringing with laughter until the very end when they take their bows.

The energy level has completely morphed. No longer is the room tense with nerves and uncertainty. It's alive and it's palpable. It reverberates in my chest. My fingers tingle as it flows through me. This, right here, is the magic of theater.

"Let's do another one. Who wants to go next?"

"Ooo, me, me!" Michelle pulls away from Tina with half her head still unbraided and bounds to the stage. I lift the basket and she chooses.

"YES!" She waves the paper in the air like she has the golden ticket from Willy Wonka. "I got a kissing scene!"

Zeb and James tumble over themselves trying to get to the stage first. It looks like James is going to prevail, but then Zeb gets a hold of the bottom of his t-shirt and yanks. James falls to the ground in defeat, and Zeb takes the stage with two hands in the air like Rocky.

Michelle giggles nervously and drops the paper on the floor.

"What's the scene?" I prompt.

"Oh, yeah." She bends over and grabs it, but her hands are shaking so much she has a hard time reading my handwriting. I take the paper and help her out.

"You're studying at the library and Michelle is really focused on the textbook and Zeb is really focused on Michelle. He keeps trying to get her attention but it's not working. Finally, he just grabs her and kisses her."

Michelle giggles again and tries to find something to do with her hands. Running them through her half-braided hair was not a great option. Now it's sticking up all over the place.

Zeb looks around. "Do we have chairs or something? Or should we sit on the floor?" He looks worried, and I don't blame him. It would be really awkward to grab someone and kiss them when you're sitting criss-cross applesauce on the dirty stage.

I start to ask Ms. B where the chairs would be, but Elijah beats me to it. He nudges Myles and they run backstage, then return with two chairs. They look at me with raised eyebrows, but I direct them to Michelle and Zeb. It's their scene, they should decide where the chairs go.

After a bunch of scraping and scooting, they are ready. Myles goes back to the audience, but Elijah stops to watch in the wings with me.

"Zeb looks like he's going to puke," he whispers in a perfect aside.

I lift my hand and shield my mouth. "Michelle might beat him to it."

After some stilted conversation and a lot of squirming, the time comes for Zeb to launch them into the kissing scene of Make-out Michelle's dreams. After a couple of false starts, a ton of hooting from the peanut gallery, and cheeks red enough to transform them both into strawberries, they turn to me.

I hurry over to them. "What's the trouble?"

"I still don't know what to do with my hands." Michelle is breathless as her hands flutter around her sides.

"Yeah, and I don't know how to grab her and kiss her when we're sitting in these dad-blamed chairs."

"Also, which way do we tip our heads and..."

A wave of laughter begins in the audience. "What's the problem, Michelle? This is your moment. Live your dream!"

"Come on, Zebby, old boy, ain't you ever kissed a girl before?"

Catcalls follow and we have pretty much descended into chaos.

I stalk over to the blow horn, pick it up, and hold it in the air.

The room is now silent as the grave.

"You guys are acting like a bunch of amateurs. Kissing on stage isn't like kissing in real life."

This is exactly why I put a kissing scene in the basket. They needed to realize how complicated this is, how much skill it really takes to make a kiss look authentic, especially when you have next to no interest in the person playing opposite. This is their lesson in taking it more seriously.

I step between Michelle and Zeb, but address the audience. "This is probably the most difficult thing you can do on stage. Whether you are an experienced kisser or not doesn't matter a bit, it's about making the audience believe that there is something between your two characters that warrants the kiss."

"I don't think I can do this." Michelle holds her stomach. "I seriously think I'm going to vomicile."

"Me also." Zeb does look a little green. "Vomicile, yes."

This might be too advanced for them. In my effort to educate them all, I think I overwhelmed them.

"Okay, look, you two sit in those chairs." I look around. "Elijah, come here." I wave him over.

He steps back. "Me?"

"Yes, you. I'm looking at you."

"Yes, but I didn't hear you say my name." Even from this distance, his smirk is the only thing I see.

"Oh, for the love of Shakespeare, *ELI*, will you please come here?"

"Yes, ma'am." He salutes and jogs over.

"I'm going to show you guys how to do this like a professional, and Elijah—"

"Eli."

"...here is going to help me."

"Wait, what am I helping with?"

"Weren't you listening?"

He folds his arms. "Yeah, I was, but it's hard to catch everything all the way over there. I thought you just wanted me to move the cord or something."

"No." I bring my hands together in prayer pose. "I need you to help me show these guys how to do a theater kiss."

The catcalls start up again, and I shake my head. "You guys, seriously, you have to be more mature about this. If you can't execute a realistic stage kiss, we might as well stop right now. Most of the best plays have a romantic interlude. You'll be stuck enacting the tortoise and the hare for the rest of your high school career if you don't cut it out."

I turn back to Elijah. "I can ask someone else if you don't want to demonstrate."

His eyes widen. "No, it's okay, I can do it."

"Can you?" I study him critically. "Because it's not like normal kissing. I need you to be professional."

"I am the epitome of professional."

I squint one eye. "Okay, whatever, let's just give this a try."

Movement catches my eye, and I turn to see Myles raising his hand. "Do you have much experience with kissing on stage?"

Beth leans forward, her hands clasped.

So, that was probably her question.

"Yes, I do, actually. I've kissed hundreds of guys on stage, but that doesn't matter a bit. That's what I'm trying to tell you. Up here, it doesn't mean anything between Elijah and Carmen or Zeb and Michelle. It's what it means to the characters that matters. You have to make the audience believe that the characters are having a moment."

Nods tell me that they might finally be getting it, so I turn to Elijah, but try to project my voice so everyone can hear.

"Now, we are always aware of the audience, yes? So, we need to stand sideways so the audience can see us both." I tug Elijah's arm so he is facing me, sideways to the chairs. "Then, the person initiating the kiss is going to lift the arm that is away from the audience to touch the other person's face. This is so the arm doesn't block the view of what is happening between the characters. Elijah, do you want to be the instigator or do you want me to do it?"

"Uh, go ahead." He swallows.

"Okay, so I'm going to lift my left hand, see, and place it on his face. But not like over his face or even on his cheek." I demonstrate, my hand suctioning at Elijah like an obsessed starfish. "It's more like a cup on his neck and jawbone. It's a nice bonus to kind of twirl his hair with my fingers. Do you see that? You guys are going to have to respond in words because I won't be able to keep looking at the audience in a minute."

"We got it," James yells.

"Thanks, okay, so, then Elijah's left hand is going to slide into place at my waist. Move slow, you want to build the romantic tension."

I turn my eyes down so I can track the movement. When his hand is nestled between my hip and rib cage, I lift my right arm. "Now, this arm rests lightly on his forearm. Tell me, can you guys still see our faces? Because in a real scene, we will probably have lines at this point and you should be able to see our expressions."

"Got it," James calls.

"Good, okay, now Elijah can make a choice."

"Eli." His voice sounds husky.

I really hope he's not coming down with a cold or something because I cannot get sick right now.

"Eli, whatever, Eli now has a choice. He can put his left hand on my waist to encircle with his right hand or he can put his left hand up higher on my back just under my shoulder. What do you want to do?"

"The, uh, the waist thing, I guess."

I wait for him to get there, then raise my voice. "Now, this is the most critical part. You have to see the tension between the characters as the audience so that means the characters need to create tension. If there's no palpable chemistry, the audience will not care what happens next. That means you have to step out of who you are and become your character. So, Elijah is a guy who has this unrequited crush on a girl that is so distracted with her schooling that he can't ever get her attention. Finally, he has a study date with her and he just loses all patience. So, that means you're going to have to be the instigator from here on Elijah, to make the scene work."

"Eli," he whispers.

"Whatever. Now, me. I'm a girl who is really into books and focused on getting into some prestigious university in Europe, but then this guy shows interest in me and I find myself wrapped up in his arms in the library. I'm not Carmen anymore so I'm going to stop talking and show you. Watch carefully."

I take a deep breath and close my eyes to help the transition. Elijah's hands are warm across my waist and the theater lights feel blazing hot. But I am a professional so I shut all of that out and picture the floor to ceiling shelves in the library and the musty smell of old books and stale coffee. I hear the rustle of pages as people study around me.

When I open my eyes, I no longer see Elijah, it's the boy I've never noticed, the one who really likes me, the one worth getting distracted for.

Instinctively, my hand that was on Elijah's face drops to his waist, and one of his hands that was on my waist moves to my neck and jawline. Elijah closes the small space between us, tightening his hand on my waist. My arm on his forearm pushes up to his shoulder. He moves slowly, watching me intently the whole time.

His eyes never leave mine, which is a little disconcerting. With most of my drama kisses in the past, the guy was so focused inward on his character motivation, he barely seemed to notice I was there.

Okay, I have to stop thinking this way. I'm not teaching right now, I'm acting. I give myself a little shake.

Guy, possibilities, impending kiss.

Elijah tips his chin to one side. I take his cue and tip mine to the other so that when our lips are ready to touch, there is nothing in the way.

I keep my eyes open as our heads move closer together so I can make notes for the others after this is done. When our lips touch, the kiss is light and airy, but then something happens that I did not intend.

A surge goes through my torso. I find myself clutching the sleeve of Elijah's shirt, pulling him even closer. His arm presses tightly into my back, and my heart is suddenly pounding so hard I can hear it in my ears. One of his hands moves to my hair where his fingers get lost and tangled.

I can't get enough of him.

I never want to let go.

A burst from the PA system jolts me away from Elijah. I don't hear a word of the announcement over the noise in my head. There's a solid two feet between us now, but I can still feel him pressed against me.

Elijah's hands drop to his sides as he stares at me in a way that I can't.

I can't.

I can't even.

I smooth my hair away from my face and try to regain some composure. It shouldn't be this hard. I am a professional. That kiss didn't mean anything. It was a theater kiss. That's all.

Just a theater kiss.

I can't look at him anymore, so I turn to everyone else. "See, it's not a big deal."

Eldon lets out a low whistle.

"Right?" Kelsie says.

Michelle shakes out her hands. "If she thinks that's no big deal, I wonder what a big deal looks like."

"No kidding," James adds. "That kiss, man, I *felt* it."

I scoff, but it sounds tinny in my ears. "Give me a break, you guys. It's just a drama kiss. All of you can do this. Michelle and Zeb, why don't you try that again, from the beginning."

I don't look at anyone as I hurry to the wings. What I want to do is bolt for the parking lot. Something I can't identify is wreaking havoc in my belly. Right now, I just need to be as far away from Elijah as I can realistically get until I calm down. My heart still slams in my chest and my lips still tingle from Elijah...

From Eli's...

Kiss.

Okay, seriously?

It doesn't mean a thing. It's this simple. We kissed on the stage, so it was a stage kiss, therefore it's nothing.

It's nothing.

It's nothing.

Act VI Scene II

I am haunted.

Not by a ghost or a memory or a tragic life event. I am haunted by a kiss.

I've tried for days to banish that moment on the stage with Eli from my memory. I've used every trick in my vast kit of tools, but I can't do it. It's there, lurking, always.

Which just makes my day-to-day interactions with him all the more awkward.

He hasn't said a word about it, but when there is a quiet moment, I catch him watching me. That alone wouldn't be a big deal. He's seriously been watching me since I moved here, waiting for me to do something wrong so he can bust my chops. Except, it feels different now. He's got the look in his eyes I saw when I pulled away from him right after we kissed.

I don't know what it means, and it is seriously messing with my mind hole.

On Wednesday, another typical, boring Wednesday, at the end of drama club when everyone has gone, I sit on the stage and mentally rehash the last hour.

I made everyone pair off and help each other with their memorization so I could brood in the wings. I have no clue if they actually did it because I was so thoroughly lost in my own thoughts. If Beth had been there today, it would have been different, but she had to stay after school to make up a test she missed when she was home with a migraine on Monday.

I should have stayed home with a migraine. I totally have one. It's exhausting to avoid Eli now. I'm aware of him even when I'm not looking at him. Like my brain is honed in on his every movement.

It is seriously the worst.

'Cause then I have to overanalyze all the things my brain picks up. Like, he scratched his cheek. Does that mean he likes me? He held his breath for a second. Does that mean he regrets that kiss?

I am cracking up here.

I sigh and lay on my back so I stare at the ceiling with my legs half dangling in the band pit. With the musty smell of the curtain and my heels thumping rhythmically against the edge of the stage, I should feel better. But it brings me no relief. I am made to suffer.

I guess the good news is, Eli is equally avoiding me. He high-tailed it out of the auditorium the second I told everyone we were done.

I use the word "good" lightly. Part of me thinks it's good news, so I can continue pretending he doesn't exist. The other part wishes he would confront me. All these unsaid thoughts are creating a musk way more poignant than whatever new celebrity perfume Skylar currently wears.

That's the other thing. Skylar hasn't called or messaged since she said we needed space. She won't respond when I call or message. Yesterday she unfriended me on social media. So, I guess we're done here?

I don't know. This is too much all at once.

Really, I should pull myself up by my boots and go home. Pamper myself with a hot bath and bubbles. The problem is, all of that requires exertion. I'm just going to lay here a little longer and obsess about life's problems. It's not like it will bother anyone. The room is empty now except for me.

I hear a shuffle of footsteps and peek open one eye.

Oh, except for me and Ms. B.

She's so quiet in her part of the auditorium, I sort of forget she's here. I hope she didn't hear all my sighing and guess what that's about.

So humiliating.

I slowly sit up so I'm not laying there like a slug when she reaches the other side of the band pit.

"Hi, Carmen." There is a half-smile on her face that leads me to suspect she knows exactly what shape my angst is. She walks around the band pit to the stairs and takes a seat next to me.

I glance over after an abominable amount of time full of horribly silent silence. "What?"

She shakes her head. "Nothing."

We swing our legs in harmony until the soft thump of our heels starts to grate on my nerves.

"I'm fine," I say through clenched teeth.

"Of course you are."

I pull my legs up and sit criss cross, then turn to face her. "It's not like it's a big deal. I kiss people on the stage all the time. It doesn't mean anything. Seriously, no thing. There is no thing between us. There is no us, even."

She nods.

I stare at her for a minute, then my shoulders droop. "But if that were true, why can't I stop thinking about that stupid kiss? I keep telling myself it was just a drama kiss. Those are so not romantic at all. I mean, it's just part of the job, you know? I once kissed the guy playing my opposite when he had a giant cold sore because that's what the role demanded. His character didn't have a cold sore, so I went forward like nothing was amiss. Of course, that meant I got a cold sore that lasted for three weeks and itched like a mo, but that's the price I'm willing to pay for my craft. When the cold sore was gone, I forgot about the whole thing until now. If I can block out a kiss as repulsive as that one was, why am I geeking out about this kiss with Eli? It was just lips touching lips. No. Big. Deal." I sigh. "Except it wasn't just lips touching lips, and it is a big deal. Ms. B, why can't I stop thinking about *him*? I don't like him. I don't like Elijah." I say his full name, accentuating every syllable because it makes me feel better. "He's a pest and a know-it-all and he has serious daddy issues. It's not just that, either. I *can't* like him. We're from totally different worlds. We have totally different goals. I mean, can you picture me wearing an apron in a rickety farm house or him on the red carpet on the way to the Oscars? In his manure boots? I mean, ew!" I groan and drop my head into my lap. "It's a disaster."

Ms. B laughs a lovely lilting laugh that sounds so familiar it makes me want my mommy. "Is that what's bothering you? Your kiss demonstration with Eli?"

"Who says anything is bothering me?" I say into my hands. "I'm perfectly fine. This is normal."

The auditorium door slams against the wall and Kelsie hurries down the aisle.

"Oh! I'm glad you haven't locked up yet. I left my lip gloss." She disappears behind some chairs for a moment and then lifts it in the air. "Found it!"

Ms. B smiles. "I'm glad."

Kelsie tucks it into her purse then gives us a second look. "What are you guys doing?"

I groan and flop back onto the stage. I lace my hands over my belly even though my instinct is to cross them over my chest like the victim in a tragic tale of woe.

Which I am.

Ms. B answers. "Carmen and I are having a little chat. Everything is fine. Have a nice afternoon, Kelsie."

I squint to the side so I can see what Kelsie does next. Ms. B's words were polite, but her tone does not invite Kelsie to stick around.

Kelsie puts a hand on her hip and nods. "Yeah, okay, you too. Bye." Then she hurries out of the auditorium.

Ms. B takes my hand and pulls me back into a sitting position.

I raise my head. "I don't like him. I can't. He's such a...such a small-town hick. There isn't a single place in my life plan that he would fit."

Ms. B nods, her face sympathetic. "You know, sometimes plans change."

"No!" I sit up straight. "Nononononono! My plan can't change! I've dreamed of this since I was, like, three. I'm going to LAAA, graduating with an agent and a contract, starring in many blockbuster movies, and retiring at the ripe old age of thirty-seven on a sprawling ranch in Sacramento with Jace."

Except, oh yeah, Jace is dating the foreign exchange student that also stole my best friend.

"Or, you know, whoever I'm in love with by that time."

"That's your life plan?" Ms. B watches me carefully, like whatever I say next matters a whole lot.

So I just nod because those rarely disappoint, and I don't know what she expects from me.

Ms. B looks at me a moment longer, then adjusts her square-frame glasses and stares off into the rafters. "You know, Carmen, that sounds an awful lot like my life plan. Except the boy was Dray, not Jace."

I laugh and then realize she isn't laughing with me. "Wait, what?"

"For the last couple of weeks, I've been watching you while you coach these kids." Ms. B waves her arm across the auditorium. "When I first met you, I thought I had a good idea who you were, but I was very wrong. There is more to you than you let others see."

"Okay." I don't know where she's going with this, and now my stomach is clenching into knots for totally non-Eli-related reasons.

I'm kinda scared to hear what she's going to say next.

"I see myself in you, Carmen, which is why I am thinking about telling you something." Ms. B takes in a deep breath, a yoga breath that makes her close her eyes. When she opens them, they are fixed on my face. She shifts so she is facing me. "I think it will help you."

Now my heart is beating like crazy. From the tense look on Ms. B's face, I now conclude that whatever she's going to say is bad.

Super bad.

The baddest ever.

I'm not so sure I want to hear it.

Her head tips to the side. "I won't tell you if you don't want me to."

Either the look on my face is horrible, or Ms. B is a mind reader. I take a deep breath to slow my heart down and consider. She said whatever it is might help me. I already know Ms. B is a nice person. It's not like she's going to ream me or something.

Right?

I nod without letting any more thoughts come through. "You can tell me whatever you need to tell me."

And then I brace myself.

She begins as if she's thinking out loud. "I don't like to talk about this. I don't want to. I don't even like to think about it, and I've never told another person in this town."

She stops abruptly and stays silent for a really long time. There's a war going on behind those square-frame glasses. She might *need* to tell me something, or she wouldn't even consider it. This is obviously a struggle for her.

After another few moments of silence, she lets out a dry laugh.

"You don't have to tell me anything, Ms. B. It's okay." Really, I am not a fan of doing hard things just for the sake of doing them.

"I know I don't have to,"—she gives a small smile—"but I think I need to. If I can spare you some of the pain I went through, then I feel like it's my responsibility as your teacher. But also, it's the right thing to do."

I nod encouragingly, even though I don't have a clue where she's going with this.

"To be honest"—she twists a ring around her pinkie finger—"there is a part of me that wants someone to know. But, Carmen, I must ask you not to mention this to anyone. It is deeply personal to me. Can we keep this conversation between the two of us?"

I am an expert at keeping things in the auditorium. I never told a soul about that time I caught my understudy making out with one of the extras in the band pit. In fact, I forgot about it until this moment, so that proves my point. She has nothing to worry about from me.

"I won't tell anyone anything," I assure her. "Your secret will go with me to the deepest abyss."

Ms. B laughs and thanks me with her eyes, then takes a deep breath. "This is much harder than I thought. I apologize if it takes some time to get the words out."

"I don't have anywhere to be."

"Thank you." Ms. B squares her shoulders and lets out a long breath. "Similar to you, I was determined to be a famous actress. I wanted to go to LAAA, knock their socks off, and become the world's leading rom-com actress."

Is she telling me this to discourage me? Because I actually think I *can* do the things I planned. If this is going to become one of those tales of things that didn't work out even though she tried, so she had to become a teacher of adolescents, then I don't want to hear it.

"And..." Ms. B pierces me with her eyeballs. "...I did all of it."

"What?" I blink. I've seen a lot of rom-coms in my day, and I can't recall Ms. Buckley in any of them.

Ms. B removes her glasses and pulls her hair out of the tight bun. It cascades down her shoulders in waves that hit the stage and pool there like gold. It's mesmerizing.

When I look over at Ms. B's face again, it's transformed. Gone is the wrinkle between her eyebrows that carries the weight of the world. Gone is the pinched look her mouth makes like she's always sucking on a lemon. Gone is the severe way that bun pulls her face upward and makes her forehead look enormous.

I draw in a sharp breath. "Holy Hollywood, you are Laura Valentine!"

The name echoes in the auditorium around us.

Valentine. Valentine. Valentine.

Ms. B's shoulders round, transforming her once again into a mousy teacher. "I am."

I pop onto my knees and grab her hands. "I have so many questions I don't know where to start! Why did you leave? What in the Grammy are you doing in this podunky town teaching math? What happened to you? What was it like filming with Brad Pitt?"

He was hot stuff when Laura Valentine was acting. I think even my mom had a crush on him. There's a 1990 something Brad Pitt calendar under the sweats in her pants drawer. He might be old now, but he's still hot snot.

Ms. B breathes deeply for a few moments. I wait patiently for whatever pep talk she needs to give herself to answer my questions. Because she has to answer my questions. I can't believe I'm sitting in the same room as Laura Valentine, the best rom-com actress this world has ever seen!

I literally have stars in my eyes right now.

Ms. B slowly gathers her hair and twists it around and around and around until she can secure it into a tight bun once more. Then she looks at me. "Please don't tell anyone who I am, Carmen. My privacy has become very important to me. I realize I've put you in a tough spot. The temptation will be there. I'm trusting you. I trust you."

I raise my hand to the square like that will prove something significant. "I don't understand why you're here instead of in California, or why you're hiding your identity, but I promise I will leave this auditorium and forget everything you tell me. No one will learn your secret from me." I wonder if she wants me to swear a blood oath. I'll totally do it. "You can trust me, Ms. B. I won't say a word. I promise."

And I mean it.

As fabulous as it would be to hop on social media and tell the world what I know, then watch my followers increase to the millions, I honestly don't have any desire to do it. There's something about her trust that takes that feeling away. It's kind of nice to be someone she can tell something this huge and meaningful. And also, I now *have* to know her story. The need itches like a huge mosquito bite.

Ms. B seems satisfied with my words. "Thank you, Carmen. I appreciate you keeping my secret."

"You're welcome." Every nerve in my body is on high alert for the moment she begins. I am aching to know. I can barely sit still. If there was a way to get information faster than mouth to ear, I would be all over it right now.

Ms. B folds her hands in her lap. "Do you know very much about my career?"

"Yes!" I shout, then look around. We are still obviously alone, but I lower my voice anyway. This is such a whisper moment. "I know about your childhood in Canada on your grandparents ranch. I know that you never met your parents. I know all about your horse, Chuckles, and your dog, Laryngitis. You put on your first play with some friends in the barn. Your grandparents and the animals were your only audience. You earned money to pay for LAAA by doing more plays in your community and leaving Canada was the hardest thing you ever had to do, oh, except for when your grandparents died and the ranch was sold to a developer by your uncle before you had a chance to buy it. Last I read, you were still trying to talk the new owners into selling it to you, but that was years ago. Did they ever agree?"

"No, they haven't yet." Ms. B looks stunned. "Carmen, I think you know more about me than I do."

I laugh. "And, also, I've seen all your movies."

"All of them?" She lifts an eyebrow, her eyes shining.

I nod. "All of them. My ex-bestie, Skylar, and I are your very biggest fans. Those are not just words. We even saw that lame movie on the deserted island."

Ms. B cringes. "Not my best work."

"No, but it wasn't you, it was the plot. Seriously, turning the deserted islands into a time travel portal to the French Revolution? So weird. What were they thinking? You, though, you did amazing with what you were given. You were magic on the screen. What happened to you?"

She ducks her head. "I suppose we should start with the accident."

My heart pounds in my chest like it does in the climax of every movie I've ever seen. I lean forward with anticipation. The accident is pivotal to this particular story. After that, Laura Valentine disappeared.

"I was filming a movie about a famous ballerina who falls in love with a stagehand. I have a background in dance so it was a very easy role. I think that's where I went wrong. I didn't practice as diligently as I should have, I was overly confident. I fell wrong after a Grand Jete and broke my ankle."

I cringe in sympathy.

"It was a bad break. It required surgery and almost an entire year of recovery. When I was fully healed, I met with my agent to discuss roles, but..." She looks at her hands.

"What?"

Ms. B now looks at me. "I couldn't walk for that year. I had to lay down almost entirely. I tried to keep up with my diet plan, but it was incredibly frustrating to lay around all day and watch my competition take over my parts. I put on thirty pounds."

I vaguely remembered something about that in the tabloids. Pictures of Laura Valentine in a bulgy sweat suit. Something derogatory about America's overweight sweetheart.

"My agent didn't want to try for any roles until I lost at least twenty-five of it. Then the pictures went viral. My face was all over everything, bloated and brushed to look way worse. Carmen, I was so consumed with my fame and what people thought of me, I couldn't see who I was without it. I really thought I looked like those memes that circulated the internet. Memes of beached whales and Jabba the Hut. And the interesting thing is, the more I tried to lose the weight, to *get my body back* as they say, the more I couldn't do it. I would do well for a few days, then see something upsetting and binge for a week. My weight climbed higher and higher, which made the media go crazy. My agent dropped me, and I sunk to a very dark place."

I rub my arms to get rid of the goosebumps.

"I had to face myself there. It was the hardest thing I have ever done. Except for maybe telling you about it." She smiles sadly. "I'd played so many roles and been so many people I didn't know who Laura really was anymore. And I knew I would never figure it out in the midst of the paparazzi circus. I had to leave. I found a small town in the middle of nowhere. I got my teaching certificate, and I started a new life as Lisa Buckley. And here we are." She spreads her hands out to the sides and keeps her eyes on the floor like she's afraid to look at me.

"Wow," I breathe out. "Wow, Ms. B, Laura, I don't..."

"Carmen," she says softly, "Hollywood looks magical and alluring, but it is heartless and cruel. I couldn't see it until I left, and then I got a clear view of the selfishness, cattiness, and greed that drives the whole industry. Now,"—she lifts a hand—"I'm not saying everyone there is like that. There are celebrities who do amazing things. They give back and donate and think about things other than themselves. I mean as a whole, Hollywood doesn't care about people. It will love you and hate you in the same breath. I went into it with stars in my eyes, and I rose to the top thinking I *was* the star. When I fell, it was hard. I want to spare you that, Carmen. If you decide to pursue your plan and become an amazing actress, I have no doubt you will do it, but I want you to go into it with your eyes open. Don't let the glitter blind you. Remember who you are and decide who you will become." She breathes heavily, like she just ran a marathon. "That's it, that's all I wanted to tell you."

Act VII Scene I

FADE IN: INT: DEEP CONTEMPLATION IN A DARK BEDROOM - OVERDUE CONFRONTATION - REENACTMENT - CAN'T EVEN WITH THIS GUY

I can't stop thinking about Ms. B's story. I've been staring at the dark ceiling in my bedroom for hours. No matter how I toss and turn, sleep is elusive tonight.

When I close my eyes, there are camera flashes and leaping ballerinas and tabloids. The beauty of Hollywood is overshadowed by a huge ugly monster with glowing green eyes.

I mean, the injustice.

Laura Valentine was an amazing actress. She made even the cheesiest movie seem better. Even if it was the same story retold a million times, she made it feel new. Everyone loved her when she was at her tippy top. I just can't understand how some extra weight would change all that.

Are we really that shallow?

I have a leaden feeling in my gut that the answer is yes.

In the back of my mind, there has been a niggling question since Ms. B began her story. I've tried to ignore it, but in the dark recesses of the midnight world, it refuses to be ignored.

Is that what I want?

Do I want to live in a world that's blinded like that? Where people don't know who they are so they look for gratification from what they can buy or from other people who are just as confused? Do I want to surround myself with people who are always pretending or looking over their shoulder to see who's watching?

Do I really want that?

Really?

I wouldn't even have had to ask myself that question only a few short weeks ago. The answer would have been a serious no-brainer. Since then, I've sacrificed time to help Beth with her stage fright, I've taught others how to act. I've sat on freezing cold bleachers, and I watched my friends chug hot sauce at an all-night diner.

I am not the person I was a few weeks ago.

I'm not even the same person I was a few hours ago.

Something shifted, and I don't know yet if this is a good thing or a terrible thing. All I know is it is a thing, and I can't unhear what I heard. I can't unlearn what I've learned. I can't undo anything that's happened.

I can't go back.

So, what if Skylar called me right now and said we are still besties? And Jace dumped his new woman and moved here to be with me until graduation? And LAAA gave me a scholarship for the fall because I'm special?

What then?

I squirm and flip onto my stomach. The lack of oxygen from breathing into my pillow has been very enlightening.

Oh my Oscars.

I couldn't.

I couldn't go back to being Skylar's friend the way I was.

I couldn't date Jace again. And LAAA...

I wouldn't do it.

This one is the hardest for me to admit to myself. It's kind of like pulling a sliver out of my fingernail, but it's also a relief. To be totally honest, I've been feeling a withdrawal from LAAA for a while. I didn't really recognize it for what it was because it happened so gradually in spurts and inches and I just didn't want to realize it.

I mean, who am I without LAAA and my fabulous life plan?

I don't know how to construct an existence without California, Skylar, Jace, and LAAA, but I also know I've changed too much to be part of those things anymore. There is so much more to life than the way I've lived. I've been so wrapped up in myself and what I want... I've made a very small package.

This is so weird. I feel like it should sting more to let the old me go. The weirdest thing is that it doesn't. Not at all. The whole world just opened up for me. It can be anything.

I can be anything.

And that is an exceptionally thrilling thought.

I wake up totally refreshed, despite my whirling thoughts from the night before. There is something deeply cleansing about being honest with oneself. It makes me wonder why I haven't done that sooner.

All of the things Ms. B told me are now tucked away in a lockbox where I can't access them. Somewhere in the remotest part of my mind with memories of wearing mom jeans and jelly shoes. Totally forgotten.

Okay, mostly forgotten.

I jump out of bed and rush to the kitchen to beat my parents. They both wander in just as I'm finishing up the pancakes I made from a very delicious mix I found in one of the cabinets. I'm not Martha Stewart, but I can add water and whisk with the best of them. We sit together at the table and talk about their research while we eat. I don't understand half of what they tell me, but they're so excited, I'm glad I asked.

I help load the dishwasher and gather my things to go to school. Instead of turning left at the mailbox, I take a right and head to Eli's house.

Becky answers the door with a scowl. "What do you want?"

I try on my winning smile then drop it for something more sincere. "Hi, Becky. I know I offended you, and I'm sorry about that. I'd like to call a truce. I'm willing to forget the milk thing if you're willing to forget I was a brat." I hold out my hand. "Deal?"

She stares at it for a minute. "You really were a brat."

"I know."

"Okay, sure, truce." She shakes my hand, her braids bouncing behind her. "Are you here for Eli?" She doesn't wait for my answer, but turns and bellows, "ELI!"

"I'm coming, keep your hair on." Eli hops into the room, trying to tie his shoe while he walks. He stops when he sees me. "Oh, hey."

"Hey, Elijah. I mean, Eli." I feel so stupid, but I'm determined not to give in to that or let it be the boss of me. "I thought we could walk to school together."

He studies me for a moment, then nods. "Sure, okay, let me get my stuff." He turns into the living room to pack books into his bag. "Do you want a muffin? Grandma made banana nut this morning."

"Like homemade?" That must be the delectable smell in their house.

Eli gives me a sassy look. "Is there any other way?"

"I would totally love one, thank you!"

"I'll get it for you." Becky bounces away.

"Get me one too," Eli says.

Becky turns and crosses her eyes. "Get it yourself."

But she brings him two and then hands one to me. It's still warm and sticks to the wrapper as I peel it away. It tastes better than I used to think fame would feel.

Eli opens the front door for me, then follows me into the sunshine. We walk down the driveway to the dirt road in silence. I wait for him to finish eating his muffins, then I speak.

"Eli?"

"Wait." He holds out one arm to block the way.

I stop walking "What?"

"That is the second time you called me Eli on your own. Are you sick? Did something happen? Is a meteor about to strike planet Earth and turn us all to dust?"

"Haha." I shake my head.

"No? Are you sure?" His eyes scan the heavens like he really thinks something is about to drop from the sky and incinerate us both. "Something must have happened. There's no way you're giving in on your own. Are you a robot?"

I start walking again, shaking my head as I go. "If you're going to be all ridiculous, that's fine. We can just leave that kiss we had on the stage in the past and never resolve anything. Whatever you want."

He jogs to catch up to me. "Wait, what did you say? I missed part of it. What are you trying to resolve?"

Yeah right, he didn't hear me. I've wondered if that kiss weighs on his mind the same way it weighs on mine, and he just proved it to me. It's obvious by the way his voice drops that he knows exactly what I'm talking about.

"Duh, Eli, we have to resolve the kiss thing. It is way too hard to avoid you in a town this small. I'm tired of the weird space, and I'm tired of thinking about what happened, so we have to talk it out until we find a way to be normal again."

"I've never been a fan of normal." Eli reaches over and takes my hand. "Have you, uh, really been thinking about our, uh, kiss?"

What is it with this guy? His touch is like fireworks going off the tips of my fingers. I still can't wrap my head around it. He's so ordinary. How is it that I feel so *extraordinary* when I'm around him?

I lace my fingers through his and let our hands swing as we walk. It's just seriously enjoyable. I forget what we were talking about until Eli speaks.

"So, how do we go about resolving this kiss thing, exactly?"

That's right, that's what we were talking about.

"Yeah, okay, so, I don't know about you, but I have kissed a lot of guys—"

"Nope."

I glance over at him. "Nope what?"

Eli grins. "I have not kissed a lot of guys."

I push his arm, throwing us both out of balance. It takes a few steps to get in walking sync once again. "Let me finish! That is not what I meant and you know it!"

"My apologies." He squeezes my hand. "Please, go on."

I check to see if he's mocking me or preparing himself to mock me as soon as I open my mouth again. He looks humble and contrite, so maybe I was wrong about that.

Or maybe he's a really good actor.

Okay, scratch that, I've seen him act. He's humble and contrite.

I pull a wisp of hair out of my mouth and tuck it behind my ear. "I'm just going to be real. Despite all those theater kisses I mentioned before, I have never felt anything like what I felt when I kissed you. Not even with Jace." I pause this time because I have this strange feeling in the pit of my stomach. I try my trick of identifying it and letting it move through me, like I taught Beth, but I don't know this feeling. I haven't ever had it before.

"Yeah?" Eli asks in a "go on" voice.

I purse my lips. "Have you ever felt like you were scared to admit something because you don't know what the other person is thinking and they might not feel the same way you do?"

I think that's what this feeling is, though I'm not sure what to call it.

"What?" Eli's eyebrows draw together. "I'm not sure...are we still talking about how we're resolving the kiss or whatever?"

Ugh, this is harder than I anticipated. I try to come up with a better way to explain, but Eli begins talking again before I find a good one.

"Okay, to answer your question, yes, I have felt that way before. I guess, I mean, I think." He shoots me a sidelong glance. "How did you feel about our kiss?"

Our kiss.

It sounds so personal when he says it that way, like we are already something. Instead of no thing. It makes my belly soar to new heights, and I kind of want it to be true, me and him, a thing. But I can't tell him what I think until I know what he's thinking.

"What?" He nudges me with his arm. "What aren't you saying?"

My brain is tired so I give it a rest and open my mouth. "I'm not saying anything until you tell me what *you* thought about that kiss. I think I've already revealed too much."

"Like, that you liked it?"

"More than liked it, I'm obsessed with it. How did you learn to kiss like that? You made me feel like I am the only other person on the planet. Like everything disappeared except for us. If you could bottle that skill, you'd be rich. You know? I totally don't get how you did that."

Oh, wow. I did not mean to say any of that.

Eli makes a noise and I look over at him, even though my natural response is to drop his hand and run for the hills. I just told him that kiss was earth-shattering for me. And it obviously means nothing to him.

Because Eli starts to laugh.

As mortified as I am, I can't leave this unresolved anymore.

I need my beauty sleep.

"Eli." I pull him to a stop and move to face him. "Did you feel anything when we kissed? Tell me the truth, okay? No messing around."

He's still laughing.

Oh my stars, I have never felt so stupid in my life. I start to pull my hand away so I can put some distance between us, but Eli grips it hard. I just succeed in a few fruitless yanks.

"Why are you laughing?" I ask in a small voice.

Eli makes a valiant effort to rein himself in. "It's not you. I mean, it's you, but not the way you think."

"How do you know what I think?"

"I don't." He half shrugs. "Okay, so it's not what I think you think."

"What?" I sputter.

"Carmen, our kiss blew my mind."

I stop trying to pull away. "Really?"

"Really."

"Then why are you laughing at me?"

Eli grins and brushes my cheek with his free hand. It's like he's moving away a wisp of hair, except his hand stays there long after the supposed wisp would be gone. "I'm laughing at this conversation. I mean, we're talking about kissing. That's weird, right?"

"*A* kiss." The back of my neck warms up, even though the sun is right in my face. "Not kissing. We weren't talking about kissing."

"Yeah, that's a mistake." Eli moves closer. His face is just inches away from mine.

"Eli?" My voice is thin vapor and he inhales it.

"Yeah?"

"Do you think we could kiss again? Just to see what happens? I need to know if that first kiss was a fluke or—"

I don't get a chance to finish my sentence.

That first kiss?

It was not a fluke.

Soooooooooooooo, not a fluke

I don't have to ask or wonder anymore if Eli feels the same way about me as I feel about him. It's so obvious. I can feel it all the way down to my pinkie toes.

Time dissolves around us again. I have no idea how long we're standing there on the side of the road next to a field full of cows, when the blare of a car horn blasts us apart.

"Come on you guys, we just ate breakfast." Beth hangs an elbow out of the passenger side of a dilapidated truck. Oh, that would be Myles's dilapidated truck since he's in the driver's seat.

Good to know.

I take another step away from Eli so there's some extra space between us. Like that will negate the fact that we were totally just making out in public.

Again.

"It's about time," Myles adds. "I conjectured that the two of you would get together a week ago, and I hate being wrong."

The back window rolls down and all the muffled hooting gets so much louder. James. Wow. It's like he's never seen people kiss before. Kelsie leans over him and half hangs out the window with her phone pointed at us.

"Can you guys do that again? I want to post it."

Eli turns his back on all of us and stalks off. The way he's walking, he's either embarrassed or filled to the rafters with regret.

Does he regret kissing me?

Great, now I'm going to wonder about that incessantly for the next forever. Unless I can catch up to him and get him to talk it out. Yeah, no, that so isn't happening in these wedges.

Oh my Grammy, this boy is making my head hurt.

And he's turning me into a quivering pile of uncertainty.

Drama, drama, drama.

I lean against the car. "Got room for one more?"

James grins and opens the back door. He and Kelsie scooch over so I can slide in next to them. Once I'm in and buckled, Myles pulls back onto the road.

Not that there's a difference, the road and the side of the road are completely identical.

"So," Beth twists her body around, "you and Eli, huh?"

Honestly, I'm still reeling from that kiss. I don't understand how that boy curls my toes and also makes me want to invent a couple of new curse words. He's intoxicating and infuriating at the same time.

When I don't answer, Beth takes the hint and changes the subject. The rest of them chatter on, while I press my nose to the window and wait for the moment we pass Eli so I can try and analyze his features to figure out what's going on with him.

But that moment doesn't come.

We are too close to the high school. By the time we pull into a parking space, I can see Eli's orange backpack bobbing through the crowd to the front doors.

"What in the heckfire darnation is going on?" James breathes out.

Yeah, I think this seems like a ridiculous amount of people too. Way more than usual.

"Are those reporters?" Beth leans forward to peer through the windshield. "Did someone let a pig in the chem lab again?"

"No way!" Kelsie puts her phone on video and points it at the crush. "That's US Stars!"

Now that we're closer, I can hear the hum of voices talking over one another. Principal Bob and the PE teacher, who looks like Kronk on the Emperor's New Groove, except he's wearing a blue sweatsuit. They try to hold the crowd at bay, but aren't having much luck. The press are pressing closer and closer to the front of the school.

Oh, wait, duh, I finally get why they're called that.

"What's US Stars?" James squints out the window, and I follow his gaze.

"A magazine." Kelsie squeals.

"No, that's, wait, that's a tabloid." I fall back in my seat without making the conscious decision. For reals, I'm pretty sure that it's hardwired into the DNA of a California girl to hide when there are tabloids present.

"No way!" Kelsie bounces out of the car, completely forgetting her school stuff on the backseat floor. "This is so major!" She runs across the parking lot and disappears into the crowd.

"What's a tabloid?" James asks.

"Paparazzi." My stomach suddenly hurts really, really bad.

"Oh, yeah." James nods, then nudges me with his elbow. "What's paparazzi?"

"Vultures." I push the car door open and step into the crisp morning air. I didn't notice how cold it was when I was with Eli, but now the shiver goes all the way to the marrow of my bones. I rub my hands over my arms, trying to get the goosebumps to go away.

The din of the crowd leaks over to where I'm standing. I can hear what the people are saying now. My heart legitimately stops beating.

No.

They're asking for Laura Valentine.

ACT VII SCENE II

FADE IN: INT: HILLBILLY HIGH SCHOOL - MORE CONFRONTATION - CRUSHED TO DUST - THE TRUTH SHALL SET YOU FREE

I have to get into that school.

Completely gone is all thought of Beth, James, Myles, and my insensible shoes. I bolt into the fray. I elbow my way through people and cameras until I get to the door of Hillbilly High School. It's still only Principal Bob and Kronk trying to talk to them. I don't see Ms. B anywhere.

And I'm too frantic to tell them to stop talking to the vultures. Everything they say is going to end up twisted into a new meaning by the tabloid, complete with highly unflattering pictures.

I yank the door open and stop only to remove my wedges before I take off running as fast as I can through the crowd of students pressed on the other side of the door. They're all trying to figure out what is going on.

"Carmen!" Kelsie's cheeks are pink with excitement. "Do you..."

I shake my head and keep moving. I wish I'd invested more time in my running skills. My lungs burn as I round the corner to the math classroom, but I can't slow down until I find Ms. B and talk to her.

The door is closed. I knock quickly and push it open. At first, it looks like the classroom is empty. It is dark and the blinds are all closed as tight as they can possibly go. Once my eyes adjust, I see Ms. B rounded over her desk with her head in her arms.

She slowly raises her face to look at me.

"I didn't!" My chest heaves, I raise both hands like I'm about to be arrested. I can't catch my breath. "I didn't...tell...I swear."

Ms. B doesn't move. All I can see in the dark is the glint of her eyes. She doesn't say anything while I struggle to gather enough air to explain myself more thoroughly.

"I didn't tell anyone who you are, Ms. B. I promise I didn't."

"That's interesting." Her voice is low and croaky like she has the flu or the onset of laryngitis. My heart wrings for her until she speaks again. Now her voice is so hard my cheeks sting as though she just smacked me with one of those thick Calculus textbooks.

I take a deep breath to steady myself. Before I can open my mouth, Ms. B shoots word daggers at me. "You do realize this school is surrounded by a mass of paparazzi who want to speak to Laura Valentine? Rumor has it, she's been hiding out in this little town as a math teacher for all these years."

This is bad. This is so, so bad.

She's right. I'm the only person she told. *Did* I mention it to someone? I try to remember. Could I have said something to someone without realizing it? I don't think so, but now I'm plagued with doubts. Her anger is so powerful all I can do is second guess myself. *Was* this my fault? Did I totally betray Ms. B?

I run through my memories of last night and this morning. Who would I have told? My parents? They were the only people I talked to after school yesterday. The thought of my parents calling up US Stars, or any other tabloid, is just laughable. Eli? Between the resolving and the smooching, there wasn't really a chance for me to spill any beans.

I didn't talk at all in the car with the others.

I didn't do it.

I *know* I didn't.

But Ms. B's stone cold face makes me feel like I did.

Like I'm responsible.

That's really unfair. I should be innocent until proven guilty, not the other way around.

But even I have to admit this looks bad. I put myself into her sensible shoes. She only told *me* and now there's paparazzi everywhere. Of course she thinks I did this. Why wouldn't she?

So, what this means is I'm innocent *and* her reaction is understandable. Now, what should I do with this information? How do I get her to believe the truth?

"Ms. B—"

She barks a laugh that is so free from humor it sends a shiver up my back. "Don't bother, Carmen. I don't want to hear your excuses. I thought I was wrong about you, but I had it right from the beginning. Well, you got what you wanted. Congratulations. The paparazzi are here. Go enjoy your moment in the spotlight. Your ten seconds of fame. I hope it's worth it."

"I—"

"Just go!" she yells.

The noise fills my head, reverberating her anger over and over and over again. Tears sting the bottoms of my eyes as I slip out of the room and close the door behind me.

I lean against it for support but find myself sliding to the floor. My head hits my knees and I start to sob. I've never cried like this before. It feels like an animal is clawing its way out of my chest.

I didn't realize until this moment just how much Ms. B's trust means to me. Is this what it's like to care about something other than myself? Because it completely sucks.

"Carmen?"

I am in the middle of a consuming ugly cry. I can't find the motivation to lift my head, much less answer Eli.

His arm slides across my shoulder. The warmth of his body combats the shivering enough that I finally take a full breath.

"Carmen?" Eli whispers as he rubs my back in a slow circle. "What's wrong? I need to know what happened, so I can help. Talk to me, please?"

He probably feels so helpless.

Well, I know how that feels.

But I can't stop the tears, I can't look up, I can't explain, even to help him feel better. My head is an iron weight and I haven't the strength to lift it. I shall remain here until I perish. My only hope is that Ms. B doesn't spit on my gravestone every time she passes the cemetery.

A new voice joins the fun. "What's going on here?"

Eli tightens up. "Nothing, we're fine."

"Well, yes, son, that's obvious." Dripping is the only way to use sarcasm. I can appreciate this, even though I am crushed by grief. "Is she hurt?"

"Don't call me son, and I don't know. I can't get her to respond." Eli's words are clipped and jagged.

I smell paint and sense a body in front of me. "Ms. Hurst, Carmen?" Arty's voice is soft. "Are you okay, sweetie?"

"She's great," Eli snaps, "as you can see."

Arty takes a deep breath. "I know you're angry at me Elijah, but it's going to be difficult to help your friend if we're griping at each other. Truce? For now?"

"Whatever, fine."

"I'll take it." Arty's hand rests on top of my head. "You don't know what happened?"

"I came around the corner and found her like this," Eli says in a hard voice. He really sucks at truces. "She's crying and won't talk to me."

"Hmm," Arty says.

"I didn't do anything!" Eli's voice rises. "Okay, so I kissed her this morning and then walked away because idiot James was making such a big deal out of it and it was that or punch him in the face. So that wasn't the best way to handle it, but I was gonna talk to her. I was looking for her right now, then I found her..." His voice trails off.

"You kissed her, huh? Is that your first kiss?"

"What? Dude!" Eli hollers. "Not a good time."

"You're right. I'm sorry. Can't blame me for the interest. I think that's the first piece of information you've told me about your life in about ten years."

Eli mumbles something.

"What was that?"

"I said I didn't mean to tell you any of that in the first place. Just forget it. I was trying to explain that Carmen isn't crying because of me."

"You're sure of that?"

"Mostly." Eli doesn't sound sure at all. "Carmen isn't the kind of girl to get all unglued like this over me walking away. I think she'd be more likely to track me down and slap me. As much as she likes using those highfalutin words and acting all drama-y, she's not really. I think the whole overly dramatic thing is a habit. Or maybe like a twitch. I don't know why I'm telling you this. Will you just fix whatever's wrong with her?"

When Arty speaks again, there is so much amusement in his voice, it lifts my weary soul a couple of notches. "Sure. I'll just wave my magic girl problem wand and she'll be alright in a jiffy."

Eli grunts.

"Keep rubbing her back, son, I think that's helping."

Arty begins to sing in a rich baritone while Eli lightly rubs my back. I don't understand the words of the song he sings, it sounds like another language, but the result is so comforting that the squeeze over my heart starts to lessen. I can finally take more deep breaths, enough to feel like I'm not going to disintegrate into the carpet.

I slowly lift my head.

Arty's face is the first thing I see. He smiles, but his eyes are sad. "Hello, there, Ms. Hurst. How are you this morning?"

"Not so good." I gulp.

"Ms. Greco, can you go get bottled water from the teachers' lounge fridge?"

Wait, who's Ms. Greco?

I follow the direction of Arty's face. Kelsie is standing behind Eli with a terrible expression.

"You may be mildly dehydrated." This last part Arty directs to me.

"Can I have my phone back?" Kelsie holds out her hand.

"You do not need your phone to walk to the teachers' lounge, Ms. Greco. I have complete faith in you."

She huffs off, mumbling to herself as she goes.

"Why did you take her phone?" My voice is gravelly, but I have to ask. At this point, I'll do anything to take the attention off myself. This is so humiliating.

"She was trying to video," Eli says.

"Me?" I gulp. "Crying?"

Eli shrugs. "She videos everything, Carmen. You know that."

Arty is very quiet until Kelsie returns with the water and I glug half of it without stopping.

"That's better, yes?" He plops onto the carpet in front of me. "Now, do you feel like you can tell us what happened?"

Eli stops rubbing my back and starts running his fingers through the ends of my hair. My mom used to do that when I was little. It brings me all the way back to myself.

"I don't really know what happened," I begin. "I mean, I do, sort of, but I promised I wouldn't say anything."

"Is this about Ms. Buckley?" Arty asks.

I nod.

"Then it might help you to know that at the faculty meeting this morning Ms. Buckley told everyone that she is Laura Valentine."

That is incredibly surprising.

"Who?" Eli looks confused.

"Laura Valentine is a famous actress, son," Arty says. "She left that behind and has been teaching here to escape her previous life."

"She really told everyone?" I break in.

Arty laughed lightly. "With all those reporters hounding the entrances, I imagine she felt like she didn't have a choice."

"Oh." That didn't make me feel better anymore. She probably thought that was my fault too. "She told me her secret yesterday, after drama practice. I promised I wouldn't tell anyone, and I didn't. I promise I didn't tell anyone." That horrible raw torture begins to climb my throat again. I take another sip of water to wash it down. "She thinks I told. But I really didn't."

"You didn't?" Eli sounds just skeptical enough to raise my hackles.

"No!"

"If she said she didn't, she didn't," Arty says firmly. "At some point, you're going to have to start trusting people, son."

Eli opens his mouth then snaps it closed.

"That's just facts," Arty adds. "I did not break the truce."

I pull myself inward, away from Eli. If he thinks I would do something like that, this thing with him and me, it's never going to work. I guess it's better to know now, than to find out after ten years of marriage and three kids, but it still stings.

Kelsie clears her throat.

"Something to say, Ms. Greco?"

Kelsie drops to her knees beside me and covers her face with her hands. "I'm so sorry."

"What are you sorry about?" Eli snaps.

Arty shoots him a gremlin look and Eli apologizes, but not very sincerely.

Kelsie peeks at me between her fingers. "*I* told, Carmen. I overheard you guys talking, remember? I came back for my lip gloss, and I got curious so I stayed outside the door and listened. I–I posted it on my social media yesterday afternoon."

I'm too drained to be mad. "How much did you hear?"

"Just the part that Ms. B used to be Laura Valentine. I left right after that. I was just so excited, I didn't really think it through."

Well, I could certainly relate to that.

"She left because Hollywood turned on her when she had her accident," I speak into my hands. Kelsie obviously feels bad and I don't want to make it worse, but she needs to know what a big deal this is. "She started a new life here, away from all the intrusiveness, and now, she won't have any peace."

I will never forget that hunted look in her eyes. Even knowing this wasn't my fault doesn't change that it happened. There is nothing I can do to give Ms. B her quiet life back. Kelsie's decision has irrevocable consequences.

"I don't know how to fix this," I whisper.

Arty squeezes my shoulder, but I barely feel it. He stands up and looks down at me. "Tell me, kids, what are you going to do next?"

I blink up at him.

Really? He's going to leave this in our hands? The girl who was bitterly accused, the girl who inadvertently ruined Ms. B's life in exchange for a viral Instagram page, and the boy who doesn't trust anyone.

That just seems like a very bad idea.

Eli stands too, his hands on his hips. He looks so much like Arty, now I can finally see how they are related. "We're going to go in that classroom and straighten this out with Ms. B."

"What?" Kelsie's eyes fly wide open.

Arty nods once, decisively. "That is the right answer, Elijah. Ms. Greco, you made a mistake. It is now your responsibility to fix it."

"I don't know if it will work." I press my lips together. "She is so angry."

"Maybe so, but we are going to try." Eli reaches for my hand. I let him take it, even though I'm not sure what to think about him anymore. "If nothing else, Ms. B deserves to know the truth."

I reach for Kelsie with my other hand.

"I really am sorry, I didn't mean to hurt Ms. B," she says in a small voice.

"I know." I squeeze her fingers.

We walk to the classroom door and Eli opens it. Ms. B doesn't say anything when she looks up, but I swear I hear a sob.

"Ms. B?" Eli leads the way.

I glance over my shoulder to see if Arty is behind us. The door closes without him on our side of it. Maybe he thinks it will be better for us to do this without interference.

Or maybe he's a chicken.

The expression on Ms. B's face is freaking me out pretty good right now, I'm not going to lie.

"Yes?" She refuses to look at me, which is slightly better than being the recipient of that horrible look on her face. I'd rather be ignored than despised.

I think.

Eli ushers Kelsie forward and gives her a nod. Her eyes are ginormous but she doesn't back down.

Respect.

"Ms. B? Carmen didn't tell the tabloids where you are. I overheard you guys talking yesterday and posted it on Instagram. I'm so sorry." Kelsie bows her head, like awaiting the guillotine.   .

Ms. B sighs.

The sound is so forlorn, I finally dare to look at Ms. B. All the anger is drained from her face, leaving her looking lined and exhausted.

"Thank you for clarifying the situation, Kelsie." Ms. B steps around her desk. "I owe you an apology, Carmen."

"No, it's okay." I let go of Kelsie's hand to reach for Ms. B. "I would have thought the same thing you did. It's totally understandable."

"Understandable, maybe, but not excusable." She offers me a smile. "Can you ever forgive me?"

"Done." I wave my hand through the air. "Wiped, gone, finished, forgotten."

The corner of her mouth raises. "You are a much better person than I am. Oh!" Her head drops to her hands and she rubs her temples. "What am I going to do?"

I wish I had a good answer for that. I glance at Kelsie, then at Eli. Neither one of them seem to know what to say either.

As I watch Ms. B struggle through options, I see a scene flash in front of my eyes. From the movie *Someday She Will*. Laura Valentine plays the role of a totally awkward, dorky woman with social anxiety. She completely killed it. It almost won her an Oscar because this character was so unlike herself. It was fire. *She* was fire.

I don't know why I'm thinking about this scene, at first, but then it comes to me in a flash.

"Ms. B?" I slide into the desk in front of her. "How do you feel right now?"

"Awful." She doesn't look up. "Terrible, horrible, no-good, pathetic, and small."

"How do you want to feel?"

She stops rubbing her temples and looks at me. "What?"

I repeat the question with the exact same tone and inflection. I wonder if she'll catch the reference. She made so many movies, can she possibly remember them all?

Ms. B studies me for a moment, then chews her lip. "I want to feel confident. I'd love to be able to walk out there and face those cameras. I'd love to tell them what they did to me all those years ago and that I don't need them anymore. I'd like to tell them to leave the school grounds, maybe suggest a specific place they can go."

Eli laughs.

I press my lips together to keep the smile from showing. We're almost there, I can feel it, but it's too soon to celebrate yet.

"Would you really go out there and tell them all to go to…" I glance around the room. "…Hades?"

"No," Ms. B says with a smile. Her shoulders straighten. "I don't really need them to go anywhere and burn there for eternity. Not really. But I would like to tell them my story. I'd like to raise some awareness, maybe keep them from printing things that have the potential to really hurt people."

I pop to my feet. "Then let's do it."

"Do what?" She looks from my outstretched hand to Eli then Kelsie as though one of them is going to explain to her what I'm doing.

"Let's go out there and face them."

"I can't." Ms. B shrinks away from me. "I can't do that."

"No," I agree. "Ms. B is pretty shy and quiet, but Laura Valentine, *she* can do anything."

Ms. B stares at me for so long I wonder if she's turned into a wax statue of herself. She stands up and walks to the window. There's probably paparazzi on the other side of it, so she doesn't lift the blinds, she just stares at them closed.

Then she starts laughing.

Uh-oh, did I just break her?

Ms. B turns around and extends her hands to the sides like she's about to hug the whole world. "It's a terrifying thing to meet your greatest fear face to face. I've imagined it a thousand times, and now that we are here, I am no longer afraid. I *am* Laura Valentine." A slow smile spreads across her lips. "And you are right, Laura Valentine can do *anything.*"

One hand whisks the ponytail out of her hair and flings it onto the floor, the other yanks the glasses off her face and drops them on the nearest desk. She flips her hair forward and then back through the air like a Pantene commercial. When she stands upright again, she practically oozes confidence.

"Let's go talk to the paparazzi." She links her elbow through mine and struts the two of us to the door. Eli still has a hold of my hand, so he comes along automatically. Kelsie hurries to catch up.

I stumble to get my feet under me without slowing us down. I don't know what Laura Valentine is about to do, but I wouldn't miss it for the world.

Act VII Scene III

FADE IN: EXT: HILLBILLY HIGH SCHOOL - A STAR
RETURNS - RISING FROM THE ASHES

Like the rats of Hamlin, we trail behind Laura as she navigates through the halls. We had to unlink and let go when we came to the first doorway which is not made for three people to walk through. Now we're single file with Laura in front, Kelsie right behind her, then me and Eli as the caboose.

Eli picks up the pace so he is just behind me. One wrong move and he'll give me the flattest of flat tires.

"Carmen?" he whispers close to my ear. "I'm an idiot."

"I know," I whisper over my shoulder.

"I'm sorry."

"I know." I reach my hand back.

When he takes it, he laces his fingers through mine. I can't see his face, but I can feel his smile through the palm of my hand.

We all hurry past the empty front office and head straight out the front doors to face the flashing lights and cameras.

Laura's steps falter for a moment as she moves into the sun. I hurry to her side and link my arm through her elbow again. She's come this far, I'm going to help her finish it, whatever *it* is.

"Is that...?"

"It's her!"

"It is!"

"Unmistakably!"

"Laura Valentine, some questions..."

"Now that you've lost weight..."

"Do you have an opinion about..."

Laura raises her free hand and waits until the crowd grows silent. It is so still it starts to feel eerie. She reaches for the megaphone that the PE teacher carries with him everywhere, not that he needs it. They can probably hear the dude *whisper* all the way in Paris. He lets Laura take his baby without any trouble. His usual smirk is replaced by a look of total and complete adoration.

And people wonder why I want to be a star.

Laura pauses a moment, then raises the megaphone to her lips and faces her fear like a boss.

"Before we begin, I want to make something explicitly clear. I will not tolerate any harassment of the good people of this town. Do you understand?"

She smiles while she speaks, so it takes a moment for the seriousness of her words to sink in. Heads bob in the crowd. Though, I'm pretty sure they would agree to anything right now if it means an interview with the elusive Laura Valentine.

"I will answer your questions, those I don't find too personal or intrusive of course, and then I expect each and every one of you to leave immediately. Without detour. Even better if you never come back. My life is not your plaything. Is that understood?"

Her voice rings through the air with such authority, I am taken aback. I can finally see the Laura Valentine she once was. The powerhouse. America's sweetheart.

More bobbing heads.

The skin around her mouth is tight, so I think she knows they won't follow her rules. Maybe she just needed to say the words and stand up to them in her own small way.

"You may begin questioning as soon as you create a path for the students to enter the building. It is a school day, after all."

The crowd parts. There's a lot of grumbling as people move from the crowd to the school. Arty appears then, with Kelsie's phone, and escorts her into the building.

I'm surprised she goes without a fight.

Principal Bob sends a glance that washes right over Eli and me. He goes inside without a word.

So, we get to stay?

I bet it's because our hands are all clasped so tightly our knuckles are white. Whatever the reason, I'll take it.

"Why did you leave?" someone from the crowd calls out the moment the school doors close all the way.

"Are you asking me why I left California?"

The returning question seems to stump the person. There's silence for a short moment, then another voice rings out with, "Why did you leave Hollywood?"

"I didn't leave Hollywood. It left me."

I am so proud of her, I want to clap. Except one of my arms is wedged into her side like a teddy bear and the other is sweating in Eli's grip.

The paparazzi don't appear to know what to do with this Laura. Some glance at each other, then another chimes in.

"Why did you stop making movies?"

"Oh," Laura's laugh rings out like wind chimes. "Do you mean after my accident and surgery, or after y'all chewed me up and spit me out because I gained thirty pounds?"

Her words are stingers, but there is no malice in her voice. She sounds sweet as caramel. She's not trying to hurt anyone. She's trying to make a point. I'm sure of it. I look through the crowd and see a number of faces where the words hit their mark.

"Surely you remember?" she says, innocently. "Those silly photos of Jabba the Hut with my face on them? The artfully doctored pictures of me eating a table full of desserts with the caption of *America's literal SWEETheart*. We have so much history together, don't we? So fun!"

A man in the front looks away. I hope it's because he's a little bit ashamed and not because he's looking for his phone so he can check his texts.

"All of you"—Laura swings her free arm out to them—"came here because you want to know why I'm in this small town teaching math when I had a glittering career in Hollywood. I can give you two explanations that I hope you will understand. The first is this: after my accident, the paparazzi made my life a living..."

She glances at Eli and I.

"...nightmare. I know you're just doing your job, and I can respect that, but do you know what it does to a person to look at a magazine with their body on it and every flaw highlighted? Do you know what it means to be terrified to step foot outside your front door because of who might be waiting there to catch you make a mistake and then tell the world about it? Do you know how it feels to be abandoned because of something you can't control, to be completely and truly alone? I know that I wasn't perfect when I was in the spotlight. I wasn't always a good person, but I did not deserve the way I was treated. No one should have their worst moments publicized for others to mock. No one deserves that. We are all the same in this way. When we are down, we need a lot less judgment and a lot more love. I wish I'd realized that sooner. I would have done a lot of things differently. I wish I could help you see that people are more important than a headline and a paycheck."

Silence fills the air. I wait for someone to ask her what the other explanation is, for why she left. I try to catch the eye of someone, anyone, to prompt them to ask, but they are all busy staring at their shoes.

Well, except for those who are trudging to their vehicles. I guess that is not the story they came for.

So, I guess it's up to me.

"What's the other reason you left?" I holler so the people in the back can hear my question.

Laura smiles at me. "Thank you for asking. The other reason I am here and not there is because I realized something very important, right around the time my agent dumped me. My fame was not real. No one really cared a bit about *me*. I thought everyone loved me. I relied on that, and I discovered that it was all a lie. I was living in a world that I had made up. Maybe others reinforced it, maybe not. It doesn't really matter. I lived there, and I thought it was perfect. Discovering the truth was hard, but it has given me so much freedom. I want you to know something. A real life might not have a Hollywood sign or a sidewalk full of handprints. Real life might be messy and ugly and freaking hard, but it is also beautiful and unforgettably sweet. In real life, people make mistakes that have real consequences, and then they fix them and make some more. I forgot all of that when I lived in your world. It's funny, I spent my time putting myself in other people's shoes, acting like someone else, in a story that resolves itself perfectly in ninety minutes. I lost sight of who I am. I was selfish, myopic, and I am mortally ashamed of it. I have rediscovered myself, and I can't go back again. So, I will say this very clearly and hope you know I mean it with all my soul. I am never coming back to Hollywood." She paused and caught as many eyes as would come her way. "Never."

No further questions.

They didn't dare.

No one can meet anyone's eyes. It's the most profound scene I have ever experienced. Laura waits for someone else to speak, but they are either clenching their jaws or leaving them slack to catch unfortunate flies.

She smiles sweetly and puts the megaphone back at her lips. "If you'll excuse me, I have a class to teach. It was lovely catching up."

Laura turns and walks away. There is only silence in her wake.

When we get inside the school, she leans against the doors and lets out the longest breath of all time. I stretch my squished arm above my head, trying to get the blood flowing again.

Laura laughs. "I feel like I lost a thousand pounds."

"That was sick." Eli holds his hand up for a high five, which Laura smacks with a grin.

"I can't tell you how good it feels to let all that out."

I am so proud of her. "I don't think they'll bother you again."

Eli's forehead is a million tiny little creases. "How can you be sure? What if they don't go away? What if they keep bugging you?"

I started shaking my head halfway through his spiel. "They won't. Paparazzi want scandal. They don't care what the truth is. She is brilliant.

By *telling* them her story, she pretty much guaranteed they won't print it."

"They might." Laura shrugs. "But they'll get bored soon and move on to something else, and you know what? I totally don't care!"

"That was pretty darn brave." Eli folds his arms.

I give her a tight hug. "I'm so proud of you." I don't think I'll be able to say those words enough times to get the meaning all the way across.

"I'm proud of me too." Laura grins. It makes her look so different, years younger, and this time I don't see the person she used to be, I only see the amazing person she has become.

Finale

AND THAT'S A WRAP

This ending with Laura Valentine finding her voice is a drop-the-mic kind of moment, triumphant and perfect to FADE OUT, but doesn't really resolve what's going down with all the other characters, does it?

So, that means this is the perfect place for a...drumroll please...yes! EPILOGUE!

(I am madly in love with epilogues)

EPILOGUE

SKYLAR

After starring in a number of fairly successful movies, she now divides her time between voice acting and facial cleanser commercials. Rumor has it she's working on a clothing line for Walmart.

JACE

Yeah, absolutely no idea what he's been up to all these years. Also, don't really care.

BETH

After a lot of late night practices and tears for fears, Beth won the monologue competition for our state. What can I say? She had the most amazing mentor. She went to California for the finals and placed second in the nation. She didn't win the scholarship to LAAA, but she did catch the eye of an agent. After graduation, she moved to LA and Ms. B is helping her negotiate the ins and outs of Hollywood. Remotely, of course, because she was serious about never going back. Beth is doing amazing!

No one is worried about Beth changing. She is so grounded. When I talked to her yesterday, she told me she was offered a role where she had to do something raunchy and she gave them a detailed description of what they could do with that script. So, yeah, Beth is going to be fine.

JAMES

The boy stuck around home to work on his daddy's pig farm. Most days I see him wrangling pigs and yelling the most skewampus phrases to get them to cooperate. I really have no idea where he comes up with these words.

MYLES

Brainiac got a scholarship to Berkley. Also Harvard, Princeton, and Yale. But he chose Berkley. Three guesses why. He and Beth got married a few months ago, and if they got any cuter, it would melt my mind.

ELDON

After college, he moved to upstate New York with the babe he met online. They bought a rambler and are having a blast fixing it up, if his Instagram account is any proof.

ZEB

Of course, stayed in Podunk forever and got a job coaching football and teaching Physics at Hillbilly High. Turns out he was just pretending to be an idiot in high school. He loves his work so much, he's impossible to talk to unless you know way too much about football or velocity. Which I don't, so I don't.

KELSIE

Went to the state university and got her degree in Social Media Marketing. I heard she has an amazing offer from Amazon, but I haven't heard if she accepted it. She might be killer good at posting, but she still stinks at communication.

MISSY

Got her oceanography club and went on to get a degree in Marine Biology from BYU-Hawaii. She lives there still, training dolphins and surfing on the weekends.

LAURA VALENTINE

Actually started dating Arty after a couple of years of putting him off. The man is persistent. I imagine we'll have a wedding in the future and Eli will have an irresistible stepmom in addition to his now almost non-existent daddy issues. He and Arty are figuring it out, with Ms. B's help of course. Really, the woman is impossible not to love. She used some of her well-invested funds from her acting career to begin a theater program at Hillbilly High. I was her teacher aide for those few months until I graduated from high school and then kept going all through college. I did most of my student teaching to finish up my education degree in her high school theater class.

ELI'S MOM

Deserves a line because she's amazingly supportive and because I'm pretty sure she's dating the guy who owns Mabel's. Becky said it's a given, and since she's almost seventeen and knows everything, I have to believe her. I hope it's true. The guy who's name I can't remember is incredibly nice and that woman deserves the best things, including all the pie she can eat for eternity.

ELI and I

Well, I could tell you, but I think it's way better if I show you. We'll have to go way back to a couple of weeks after the whole hoopla with the press and Laura Valentine. That's when I finally decided to talk to Eli again after he was such an idiot.

AND...FADE IN:

The crackly PA system interrupts the tail end of a math test to announce an assembly. I'm crunching the numbers, or, depending on how you look at it, they are crunching me, so I don't really listen to what the announcement says. There are three problems left on this stupid test and I am so done with the whole thing.

When Ms. B asked if she could give me college work to supplement the high school curriculum, I was like, what? And now that I am knee-deep in it, I'm like, bleh.

When I finally reach the end of the test and look up, the entire classroom is empty except for Ms. B and me. Talk about in the zone. I didn't hear any of that.

I throw my pencil on the desk. It bounces by the eraser to the floor and skids across the room. Not that I care. After toiling through the numbers together for this long, I never want to see it again. The pencil is dead to me.

Ms. B chuckles. "How'd it go?"

I groan and slide from the desk to the floor, letting my body fold over until I lay there face down. It is not my best moment. For one, carpet lines do nothing for my complexion and for another, either someone threw up in this spot at some point and the smell is ingrained in the fibers, or the carpet has never been cleaned at all. Either way, it is so not good.

I flop over to my back and fling an arm over my face.

"That good, huh?"

"Horrible," I croak, peeking out from under my arm to where Ms. B is sitting at her desk. Her hair flows over her shoulders like spun gold, and the navy pencil skirt she wears does wonders for her figure. So much better than those oversized sweaters and baggy slacks she used to wear.

Ms. B laughs and gets to her feet. "Well, I am always a fan of languishing, but there is an assembly starting in"—quick glance at the clock above the door—"five minutes. How about we go to that instead?"

I reach for the hand she offers and let her help me to my feet. "Is it about math?" I brush goobers off my clothes and fluff my hair.

"The assembly?"

I nod.

"Well, I'm not entirely sure, but I'm pretty sure the announce-ment said we have a guest speaker."

"Does the speaker like math?" I swing my backpack over my shoulder.

Ms. B holds the classroom door for me. "I haven't had a chance to ask them that question, but I definitely will at the first opportunity." Her eyes twinkle as she shuts the door, then gestures down the hall to the auditorium.

I slump along beside her, grumbling about everything that has to do with numbers. It's not entirely my fault. There are numbers everywhere. I never noticed how many before. Now it's like they mock me at every turn.

Classroom numbers, posters, numbers on clocks.

Boo!

"You know, Carmen, you don't have to do this college work if it's too challenging. I have full faith in your capabilities, but if *you* don't, it's not really necessary."

I stop walking. "What are you saying?"

"We can go back to normal math curriculum if you want." She pauses just outside the auditorium door to glance over her shoulder at me. "A challenge that crushes you ceases to be a good thing."

I jab both hands on my hips. "Are you kidding me? I'm not quitting. I'm just belly aching. You should know the difference."

A smile breaks over her face. "Oh, I do. I was just giving you options."

"Well,"—I toss my hair over my shoulder—"I don't want those kind of options. I'm going to conquer this math and make it cry for its mommy. Also, I'm going to complain about it the entire time. Just so you know." I march by her and pause inside the auditorium to let my eyes adjust.

Her trademark "Laura Valentine" laugh floats back to me as she heads to the rows of seats reserved for teachers.

I can't see where Beth or any of the others are sitting, so I slip into an aisle seat next to a fairly empty row and get comfortable. The assembly is about technology with some bigwig from somewhere so, yeah, I'm prepared to take a little snooze.

"Hey, Carmen!" Beth is out of breath and she scoots over my legs to take the seat next to me. "I'm glad I found you."

"Why are you late?" I stare at her flushed cheeks. "You left math before I did. You should have an amazing seat in the front row."

"Yeah." She tugs at the end of her ponytail. "I had to stop somewhere and do something."

Wow, that explains everything.

I let it go because the super important tech guy just took the microphone and it is officially my nap time. I scooch into the back of the seat, trying to get comfortable. The back of my head bumps against a metal rim that lines each chair, but other than that, I'm almost cozy. I close my eyes and let myself drift off. I've almost reached that lovely place of incoherency when Beth pokes my arm.

"Hey, Carmen?"

I peek one eye open. "Yeah?"

"Um, I was just wondering something."

I try not to feel irritated that she's wondering something now instead of thirty minutes from now when the talk and my nap have concluded simultaneously. "What's up?"

She twists her fingers together in her lap. "It's about Eli…"

Eli. Ugh. She must mean the guy who acted like an idiot when he didn't believe me about tattling on Laura and then ignored me for like a week afterwards because he was embarrassed, which means he needs to figure out a better way of processing his emotions.

I hiss. "I thought we agreed on he-who-must-not-be-named."

"Right, him. So, I guess that means you don't really want to talk about him?"

I flick my index finger in her direction.

"Does that mean yes, you don't want to, or no, you don't want to?"

I roll my head across the back of the seat. "It means you're right, I don't want to talk about him."

"So, you're still mad?"

I groan so loud that every person in the five rows ahead of me turns around to glare at me. I ignore them and sit up. No use pretending I'm going to be sleeping anytime soon. "Beth, I'm not mad at him. I forgave him for being a butt. I just don't get him and I'm not sure if I can trust him to be consistent. He's not consistent, like, ever."

"You know that's because he doesn't get himself, right? He's so mixed up and confused. He loves his dad, but he's so mad at him he thinks he hates him…"

"That's fine, he can be mixed up and confused all he wants. He can live every one of his trust-issue dreams to his heart's content, yay. I'm not going to be his emotional punching bag while he figures things out, though. I'm more than happy to talk to him after he works through all that garbage."

"So, you think he should have to work through his garbage alone?"

I glare at her, but because it's dark, I don't think it matters. "That's not what I'm saying." I lean forward so I don't broadcast my feelings to this section of the auditorium. "It ripped my heart out when he didn't believe me about Ms. B, Beth. Seriously. And then it ripped out again when he wouldn't talk to me about it. How can we have a relationship, or whatever, under those circumstances?"

She stares forward for a minute. "Last weekend, Eli went out to lunch with his dad. They had a really good talk. They're working on it."

"I'm very happy for them both."

Beth peeks at me. "That's it?"

"What do you want me to say?"

She looks over the top of my head, and I suddenly get that creeped out feeling like someone has been staring at me for a really long time. I slowly look over my shoulder.

Eli stands by my side. "Hey, move over, I'll sit by you."

"No." I put my hand on Beth's arm to get her to stay still.

He bends down slightly to whisper, "Seriously?"

I look forward like the speaker on the stage is actually Taylor Swift in concert. Rapt attention, y'all.

"Carmen—"

"I don't want to and you can't make me."

Eli lets out a rough breath that blasts my arm with hot air, then plops into the aisle seat behind me.

I twist around. "Why are you sitting there? You can't sit there."

"I can, actually, it's a free country."

So mature.

I glare at him, then face the front again with all my might. I don't have a clue what the speaker is talking about, but I'm going to tune out everything except him from now on. By the end of this assembly, I will know his spiel better than he does. If the opportunity arose, I'd be able to give it in his place. I could travel the country regurgitating his talk for high schools everywhere.

Beth pokes my back.

"What?" I snap at her, then sigh and roll my eyes. "Sorry, that was harsh. What I meant to say is yes, darling Beth, friend of mine. What can I do for you?"

"Eli wants to know why you won't talk to him."

Really? He's asking her to ask me? Because we're in kindergarten now?

"Tell Eli he knows why."

Beth turns around and relays my message. All the hairs on the back of my neck are at strict attention, waiting for Eli's response.

So much for listening to the tech guy and doing school tours. I don't know why I'm pretending. Even the hairs on the back of my neck know I want things to be good with Eli. It's true he's full of issues, but I really like the guy.

It's just one of those things, I guess.

"Eli says he really doesn't know why you won't talk to him, because he screwed up so much there's too many things for you to be mad about to choose from. He'd like to know which one you're talking about specifically."

For real?

I glance over at him and my heart kind of melts. He looks so miserable. And sincere. He's not a good enough actor to do that without feeling it.

"You have two minutes," I say.

Eli grabs my hand with the speed of a viper. "Carmen, I was a jerk."

"I know. I was there. You have one minute and forty-five seconds. I don't want to miss any more of the assembly."

"It's about wind power." He gives me a skeptical look.

I huff. "And? If you knew me at all, you'd know I'm fascinated by will power."

"Wind power."

"That's what I said."

Eli laughs and leans forward. His breath warms my skin, sending shivers down my arm. "What's it going to take, Carmen? What do I have to do to make this good again?" He holds up his hands and starts ticking off his fingers. "I've been eating lunch with Art...I mean, my dad, I had lunch with him last weekend. I helped Nana milk the goats even though they are evil and hate me. I turned in all my homework on time. I brushed and flossed my teeth—"

"I am not your mother." I grin. "I don't actually care if you do those things, did you know?" I pause for a second. "Except for the brushing and flossing, that actually does matter to me."

"Why?" A smile tickles the corners of his mouth.

I narrow my eyes. "Because kissing with bad breath and food lodged between your teeth is disgusting."

"So, you want to kiss me? Is that what you're saying?" He looks at Beth. "Is that what you heard?"

She raises both hands. "I'm staying out of this from now on. I know when I'm in over my head. From this moment forward, I, too, am passionate about wind power."

"Will power," I say.

Eli tugs my shirt sleeve. "Come on, Carmen. Give a guy a break. I brought over banana bread and Nana's chocolate cashew bark—world famous. I even sent you apology flowers. Help me out, truly, I'm out of ideas."

My eyes dart to his face. "I never got banana bread or flowers." I did get the cashew bark. It was totally amazing, but I'm not about to tell him that.

"I gave the bread to your parents and left the flowers on your back porch."

"All on the same day?"

"No." He looks at the ceiling. "The bread was two days after the whole paparazzi thing and the flowers were two days after that."

Well, that explained it. If he gave the bread to my parents they probably ate it without telling me because they are suckers for homemade stuff, and the flower thing would have been on the day Kelsie's grandpa's prize pig escaped and ran amuck in our yard.

I hope my flowers gave it indigestion.

"Carmen," Eli pleads. "The thing is, I know I handled that all wrong. I believed you didn't tell Ms. B's secret once I thought about it for two seconds. I know you wouldn't do something like that. I'm seriously sorry."

Before I could open my mouth to tell him I already forgave him that day at the school when I let him take my hand, he moves his face close to mine. "What's it going to take for you to forgive me, Carmen? What do I have to do?"

"I—"

"'Cause I'll do anything. I'll go up on that stage right now and sing a boy band song with background dancers if it means you forgive me."

"Wh—"

"I'll drop balloons from the ceiling filled with apology notes and then beg for your forgiveness in front of all these people. I'll do it."

"You—"

"You don't believe me? That's fair." He sets his mouth into a line and stands up. "You just watch this, Carmen Hurst."

"Wh—"

But he's already gone, striding that confident cowboy stride up to the stage where the speaker is beginning to wrap up.

I half rise, trying to figure out if I should run after him and tackle him before he does something weird, or if I should run the other way before he does something embarrassing.

Beth puts a hand on my arm. "Wait a bit longer."

Eli pauses to talk to Principal Bob and then to shake the tech guy's hand, then he takes the microphone. His confidence wafts off him like fancy cologne.

It suddenly occurs to me that drama training is a dangerous thing in the wrong hands. Without it, I don't think Eli would have ever strutted up to that stage in the middle of an assembly and commandeered the microphone.

What the Grammy is he doing up there?

Also, the stage lights glisten off his hair as he leans to one side a little, adjusting the microphone stand.

He has never looked so hot.

Like, ever.

"Hey, peers," Eli says in a jaunty voice.

He pauses to let the various responses fade.

"Yeah, love you guys too. That was an awesome assembly, wasn't it? I was sitting down there thinking about how all it takes to change something is to see a need and then persist until you get where you want. So, that's why I'm up here. But first, I *need* Carmen Hurst to come join me on the stage."

Okay, I have never had a problem joining anyone on stage, but I admit I hesitate now. Beth pushes the backs of my legs until I have no choice but to walk into the aisle. Somehow I get the rest of myself coordinated and make it onto the stage.

Butterflies invade my stomach until I step into the stage lights and then they scatter. This is my place. I grin and stride to Eli with my shoulders thrown back. "What are you up to?"

"You just watch." Eli flicks his wrist at the lighting booth and the whole auditorium goes dark. A bright spotlight illuminates Eli, now standing in a staggered line with Eldon, James, Myles, and Zeb. The opening notes of *I Want It That Way* by Backstreet Boys fill the airways.

I can barely keep my stuff together as I watch them twirl and hop and boy band it up. It's stinking hilarious! I stagger to the edge of the stage so I don't get trampled by James, who has no concept of personal space normally, and much less when he's dancing like a maniac.

I bump into someone near the curtain. "Sorry!"

"Carmen, is that you? I think the lights blinded me, I can't see anything."

"Kelsie?"

"Yeah, it's me."

"What are you doing back here?"

"Manning the curtain," she says in a *duh* voice. "Oh my gosh, look at Myles, who would have thought, right?"

She's right, I never would have pictured him shaking what his mama gave him the way he is right now.

"You are so lucky! I hope I meet a guy like Eli someday," she says in a wistful voice. "You know? Someone who is so crazy about me that he does something like this. He's been working on it for like a week. Driving everyone nuts, wanting it to be perfect. It's seriously the sweetest thing ever. Irresistible, right? How can you not forgive him?"

"Irresistible," I repeat, my eyes glued on Eli.

The crowd cheers as balloons start falling from the ceiling. Kelsie reaches out a hand to bop one away from us while I think obsessively about her words.

I can't believe Eli did this for me.

He *is* crazy.

In the best possible way.

There's like a billion balloons everywhere. Floating down over the crowd. How did they even get them up to the ceiling? I grab one that wafts my way and pull out my keys to make a hole in it. The air oozes out slowly, then I pull the latex apart to reveal a strip of paper. I step closer to the spotlight so I can read it.

"I'm sorry I didn't have the guts to tell you I liked you from the second I saw you, even after you pepper sprayed me in the face."

I burst out into a laugh no one can hear except for me. The music reaches a crescendo and Eli's head starts whipping around. He sees me and slides across the stage on his knees.

Luckily he stops at my feet instead of slamming me back into the band pit.

That would be tragical.

"Carmen," he takes my hand, and for half a second I wonder if he's about to propose. "I was an epic jerkward from day one and I'm sorry."

Tears come from nowhere and run down the sides of my face. I think they are happy tears, but I don't know. This has never happened to me before.

I shake my head and pull him to his feet. "I was an idiot too, Eli. *I'm* sorry."

He wraps me up in a good old-fashioned bear hug. "Dang you smell good," he says into my hair.

I step back so I can see his face. His hands drop to his side, along with his hopeful smile.

"It's not enough is it?"

I smack his arm. "No, you moron, it's more than enough. I just remembered I thought you said you would rather eat pickled pigs feet than stand in front of people and dance."

A slow smile spreads over his face. "I did say that. I remember. That's why I had to do this, girl. I wasn't joking earlier when I said I would do anything to show you I have changed. Did it work?"

"Yeah, it worked, you proved it." I purse my lips and run one hand up his arm and across his shoulder to the back of his neck. "But, I don't want everything about you to change, you know."

"No?" His voice is low as he wraps both arms around my waist again. Whoever is manning the spotlight swings it over to us so Eli and I are surrounded by a perfect circle of sunshiny light.

"No." I rise to my tippy toes so my mouth is level with his. "No way, Eli, you are a *really* good kisser."

"Yeah?"

"Yeah." I nod.

"Better than alllllll those bazillions of drama kisses?"

"Mmm hmmm."

"I don't know." He grins, showing that adorable dimple in his cheek. "I think I better prove that to you too."

FADE OUT:

Eli and I dated through college and graduated at the same time, me with a teaching degree, minor in theater, and him with a business degree. Then we moved back to Podunk to start a community theater.

On opening night of our very first community play–that would be Annie cause I know you're wondering—he did a little reenactment of that apology dance in high school. He even brought the boys back as background dancers.

Usually, I don't love sequels. It's like a watered-down version of the first. But Eli outdid himself on this one, once again busting my expectations. When he hit his knee under the spotlight with the whole crowd watching, and opened that little black box with a diamond ring inside, well, that was a million times better than any part I've ever played.

Because it was real.

Acknowledgements

There is nothing more fun then taking an average, every day experience and amplifying it into something dramatic, absurd and awkward. I actually think that's my favorite thing about writing high school novels. Awkward is my battle jam! Which means this book was probably the most ridiculous fun I've had writing, like, ever.

Carmen needed a lot of work though. It's easy to run away with the Drama - or, you know, let it run away with me! I super relied on my Story Squad readers, Lily Chambers and my no drama Mama, Shannon Farr, to keep me and Carmen in check. Their google form input helped me make this story so much better than I could have done on my own - so THANK YOU and thank you!

SUPER HUGE thanks to my publishing team, Apeiron, and the amazing individuals who keep me going. Five star rating. You guys seriously make the world a better place!

To my girlies and their flare for the dramatic. (I swear they didn't get it from me). Also to my boysies who will never admit to having their own little drama moments. (Just wait for them to get hangry). You weirdos are life with the sauce and I love every minute of it!

I'd also like to thank our cat, Willow, for trying to sit on my face every time I went to work on this story. I swear it's her fault I had so many grammatical errors and not at all because punctuation is my Waterloo. Me and punctuation are like this. (Insert emoji of fingers crossed).

I think that's legit called 'denial', but we're going to go with it.

And to you, dear reader, wherever you are and whatever else you do, THANK YOU for showing up here to share these stories with me. This is the funnest thing ever. I love it SO much!

And you!

ABOUT THE AUTHOR

High School Cori once dreamed of becoming a famous actress, until her first real play where she was almost cast into a kissing role. That's when she realized she super lucked out because acting meant kissing random guys. Some she'd known since elementary school. Some she didn't know at all. Some with questionable hygiene. Some she'd seen spit super huge and disgusting loogies in the school parking lot.

That really took the glamour out of it.

So, instead, she focused on having a blast with her friends so she now has a boatload of awesome and cringey experiences to make into stories. Which is actually her real dream. Creating stories. Best. Job. Ever!

Besides that fun, she loves to watch Jane Austen movies with her teen daughter, trade witty puns with her teen son, send spam levels of video messages to her adult daughters, and gaze adoringly at her husband, who after twenty five years of real life, is still her very most favoritest thing in the entire world!

CONNECT WITH CORI

INSTAGRAM, BOOKBUB, GOODREADS, PINTEREST, FACEBOOK AND HER WEBSITE, WWW.CORISTORIES.COM

If you like this book - be sure to check out the others!

The Bake Believe Trilogy:
Bake Believe, Bake Off, Bake Happy
Ways to Improve Bailey
Sage Advice
One Quarter Villain
Tears into Gold
A Tale of Two Crushes
Darby's Cafe
The Importance of Being Roxie
The Perfect Girl For Kai